MW00875964

*Sometimes falling in love
means letting go of the past . . .*

SOMETHING

WONDERFUL

M. CLARKE

Dedication

To my loves—hubby, Joshua and Kaitlin—thank you for all your support, especially when I'm on Facebook...lol!

I would like to thank my street team. You are amazing and I can't thank you enough, especially my admins-Janie Iturralde and Elliot McMahon

To Kim Rinaldi—Your feedback means the world to me. You're not afraid to let me know. I appreciate your honesty for helping me make this book awesome.

To my PR, Damaris Cardinali—What would I ever do without you? Thanks for EVERYTHING you do and will do to get me out there. We make a great team!

To Alexandrea Weis—For giving me great feedback. I love sharing our crazy book ideas. And thank you for taking your time to look over mine when you could be writing.

To Jennifer Miller—Thank you for swapping teasers with me, but most of all for your friendship.

To Sam Stettner—for your continuous support in everything I write. I love you to the moon and back!

I want to give thanks to Lisa from The Rock Stars of Romance for hosting the best blog tours!

To Laura Hidalgo, who does amazing book covers. She has done all of mine. You are truly talented!

To Esperanza Duarte and Jodi Shaw for being great editors and for polishing up my book.

To Jane Soohoo—for taking the time to make sure my book is polished and ready to go. Thank you for everything!

To Kitty Bowers—for being my number one cheerleader. I can't thank you enough for spreading the love of all my books.

To Jenny Brewer—for loving this series so much, she runs Something Great Fan page. I can't thank you enough. How cool is that!

To my breakfast club moms—thank you for ALL your support in books and in life—Rosie, Michelle, Gracie, Hung, Holly, and Patricia.

Extra thanks to the three amazing friends. I'm excited to have their made-up quotes as part of my story.

"Books! The other soul food." –Vanessa Strickler

"Book hangovers, a girl's worst nightmare." –Ashley Garland

"Book boyfriends are better because they are always there when we need them." –Pamela Joy Pope

To my readers and bloggers—I can't thank you enough for falling in love with my characters. It means the world to me that you want to continue this journey with them. I hope you'll love Something Wonderful just a much, or if not more than Something Great. Thank you for your continued support. Your support means the world to me and I thank you from the bottom of my heart.

Praise for:
Something Wonderful

"Something Wonderful is truly something wonderful. M. Clarke captures love, romance and forgiveness beautifully. One of 2014's MUST READS!" **Sammie's Book Club, for Book Lovers**

"Be mine, because I want to be yours. I want to give you forever. It doesn't get much better than that. Something Wonderful from M. Clarke is an amazing sequel! Everyone will wish they had the epic love of their lives like Max and Jenna." **Vanessa, Fairiechick's Fantasy Book Reader**

"Something Wonderful heats up the series with its undeniable need, want, passion, incredible characters and intense heated plot. New Adult at its BEST!" **Michele, Insane About Books.**

"Something Wonderful is amazingly brilliant! Sexy, Romantic, Page turning good. Could not put this book down." **Janie, Crossangels**

"Just when you think the art of storytelling couldn't possibly get any better, M. Clarke paints a delicate and refreshing masterpiece that will inspire, electrify, and melt your heart. Her exquisite and unforgettable talent is a rare jewel that you will treasure and enjoy over and over again." **Amber, The Wonderings of One Person.**

"In the darkest times, when your trust is tested, love will conquer all. Something Wonderful gives us two stories of love, passion, and the ability to save someone who was once broken." **Brittany, Spare Time Book**

"M. Clarke has done it once again. I am officially addicted to this series!" **Delphina, Delphina Reads too Much**

"If you are looking for love, heartache, hot steamy sex and brothers that will rock your world this is the read for you!" **Bella, Paranormal Book Club**

"This title says it all. It's so fitting for this book! It truly is Something Wonderful!" **Jennifer, Jeni's Bookshelf**

M. Clarke has done it again with the sequel to Something Great. It was better than the first. I highly recommend it! **Victoria, Novel Reality**

Enjoy a Sneak Peek of:

My Clarity by M. Clarke

Prologue
Becky

What a crazy night. Everyone was wasted, including me. Beer bottles and red cups littered the place. Couples made out every way I turned. Most of the party guests were juniors in college, including me, but the senior who had invited us passed out on the sofa and had no idea about the mess he would find in the morning.

As it was past two in the morning, and I didn't want to spend the night there, I decided to go home. As I looked for my roommate, everything moved in slow motion. I wouldn't have gotten so buzzed, but since it was Amber's turn to be the designated driver, I let myself go and drank as much as I wanted, even knowing I would regret it the next morning.

Since I had just broken up with the guy I had been dating, I needed a night out. He turned out to be a jerk, but as far as the guys I'd been attracted to, that seemed to be my pattern lately. I was an asshole magnet.

"Amber!" I yelled. The music pounding in my ears made it difficult to figure out if my voice carried. I opened the nearest bedroom door. Smoke filled the space and they held a joint in their hand, so I slammed the door.

"Amber!" I called again by the bathroom.

When I heard my name, I rushed in.

"Amber?" I stopped from going in any further.

Her hair snaked over to one side, and her hands rested on either side of the toilet seat bent over. "I need a minute." Her words echoed inside the toilet. A few seconds later, whatever she drank and ate poured out of her mouth.

"Amber, you okay?" I grimaced and dropped next to her.

"Yeah," she managed to say, flushing the toilet. After wiping her mouth with the back of her hand, she collapsed beside me. "I feel...awwwful. Let's go home."

"You said...you weren't supposed to drink, remember? You drive. Me drink." I pointed at myself. I didn't feel sorry for her anymore. Anger rose to the surface. "What the fuuuck, Amber?"

"Sorrrry. I saw him...with...her," she sighed, somberly. Holding on to the sink, Amber stood up, stumbling until she got a hold of herself. "Come on."

When I didn't respond, she grabbed my arms. With an irritated sigh, I pulled myself up. "I don't..." I started to say, but I lost my words and finally understood what she meant by seeing him.

Her boyfriend had broken up with her and had started seeing some other girl right away. I sympathized, but it didn't matter. We were both wasted, and we had no way to get home. Amber tugged my arm. I had no idea where we were going as I let her lead the way. We passed the kitchen, the living room, and oh, crap...passed her asshole ex-boyfriend and somehow, we burst out of the house with our purses.

The cool wind whipped against my face and made me alert, reminding me I'd left my jacket inside. Not only that, a few drops of rain landed on my arm, falling faster by the second. Shivering, I glanced at Amber, struggling to get her keys out of her purse.

"We can't," I said, a bit more aware of the situation. "We're both wasted."

"I feel better," she argued, pushing me aside to get in the car.

I held the door open, hoping to calm her down. "Forget him. He's not good enough for you."

Amber had already started the engine. "Get in," she barked, as tears dampened her eyes.

"Please...get out of the car. We're both too drunk," I said forcefully, trying to snap her out of the buzz and make her come to her senses.

"I can't be in the same room with them." The tears she held at bay streamed down her face. "How could he just move on like that?"

Feeling her pain, my heart ached for her. If we were home, I would cry with her. "We'll stay away and hide in one of the rooms."

Amber wiped her tears, and then she peered up to the sky. "I'm getting wet. You coming?" She reached for the door and missed, her coordination lacking. Finally, on her third try, she managed to grab the door, forcing me to jerk back as she slammed it shut.

"I'm serious. You can't drive." I desperately pounded on the window. My words didn't get across the urgency of the situation. I thought I had convinced her when she looked up at me again, but her mind apparently had been somewhere else. When your heart broke with that intensity, nothing mattered. You want the pain gone, even if you have to physically distance yourself from it. I understood. I had been there before.

"It's not that far," she said.

"Please...stay with me."

When she realized I wasn't getting in the car, she sped away. Drenched from head to toe, I ran back into the house. Warm, smoky air wrapped around me, and I shivered from the drastic temperature change. I fumbled through my wet purse and took out my cell phone to dial Amber's cell.

The pouring rain, the booming thunder, and the worst reception from her Bluetooth made it difficult to hear her voice.

"Amber, come back. It's dark, it's pouring, and you're freakin' wasted." She was risking her life over a loser who wasn't good enough for her.

"He broke my heart," she bawled.

Her cry pierced my heart. I knew that cry. I've cried like that several times myself. I also knew it would be difficult to drive in that condition, not to mention the other reasons why she shouldn't be behind the wheel.

"Amber!" I snapped. My heart pounded against my chest. I had a terrible feeling and I couldn't shake it. I was scared out of my mind and I didn't even know why. "Pull over. I'm coming to get you." Looking around the living room, I urgently searched for someone sober…anyone.

"He's such an ass and I—"

The next sound tore my world apart. It was worse than a boyfriend break up, worse than failing a class. You never think it would happen to anyone you know because at that age, you think you're invincible… untouchable… unbreakable. She yelled my name, then a loud screeching caused immense pain in my ear, and then silence fell as the call disconnected.

It happened so fast it felt like a dream. My phone slipped out of my hand. I couldn't speak. I couldn't move. Then I knew. I just knew I'd never speak to her again.

Matthew

Sometimes life is cruel and fate doesn't work in your favor. I wondered what the hell I did to deserve this. Her family certainly didn't deserve it.

As I sat there on a chair next to the hospital bed, my heart pumping into overdrive, I gazed at my Tessa hooked up to a bunch of machines, the only things keeping her alive. She was already brain dead and bleeding internally. Tessa...my Tessa...was gone, and yet her hand was still warm as I held it to my cheek. My lips quivered and every cell, every nerve, every muscle in me shook. Panic gripped me...so tight, constricting, preventing me from moving, preventing me from breathing. I was running out of time; *she* was running out of time.

I spoke to her, desperately praying for a miracle. "Tessa, baby. How am I supposed to let you go? How do I breathe without you? Don't do this to us. Come back to me. I know you can hear me."

I didn't think I had any tears left to shed, but when I realized that would be the last time I would ever see her...touch her...speak to her face to face again, I lost it. "Why did you run off and get in that stupid car?" I reprimanded. "And why the fuck did it have to rain that day? If you leave me, you're taking everything good in my life. You're going to take my heart...my soul...my will to live. Do you hear me? Your parents need you. Your sister needs you. I need you. If you want to punish me, then fine. Just...come...back."

I let go of her hand and rubbed my face with my palms. My throat made an awful grunting noise, but no tears came. I was utterly drained, dried out. The life had been sucked out of me and all my will had been spent. Letting go of what I loved hurt, but holding onto something I thought was meant to be forever was killing me. Though I knew it was time to let her go, I couldn't...I just couldn't.

"You know what's really fucked up?" I continued. "Your parents have to decide whether to pull the plug and let you die. How the hell are they going to live with themselves knowing they gave up? How the hell am I going to live with myself knowing that I stood by and let it happen? You tell me?"

Standing up, I hovered over her and gave her one last soft kiss on her lips. It was the most painful kiss I'd ever given anyone. I lost it again when I buried my face into the side of her neck to inhale her scent. I needed to memorize her smell, memorize the feel of her soft skin, memorize...*her*. I was afraid I would forget her, afraid she would disappear in my mind. I was terrified I would forget how much I loved this woman. In desperation, I started shouting at her. "Wake up! Wake up!"

"Matthew." Max placed his hand on my shoulder. "It's time to let her go. The doctor is on his way."

I didn't know what I would have done if Max hadn't been there. Even understanding what he had said, I didn't budge. My body refused to listen.

"You need to step aside. You had your time. Her family is waiting."

"I can't, Max. I fuckin' can't. How am I supposed to walk out of here? This is where I belong...with her. The moment she dies, I'll die with her." I looked at Tessa again.

Hoping...

Wishing...

Praying...

I waited for her to open her eyes, staring at her so the

first thing she would set her beautiful eyes on was me.

"You'll make it through, Matt. I promise. You have your family; we'll help you get through this. You're not alone." Max's shaky voice didn't help the situation. He hurt too, but he was being strong for me.

Max meant every word he said, but it wasn't enough. The pain cut too deep and it had sliced through whatever faith I had left. When the doctor came in, followed by Tessa's family, Max grabbed my shirt and pulled me to the other side.

"Please…let's wait one more day," I pleaded wearily.

"Matthew," Tessa's father started to speak in between taking small breaths. He tried to contain himself. "She's gone. And even if somehow there was a miracle, she wouldn't be the same Tessa."

He was right, but I hoped he would change his mind. "No," I said quietly as I watched the doctor do his thing in horror. "No…no, no, NOOOOO!"

Max dragged me out of the room. He knew I would've attacked the doctor if he hadn't restrained me. Through the window, I watched her family sob, and I did the same in Max's arms, feeling helpless, like someone had ripped out my heart.

"It's my fault, Max. It's my fault. I…let…her…go." I bawled. My body trembled in Max's hold as I let out a gut-wrenching cry that poured out of my soul until nothing was left of me. My body and mind had disconnected and I became lost to the emptiness.

Air…no air.

I needed air.

I couldn't breathe.

My air, my purpose, my will to live had been sucked out of me. My world shattered that day. In some ways, it broke me forever. I cursed at life and I cursed at God. I had been damned to hell, but I didn't care. I was dead anyway.

Chapter 1
Jenna

"Becky!" I exclaimed, running toward the open front door. "Let me help you with that." Grabbing the tail end of the Christmas tree, I lifted it up to my waist and helped her carry it to the living room next to the television. Thank God we had wooden floors. The pine needles left a scattered trail and my head spun at the thought of having to sweep them up.

"You okay, Jenna?" Becky asked worriedly, placing her hand on my shoulder.

I must have looked flustered. "Yeah…just…nothing." I smiled, inhaling the fresh scent that spiraled into my nostrils, imagining myself in an enchanted forest.

"Doesn't that smell heavenly?" Becky proudly looked at the tree with her arms crossed as I mimicked her stance.

"Yeah, it does." Gazing at her, I scowled. "Why didn't you ask me to go with you?"

"You had company. Speaking of which, is Max still here?" Taking off her red scarf and black coat, she flung them on the sofa.

"No, he left a little while ago. He's going to stop by the office, then come back around noon."

Becky headed to the kitchen, coming back with a broom and started to sweep the pine needles into a pile. I wanted to help her, but we only had one broom, so I became creative and tore off some paper towels, got down on my hands and knees, and swept up some needles.

"Jenna? What are you doing?" From her tone, she didn't like my ingenuity.

I stopped and peered up to her. "Helping, silly. We only have one broom."

"Get up," she demanded, sounding a little irate. Her intonation softened. "Stop. I can do this. It's no big deal."

Standing up, I met her stare, baffled by her expression. Without a word, I headed to the kitchen and threw the paper towel in the trashcan. As grateful as I was, part of me felt helpless. Max had been there day and night taking care of me, though I felt much better since the car accident. What I needed to do was get out of the apartment. I wasn't the type to mope around and have everyone treat me as if I couldn't lift a finger.

"Jenna." Becky stuck her head into the kitchen, looking guilty for slightly blowing up at me. "I'm sorry. I'm not mad at you. I just didn't want you to overdo it."

"I'm fine. I wish everyone would stop treating me like I just got out of the hospital." I rolled my eyes.

Becky's eyes popped open in disbelief. "But... you...did." Then she went back to sweeping.

Leaning back against the kitchen cabinet, I crossed my arms in annoyance. "Is that the reason why you didn't ask me to go pick out a tree with you?" I asked loud enough so she could hear me. I was trying to brush the hurt aside, but I couldn't help the way I felt. We had always gone tree shopping together. It was a tradition. How could she go alone?

Becky came inside the kitchen and stood in front of me. "I'm just thinking of you, dummy." Draping her arms around me, she squeezed me tightly and spoke with sincerity and tenderness. "Don't ever end up in the hospital again. I thought I'd lost you."

A sudden pang pierced my heart. I could imagine how she felt. If she had been the one in the hospital, I would have felt the same. Tears pooled in my eyes and one drop managed to escape at the corner. When she released me, I quickly wiped it away and she did the same when she turned from me. "Anyway," she continued. "Who would pay the other half of the apartment cost?" she snorted, trying to hide the fear and sadness as she walked out of the kitchen.

I was deeply touched, and though I was the one who had physically suffered, I understood — Becky, Kate, Nicole, Max, and especially Matthew — what they had been through because of me. I felt guilty for being so stupid, driving while clearly incapacitated by gut-wrenching sobbing, hurt, and anger; all because I thought Max had cheated on me with his ex, Crystal. I still hadn't even told my parents what had happened, since they were on a cruise.

"Is that all you care about?" I followed behind her, stealing the broom away so fast she had no idea what was coming, and started to sweep.

"Good. My cleaner is back." She didn't try to stop me this time. Maybe she just needed a hug or assurances that I was fine. "I need to run some errands and head to Starbucks since I ran out of coffee. I'm going to bring my laptop and read some query letters while I'm there. Do you or Max want anything?"

"No, we're good, but thanks."

Becky looked deep in thought, then dashed into her bedroom, made some noise, and came out with several small boxes in her hands, as I finished sweeping the last pine needles into a pile. "Let's decorate the Christmas tree before I go."

"Sounds good." I steadied the broom against the wall.

Placing the boxes down, Becky went to the kitchen and brought back a bowl of water as I opened the boxes. Kneeling down, she poured it into the container surrounding the base of the tree. "There, now drink up and stop shedding your greens and make our place smell like we're in the middle of the forest."

"Here, you get to put up the first one," I said, handing her an ornament. It was a frame with a picture of the two of us. We had taken it when we first moved into this apartment.

Taking it from my hand, she looked at it with soft eyes. Then, she looped the string on a section of branch. After putting the first ornament in place, we draped white lights around the whole tree. This was kind of tricky, since they always seemed to tangle. We hurriedly hung the other ornaments. We finished by placing the angel on top, and decided not to turn on the lights until that night.

After Becky and I hugged, she went out with her workbag, while I headed straight to the computer, waiting for Max to return. While I was surfing the Internet, my phone buzzed with a text. Surprisingly, it was from Luke. Not only did he apologize again for the way he acted when we broke up, he asked to see me. The last text I'd sent to him, I told him I was seeing Max and that there could never be anything between us. I guess he wasn't giving up. I didn't know what else to do except to ignore him.

Chapter 2
Becky

Jenna had no idea how difficult it was for me to see her lying in a hospital bed, so helpless. She didn't know I had lost a good friend before; a friend who happened to have been my roommate. I was too embarrassed to tell Jenna because Amber had been under the influence of alcohol when she wrecked.

I should've been a better friend and forced her not to drive. Not only did she die in that accident, but she had taken someone else's life as well. That was unforgivable, but it wasn't my story to share. My friend had passed away because of a terrible mistake, and I know somewhere she's feeling a whole lot of guilt and making amends for what she had done.

Selfishly, I was glad I wasn't the one who took someone's life. I'm also glad my friend would never know what she had done. I don't think she'd have ever forgiven herself, so in a way, fate somehow spared her, but not her parents.

That made me sober up right away. Since that day, I had never allowed any of my friends to drive drunk, even if I had to steal their car keys. I spent many days missing her and I drowned my sorrows, sometimes not in a good way. So, I decided to get a roommate, hoping that would help me move on. Not that I wanted to forget her; I just wanted someone around. I had friends, but they were mostly party friends.

When Jenna became my roommate, her goody-two-shoes ways made me reform some of my behavior. I stopped cussing around her, because she would flinch or become edgy when I did. She was so innocent and naïve, it made me like her even more, not to mention her "goodness" rubbed off on me...somewhat. Nicole and Kate also came into our lives shortly thereafter when we ended up on a group project together. We were great friends who were meant to last, even after college.

Though I still partied during our senior year, I didn't party as hard as my junior year. I didn't have a good reputation with the boys like Jenna did. Guys went after her, not only because she was beautiful, but also because she wasn't the type to go out with just any guy. She was like a trophy they would try to win, but couldn't. So conquering her meant they would have to be someone pretty special.

As for me, I made out with enough guys to lose count, but I wasn't a slut. I'd had two actual boyfriends, though not long term, so I was more experienced in the "making out" department than the "long-term relationship" department. I always hoped one day, I would meet that guy who would lift me off the ground and never put me back down again. That was how Jenna told me she felt with Max. I was so happy that she found her forever—hopefully.

Starbucks was packed with a line to the door. I thought it would have slowed down, but the cooler weather attracted more customers. The thought of leaving entered my mind, but I realized I was practically high from the first whiff of the scent of coffee. I didn't care if I had to stand in line all day. I had to have my coffee fix. I was totally addicted to caffeine and my favorite latte.

After I picked up my drink, I headed toward the table in the corner near the front door. Since it was difficult to find a table at Starbucks no matter what time of the day, I was more than happy to find a table with two chairs. Perfect! Hopefully, nobody would sit across from me.

Taking out my laptop from my oversized bag, I opened it up and clicked on the file I'd named "query." I was so behind it wasn't funny. I had put work on hold while Jenna was in the hospital. Unable to think clearly that whole week, I stopped trying to read since I couldn't give it my full attention, and that would be totally unfair to the authors.

Before I even opened my first file, a group of women who started giggling like schoolgirls distracted me, whispering things like, "He's hot...let's get his attention...ask him to sit with us."

I couldn't help laughing, and being the curious type, I had to look. Shifting my eyes away from the screen, I peeked up to see him standing in line. He was wearing an Angels baseball cap, a dark gray sweater, and jeans. Nicely built, he was tall with broad shoulders, and an ass anyone would love to squeeze. He was definitely swoon-worthy from the back. He reminded me of someone, but I couldn't figure out who.

When he turned to the side and winked at the ladies who were ogling him, my heart did a funny flip and I died right then and there. Actually, I wanted to bolt out the door, but he would see me. Oh God! I didn't want to see Matthew again after our last encounter. That's when he had told me to wash his sweater after I purposely, though I made it look like an accident, dumped the leftovers on him.

Not only that, he had the audacity to ask me out. If he looked a little more to his left, he would see me staring at him, so I shot my eyes down to the screen. Ducking my head as low as I could without making it obvious, I prayed that he wouldn't see me.

I didn't know why I felt this way around him. My heart fluttered and butterflies danced inside my stomach. In all my dating years, I had never been like this in front of a guy. In fact, I made the boys feel like how I'm feeling right now. Damn! I had to break out of it somehow. This feeling was too much for me to handle and I didn't like it at all.

Hearing the cashier giggle meant only one thing. She was flirting with him or vice versa, but I didn't care. I just wanted him gone. When I heard his footsteps, I held my breath, hoping he wouldn't notice me. I didn't know what he would say or do, but from what I recalled of our last confrontation, he would probably say something egotistical and get me all riled up.

When he passed by, I slowly exhaled the breath I was holding, knowing he would be gone as soon as I felt the cold breeze from the door swinging open. I couldn't understand how his mere presence sent blazing heat through every inch of me. Just when my heart had settled down, the chair across from me slid out. How rude!

He or she didn't even ask if the seat was taken. Great! Playing the same game, I refused to look up and acknowledge the uncouth person. After a few seconds, a sound vibrated through my ear. He was definitely male judging from the deep sound of him clearing his throat. Thinking he was doing it out of impulse or simply something in his throat, I ignored him until he did it again, begging for my attention. He nudged his feet lightly against mine at the same time.

With a huff, I flashed my eyes directly into his and heat infused through me. I couldn't look away; I think I even drooled a little. As I desperately tried to break away from the spellbinding trance he had over me, I couldn't move or speak until his deep voice and that sexy grin snapped me out of it…somewhat.

"Hello, Becca." He dragged the last sound of my name out as if it was the ending of a song. Leaning toward me, he crossed his arms on the table and checked me out. I wore a fitted black sweat suit from Victoria's Secret, and my hair was tied in a high ponytail.

Feeling his eyes practically undressing me, and irate that he called me by the wrong name, I spoke out. "I don't know who you have confused me with, but I'm not Becca. My name is Becky," I scowled.

"Don't worry. I remember your name, and I never forget a pretty face. I just like to call you Becca. It's cute. It has a nice ring to it."

"Then don't expect me to answer." Did he say I was pretty?

Matthew ignored my last comment, reached over to grab my cup, and took a long whiff. "Hazelnut, such a girly drink." Then he placed it down and took a sip of his. Watching him made me thirsty, so I took one too. "Becca, what are you doing?" His eyes burned through the computer screen…actually through me.

"None of your business," I snapped lightly, so he would get the point that I didn't want to be bothered.

Matthew beamed a mischievous grin that caused all sorts of funny flips in my stomach. He was simply gorgeous. "I made you answer when I called you Becca."

Grrr! He was right; I did. Knowing he had the upper hand, I changed the subject. "Do you mind? I have work to do. Some of us actually have to work."

His eyebrows narrowed together, pinching in the center. A part of me felt bad. I shouldn't have said that, but then again, that's what he got for being an ass—albeit a *hot* ass.

"You shouldn't read on the computer screen so much. It's not good for your eyes." Matthew leaned back into his chair, spreading his long legs, while his eyes continued to fixate on me.

Not knowing how to respond, I decided to ignore him and shifted my eyes back to the screen. I'd hoped he would get the point that I wasn't in a talking mood. Actually, my nerves were unsteady and I didn't know what to say, but he kept right on rolling with whatever he thought this was. Matthew tapped my shoes with his, making me look up at him. "You didn't answer me," he said, giving me that sly grin.

I pulled my legs back so he couldn't touch me again. "Why don't you talk to those ladies behind you instead? I'm sure they have nothing better to do. Go bug them." I pointed to the table where the group of women sat. Their eyes never left him, and I could tell they were homing in on our conversation. Matthew didn't even bother to look in the direction I pointed. He didn't seem interested at all.

"I'd rather stay here. I think you like me here too." With his eyes intentionally locked on mine, he took a big gulp of his drink, and EVER so slowly, licked away some that escaped with a long, seductive stroke of his tongue. Watching him made me quiver *everywhere*. My face became as hot as my drink, and naughty thoughts rushed through my mind...I wanted to be the cup he just licked.

Managing to snap out of my trance, I said hastily, "Fine. Suit yourself. I'm not going to talk to you." My eyes went straight to my laptop, but since I was dying to know, I asked him a question. "Why are you even here? You don't live near here."

"I thought you weren't talking to me?" he smirked, but he continued. "Max asked me to stop by your place and bring some files over. We have some business to discuss." He leaned over. "I actually work for a living, too, in case you didn't know, but I also like to have lots of fun. I could show you what I mean someday."

I stared at him as my jaw dropped. Show me what fun meant? I didn't need him to show me. I practically invented the word. No way would I allow this arrogant jerk to show me what he meant by fun.

"I don't think so," I replied with a sting of attitude.

Without a comeback, Matthew stood up, shifted his baseball cap and quietly pushed his chair back in while I watched his every move, trying not to make it obvious. "Gotta run. Duty calls. Have a nice day."

"How long will you be in my apartment?" I asked casually.

"Couple of hours, I suppose. Why? Would you like me to stay longer?"

"No. I just wanted to calculate how long I need to be here so I don't run into you again," I said in monotone, with a twitch of a brow — playful yet serious.

He let out a chuckle. "That's a first."

What did he mean by that? When I thought he was out the door, I took in a deep breath. He was stealing my oxygen and I didn't even know it…that thief. He even took a piece of me with him, but I didn't know what it was. All I knew was that I kind of missed his presence and our awkward, not-so-friendly conversation.

I was just about to click on a query letter when a

shadow loomed over me, getting smaller. "Looks like an important document. I like what you're reading. The file must be called the blank screen," he whispered in my ear. His hot breath brushed against the side of my neck and heat rushed to the core of my being, making me dissolve into the chair. I didn't want him to stop.

When he opened the door, the cool draft took his warmth away. I was upset at myself; now he knew I had nothing on my screen. I was also sure he knew I was too nervous around him to even *think* of work. Freakin' great!

Chapter 3
Jenna

It had been a week since I was released from the hospital. Max came over every single day to take care of me, even though I was perfectly fine on my own. I also had Becky if I needed anything. Max threatened to hire a full time nurse if I didn't cooperate, which would have been a waste of money, so I agreed. My sweet Max; he was too good to be true, but sometimes too much to handle.

Matthew came over on several occasions to discuss work, but somehow Becky always managed to have scheduled a meeting or something. I had a strange feeling she purposely avoided him, and I knew why. I assumed she had a crush on him, since I had never seen her act so nervous around a guy before.

Max and Matthew decided I should transfer to Matthew's department, which I was thrilled about. I would be helping him with the layout of the magazine and I couldn't wait to get back to work. Since I would be under Matthew's supervision, Max agreed that I could start as soon as he felt I was ready. I was one hundred percent ready to get out of the apartment and get back to reality. I just needed a car.

"Ready for car shopping, Jenna?" Max asked, standing against the doorframe, looking as handsome as ever.

Max dressed casually today—a pair of jeans and a V-neck brown sweater that hugged his firm chest nicely. Since Max hardly wore a jacket, the fact that he wore one today indicated it must be freezing outside.

As if time stood still, I took a moment to stare at this gorgeous man, taking a mental picture of him in my mind. He was too good to be true; not only did he have the most generous heart; he was so good to me. Occasionally, I would wonder if I had dreamed him up.

Perfectly combed, Max's hair was never out of place. His smooth, clean-shaven face made me miss that gruffly, sexy, I-don't-give-a-crap appearance, but then again, he looked delicious either way. Every time I looked at him, I saw a respectable, genuine, powerful, possessive, and sexy man. To put it in easy words, Max was hot, and I could never help the direction my thoughts took around him. I loved the way he made me feel when he kissed me, touched me, and especially when he was inside me. I could already feel that electrifying sensation, and he hadn't even touched me yet.

"Ready as ever," I cheered.

Max helped me slip into my long coat. After grabbing my purse, I shouted goodbye to Becky, though I didn't know if she heard me since she hadn't come out of her room.

Several days before, I had explained to Max what kind of car would fit my budget. He had agreed, but somehow we ended up at the BMW dealer. Was he looking for a car for himself? Surely, he remembered we were supposed to be shopping for me.

"Max, what are we doing here?" I stepped out of the car and gladly took his extended hand.

Without answering, he wrapped his arms around me

and tried to block the freezing wind that whipped around us while he led the way. An employee held open the double glass door for us as we entered. Talk about customer service.

"Good morning, Mr. Knight," a salesman greeted, coming toward us with a huge, warm grin. He offered his hand to Max. "It's good to see you again."

"Kenny," Max said, shaking his hand, then he turned his attention to me. "This is Jenna." From their friendly greeting, I assumed Max had been there many times before.

"Hello, Jenna." Kenny took my hand and gave me the biggest grin. After the polite professional greeting, he led us toward the back.

"Max, where are we going and why are we here?" I narrowed my eyes at him. He was up to something and he didn't let me know what. Lacing his fingers through mine, we followed behind Kenny.

"I'm leasing a car for work…for you," he whispered in my ear.

I halted, but my body weight did nothing to anchor him. Pulling me to his chest, he tried to calm me down by caressing my arm as we continued to follow Kenny.

"I can't take the car." My tone was intense, but soft. I didn't want to make a scene.

"It will belong to the company. You'll be driving around for meetings. It's the company policy. We'll be paying for your gas and insurance too."

Though I liked the sound of everything he told me, I wasn't sure if it was the company's policy or his. "Then why didn't you let me know?"

"Would you have come if I told you?" He planted his lips on my forehead when I frowned.

"No." I pouted as we stepped out to a lot full of cars.

"Don't pout, Jenna. You make me all crazy inside and if you don't cooperate, I'll make a scene." He winked, giving me that wicked sexy grin.

Already weakened by the wink, I didn't say a word.

"Here is the beauty," Kenny exclaimed, opening the passenger door, and giving us space to peek inside.

"What do you think, Jenna?" Max asked. He looked so proud; I couldn't break his bubble.

"It's beautiful," I replied, and it was. "It's perfect." It was sleek, black with black leather interior.

"Come sit inside with me," Max ordered politely, forcing me into the driver's seat. "You need to feel the car."

I never knew what it was about men and their cars, but for me, I only needed something reliable and I'd be perfectly happy. After admiring the inside — the dashboard, the high tech gadgets, and the smooth steering wheel with wood trim, Max asked me to turn on the engine and we went for a test drive. I had to admit, I didn't want to let go of this car. The ride was smooth, sturdy, and it turned the corner as if it were gliding on air. Yup, I liked this car way too much.

If I compared the car to a woman the way most men did, I would say the curve of her luscious body would make any man stop dead. Just one look would leave him greedily wishing for one. The engine purred softly like a kitten, but roared like a lion when at full speed. The tantalizing package could make someone explode with hunger and want.

Max never took his eyes off me as I drove. I think I know why. I knew for sure I had the happiest grin on my face. I must have looked like a little girl who'd opened up a brand new beautiful doll and it wasn't even Christmas. After I parked the car back at the dealership, we headed to

Kenny's office.

After pulling out a chair for me, Max pulled out his. I thought about how we were still at the dating stage and wondered when or if Max would stop pulling out chairs for me like a perfect gentleman. Most guys I'd seen stopped acting charismatic when they officially became a couple, but I hoped Max never would.

"We just need to take care of some little details. We can finish the rest of the paperwork with your secretary, Mr. Knight, if that is what you prefer." Kenny muttered, shuffling papers in front of him.

"Thank you," Max said. "We do have things to do."

"Great. I just need to know what color."

Max looked at me for an answer, but instead of giving him one, I kept my lips sealed. Feeling somewhat annoyed at him for not letting me know about all this before we came, I decided to be a little naughty and playful.

"What color would you like, Jenna?" Max asked.

"Orange," I said, crossing my arms.

He raised his brow at me while the corner of his lips curled, and his expression stayed there longer than I had expected it to. Turning to Kenny, he said, "Black."

"Black," Kenny repeated, typing something on his computer, then turned to Max again. "How about the color of the interior?"

"Lime green," I sputtered.

Max tilted his head and gave me a hot, evil grin, as if he was going to punish me. "Black," he said to Kenny.

"Black," Kenny repeated. Then he asked a bunch of other short questions about window tinting, navigator, and other requests I had no desire to pay attention to. Since I wasn't cooperating, Max stopped asking me what I wanted. I couldn't believe I was acting like a child, especially in front of Kenny.

After they completed the deal, Max and I shook Kenny's hand; he held the most amusing grin on his face, as if he had just watched a comedy show.

When we got to Max's Porsche, he opened the passenger door for me, and then walked around to get into the driver's side. "I hope you like your orange car, babe," he said, chuckling lightly.

I wanted to thank him, but at the same time, I felt so guilty. "Max, I can afford my own car. Was it because I told you I could only get a specific kind? You've already done so much for me. I can't take this, too. I feel awfully guilty."

Max cupped my face with both of his hands. "Don't feel that way. I want to take care of you. Let me make you happy; that makes me happy too. Don't take it away." Sighing, he placed his forehead on mine, then his lips tenderly stroked mine. It was so soft and gentle, yet powerful, making me want more. When he pulled away, I slowly broke out of my daze and watched him do the same, as his eyes set on mine with lust, waiting for my reply.

After what he had just said, how could I refuse? I wanted to make him happy and if a car was one way, then I would have to let it go. "Okay," I sighed, but I barely got the word out. Max was already devouring me with his lips again. Shortly after, he let go with the pull of his teeth on my bottom lip. A soft, sensual growl escaped his mouth while his hand ran over my breast, and then stopped.

"I don't want to give them a free show," he said. "Let's get out of here before I really give them one."

"Where are we going?" I asked, feeling electric tingles throughout my body.

"Back to our place, Ms. Mefferd. You've been very naughty today. You have no idea how turned on I am right now. I'm going to have to punish you until you can't take it anymore." Then he drove off with the thunderous roar coming from his car.

Holy Jesus! I thought I'd just combusted from his hot words and the anticipation of what he was about to do to me.

Chapter 4
Becky

Max and Jenna had gone car shopping so I had the apartment to myself. I didn't mind having Max over, but it was nice to have some solitude.

I hadn't planned on going out, so I stayed in my PJs and didn't even bother to brush my hair. Looking at myself in the mirror, I saw my hair was wild, kind of sexy, and made me look like a hooker. Laughing, I grabbed my empty water glass from last night and headed toward the kitchen. The aroma of my favorite thing to eat for breakfast filled my nostrils, and my stomach cramped deeply with hunger.

Wow, how strange! Someone was cooking. Had I misunderstood Jenna? I could've sworn they'd left. Feeling groggy, I didn't even bother to reply back when she had said she was leaving. I figured she would assume I was asleep since I didn't answer.

"Jenna?" I murmured. I started blinking, wondering if what I saw was real. A stranger loomed in front of me, I was about to scream when I realized I knew that masculine figure. I took in how good he looked in dark navy slacks and a pin striped, black and blue dress shirt. He had the sleeves rolled midway up his arms. The shirt clung nicely to his upper body, and he was way too sexy for my eyes. Matthew was cooking. He was using my kitchen utensils and my food without even asking.

"Wh…wh…what are you doing here and h…how did you get inside?" I stuttered. Then the empty glass slipped out of my hand, crashing onto the floor and splattering glass shards around me.

He flinched, and then his vision went straight to my top, then down to the floor. Shit! I wasn't wearing a bra and my T-shirt was form-fitting and midriff-baring.

"Sorry to scare you." He reached for the broom that was in the space between the refrigerator and the stove. "Max and Jenna let me in. I stopped by to bring you a cup of hazelnut, and since I hadn't eaten breakfast, I assumed you hadn't either. I thought I'd cook some for us."

He brought me a cup of my favorite coffee and he cooked me eggs? No guy had ever cooked for me before. No guy ever bothered to find out my favorite coffee either; recalling when he smelled my coffee at our last encounter…that was smooth.

When he came toward me, I crossed my arms and retreated, uncertain how much of my breasts he saw. That's when I jerked my leg up and yelped in pain. I had stepped on glass while barefoot.

Matthew's expression turned from boyish grin to a look of concern. "Don't move. Let me help you."

I wanted to refuse, the blood pooling under my foot made me so nauseous I had no other choice. Planting my hand on the cabinet door for support, I waited for Matthew's help. Quickly he swept a clear path on the floor. With one effortless move, he picked me up and headed for my bedroom.

As he carried me, I held my breath in fear that somehow I would let him know I was attracted to him. His bulging muscles flexed against my back as he held me steady. When he laid me down on my unmade bed, I thought about pulling him on top of me and making it look like I had accidently done it, but I resisted by looking away. If I looked him in the eyes, I would never want to look away.

Since I still had my arms crossed over my breasts, he covered them with my blanket. That was considerate of him, since most men I knew would be gawking. Especially since I'd been told I had a "nice set" that many women envied. I was also impressed at how calm he was and how willing to take care of me.

"Where are your medical supplies?" Matthew raked his hair back, causing his hard toned muscles to flex as he looked concerned.

I hoped he wouldn't do that again. He did it so appealingly. "In the kitchen. Top right cabinet over the sink."

Matthew headed to the kitchen. After the sound of a few cabinets opening and closing, he came back with a small bag and some paper towels.

"This is going to hurt, just a little. I'm going to have to take out the glass."

"Okay," I nodded. Though the pain was bearable compared to the first initial stab, the sight of blood got me all riled up. I could never be a nurse or any profession that involved seeing blood.

After Matthew took the glass out, he cleaned my wound, wrapped a bandage over it, and left the room. I heard him back in the kitchen, so I assumed he was cleaning the mess for me. He wasn't a big jerk after all. After I changed my top, I hobbled to the table where he set the dishes of eggs and coffee. "Thank you," I said sincerely, getting lost in his hazel eyes.

Looking through his thick, long eyelashes, he winked at me, making my heart skip a beat. I had to stop allowing myself to feel these feelings. He was Max's brother and he would be around a lot, so I would have to get used to his presence and try to be his friend.

"Becca, what do you do exactly? I mean I know you're an agent, but I really don't know what agents do," he asked, giving me his full attention after he shoved a forkful of eggs in his mouth.

After swallowing the rich, sweet coffee, I explained. He asked me if he could read some of the query letters, and of course, I told him they were confidential. He gave me a frown that was too adorable, so I focused on his chest. Big mistake. Then I couldn't stop staring at his pecs.

When he probed with more questions about what I looked for in query letters, I told him I liked romance novels and that I basically looked for potential book boyfriends.

"Book boyfriends?" He chuckled. As I watched, his chest moved to the rhythm of his laugh. "Really?" He took his last bite and chugged his coffee.

"Yes, really." I had already finished my plate since I was too nervous to talk.

"Is that like for people who can't get one in real life?" He was totally amused by the notion.

"No, silly." I giggled. "Readers want books that help them escape from the daily routine of life. Many of these romance books have a swoon-worthy, gorgeous guy with six pack abs, who can deliver wild, hot sex." The thought made me turn red, and I froze when he gave me a heated look. Then his eyes concentrated on my lips, shifted to my breasts, then back up to my eyes. When I said 'wild, hot sex,' I just described him and what he could potentially do for me.

Gravitating toward me, his eyes locked lustfully on mine. His lips were inches away as they parted to speak, and I didn't know how he got so close to me. "I would like to be your book boyfriend," he said with the hottest sound that could sing out of his luscious, lick-able mouth. The puff of his breath on my lips sizzled way down to my sex. He reached out to my face, his thumb sensually sliding, feather-light to touch my bottom lip with one long, slow stroke. As I watched his tongue glide over his bottom lip at the same time, I quivered beyond control.

Completely dumbfounded, I sat there staring at him and in my mind, I had already taken off my clothes for him. Blinking because that was all I could do, I wanted to say yes, but my pride and my head knew better and stopped me.

He broke his gaze and it felt like he had dumped ice water over my head. "Is that what a book boyfriend would say and do?" he chuckled as he picked up our plates and took them to the kitchen.

What just happened? My face must have been deep red, because I felt it down to my toes. Was this how Jenna felt when she drank alcohol? Matthew came back and leaned against the wall by the television, looking so dreamy with his hands in his pocket. "I think you'll be fine, but if it doesn't start to heal or if the bleeding gets worse, you should ask Jenna to take you to the hospital. If she's busy, then you can ask me."

"I'm sure it's fine," I said, thinking how sweet that he'd offered. "I'll just be hopping around for a couple of days. Thanks for the eggs and the coffee, and thanks for helping me. I'm not good with blood." Though I wouldn't have broken the glass if he weren't here in the first place, so it was his fault, but I sure didn't mind him carrying me.

"I noticed." His lips curled into an amused smile, flashing his white teeth. "Anyway, I'd better go. Max and Jenna are taking too long. They should have been back by now. Max had already set up the whole deal before they went to take a look." He paused and a brow lifted. "Unless…they took a detour."

Looking at my confused expression since I had no idea what he was talking about, he put on the suit jacket that was slung on the sofa and started to step toward the door. "If they stop by, can you tell them…never mind, I'll just text Max." Placing his hand on the doorknob, he turned to see me right behind him. "So, book boyfriend, huh?"

"What?"

"You like wild, hot sex?"

"What? No. I didn't say me," I stammered and laid a light punch on his arm.

He chuckled at my effort. "Well I don't need a *book* girlfriend, that's for sure. See you around, Becca. Some of us actually have work to do and don't get to stare at blank screens. Oh, and don't look at my ass while I walk out the door. You'll turn me on." After he winked, he left.

His words should have annoyed me, but instead, I was turned on; and guilty as charged because he was right, I looked. He looked so damn hot in that suit that I would have to be a freak not to look. I wanted to peel it off him slowly and enjoy every inch of him. His last comment seriously gave me hot flashes. From the moment we met, he turned me on, but I would never feed into his ego. Oh, but what an arrogant, sexy, hot ass!

Chapter 5
Jenna

Christmas was just around the corner and I still hadn't gotten anything for Max. I had planned to go visit my parents, but Max was adamant that I shouldn't fly, so I persuaded my parents to come to Los Angeles. I was glad Max convinced me to ask them to come. Since Becky wasn't traveling to her parents, it would mean we would get to celebrate together with Nicole and Kate, too.

It had been a while since the four of us went out to dinner, so we agreed to meet tonight. It was the first night Max wouldn't sleep at my apartment since the accident. Becky would be happy about that. Not that she minded him coming over, but it would give us time to catch up and hang out.

"So...he leased a 740 Beemer for you?" Nicole exclaimed, twirling her straw. "That is so sweet. Those cost a fortune."

"I wouldn't have protested, but knowing Jenna, I'm sure she did. Didn't ya?" Kate asked.

"Of course I did, but somehow Max always gets his way. I mean, not always, but with things like this. He said it makes him happy," I explained, looking at my menu. I was so full of excitement and nervousness about my new car, my stomach might not have room for food.

"Don't worry and don't feel guilty. It's leased, anyway. Make him happy," Becky said sharply.

We all looked at her, giving her the "what's up with you" look.

"What?" Becky snapped. "Why are you all looking at me like that? I'm just saying..."

Becky almost never used such a harsh tone.

"Are you okay?" Nicole asked.

"I'm fine...fine. Just a little stressed. I'm behind with my work," she said and hid behind her menu.

Something was bothering Becky for sure, but I couldn't tell what. She usually confided in me, but I hadn't been available much lately, and for that, I felt awful. I made a mental note to ask her later.

"Enjoy it while it lasts, honey, cause when you get married, it will be different." Kate paused. "Take the advice from a married woman, nothing stays forever. Things change, especially once you have a child."

"Like what?" Nicole inquired, breaking her eyes away from the menu.

We all leaned in closer with curiosity. "Well for one thing, Craig used to take care of me; he was always so attentive all the years we dated. Once we got married, I was the one taking care of him. Not only do I have a daughter, I've apparently gained a son, too."

"Have you spoken to him about it?" Nicole asked. "You already know Keith and I had a long talk and everything is better now. Men are what I would call non-intuitive. You have to tell them everything; spell it out. They don't understand. They are not the same species."

Kate looked flustered. Instead of responding, she continued. "I mean, is it so difficult to wash the damn dishes while I feed Kristen, change her diaper, and bathe her?" she huffed. "He just sits on his ass and watches television. His dirty socks are all over our bedroom and he leaves the newspaper on the couch. Do you know how much dirt and ink a newspaper leaves on a couch? I know he's had a long day at work, but it takes two people to raise a child, not just one. Sometimes I feel like I'm a single mom. I love Kristen, but I need a break too. Just because I don't work doesn't mean I'm not keeping up with my share of the responsibilities."

Kate's voice softened toward the end and her expression changed from being intense to relaxed. I guess she just needed to let off some steam. We all looked at her, but we couldn't give her any good advice, since none of us had been through it.

Nicole draped her arms around Kate. "Just talk to him. He doesn't know how you feel."

"I so needed to be here with you guys. I need my girlfriend therapy. I love my life right now, even with these small problems, but sometimes I miss our college life," Kate continued.

"I know what you mean," Becky seconded, apparently thinking about those years too. "No responsibilities, no work...just going with the flow, living one day at a time, and definitely, all the parties."

"I hear ya," Nicole agreed. "But we've gotta move forward."

Our waitress came to take our order, interrupting the conversation.

"What do I feel like tonight?" Kate mumbled under her breath.

"I'm not that hungry. Let's do family style," I suggested.

"Sure," they all said in accord.

We placed our order and the waitress left.

The ride to our apartment was quiet. I was too busy concentrating on driving, while Becky had focused her attention outside the window. Feeling the tension in the air, I wasn't sure how to start the conversation. When we stepped into the apartment, I didn't want Becky to go straight to her room, so I asked her if she'd like some tea. Accepting my offer, Becky sat at the dining table while I prepared the drinks.

Placing the hot mug in front of her, I sat in the opposite chair in front of beautiful red roses in a vase with a big red bow tied around it. I loved how they filled the room with their sweet scent. "Are these yours?" I asked.

"Oh, I completely forgot." Becky ran her fingers through her hair, looking tired "They were delivered this afternoon. They're for you."

"For me?" I questioned. Only one person would send red roses to me, but they didn't look like the roses he usually sent; these were much smaller. Still smiling, I opened the envelope and began to read the card.

Jenna,
I've made a huge mistake.
Please give me another chance.
Think about it.
Miss you,
Luke

"What's wrong Jenna?" Becky asked quickly. She must have seen the disturbed look on my face when I crumbled up the note.

Matching her eyes, I sat on the cushion and mumbled unhappily, "They're from Luke."

Becky had the most disgusted expression on her face. "Now he sends you flowers? He should've treated you better when you were together. Just tell him to get lost! You're not thinking of giving him another chance, are you?"

"No, of course not," I shook my head. "I would be crazy if I did. Max is wonderful. He is everything I could ever ask for. Luke has been texting me almost on a daily basis. I told him I was seeing Max, but that doesn't stop him. I ignore his texts, but I don't know what else to do."

"It's a good thing Max isn't here right now. He would totally flip out."

"True," I agreed, then took a sip of my tea, which warmed me up. "I don't want to throw them away. It would be such a waste, but I don't want Max to see them."

"Then keep the flowers and throw away the card. If he asks, tell him they're for me."

"Are you sure?"

"What are friends for," she winked.

Speaking of being friends, I needed to change the subject. It had been about me since Max entered my life. I needed to be there for her now. "Becky," I called softly, getting her attention once more. "What's wrong? You hardly said a word in the car."

"Nothing."

"I can read you like a book...well, almost."

"Really, it's nothing." She said it as if she meant it, but I knew better; and I wasn't going to give up. "I just have a lot on my mind," she continued. "I go through this guilt trip when I turn down a potential author. I feel like I'm taking away their dream." She brought her mug to her lips and blew away some steam.

"I'm sure they'll get picked up by another agent." I had no doubt this wasn't the reason for her foul mood, but I played along. "You can't say yes to all of them. It's like interviewing for a job. One person gets the spot."

"Yeah, I know," she sighed, shrugging. Taking a sip, she seemed to relax as the warm tea went down her throat.

"So I've been meaning to ask you about Ryan."

"Who?"

"You know, the guy you were so excited to see over Thanksgiving? Did you two hit it off?" I plopped my feet up on the seat and pulled my knees closer to me as I shivered. It was freezing out today and we had just turned on the heater as we walked in.

"Oh, him. He asked me out, but"—her finger slid around the rim of her mug while her eyes followed—"there was no spark, no chemistry…nothing. Shoot, my book boyfriends were even hotter than him," she giggled, evidently thinking of something or someone else.

She stared off, lost in thought. "Are you okay?"

Becky didn't answer my question, but instead she asked, "Do you know why I needed a roommate?"

"No, I didn't care about why. I was desperate. You and I had just met and I really needed a place to stay. I couldn't stay at my apartment after what had happened with my roommate and my ex."

"I needed one because my roommate got into a car accident. She died in the hospital."

The blood drained out of my face, probably leaving it white as the wall behind me. Not too long ago I was in the hospital. Becky must have gone through such a rough time, especially since it must have reminded her of the tragic loss. Maybe that was the reason Becky's mood had been so unsteady lately. It started the day after I came home from the hospital. "I'm so sorry, Becky." I ran to her and held her tightly.

"There's more." Her head stuck up from the empty space around my arm. Releasing her, I pulled out the chair next to her and listened intently. "She died because of me. I let her drive drunk. It was my fault." Tears started to flow down her cheeks. "I was pretty wasted myself, but I knew enough not to get in the car with her. I tried everything to get her out of the car, but she wouldn't listen and I couldn't think straight. I realized too late that I should have taken her car keys."

"Becky, it's not your fault. You can't blame this on yourself. That is too much of a burden."

She wiped her tears, brought her knees up to her chest and started to rock slowly.

"I know…but I know you wouldn't have let me drive," she said with conviction, looking right at me.

"Of course I wouldn't now, but who is to say what I would have done back then? We're more mature now and we know better. There are things that we'll always regret. Hopefully not too many; but in the end, it all comes down to the decisions we make as individuals. You tried to stop your friend, but she chose to drive drunk. Just like you didn't force me to give Max a chance, but I did. You were certainly an influence, but you didn't make me. We learn from the past to make the future better, okay?"

Becky nodded, but I wasn't sure if she believed me. "I didn't tell you because I didn't want you to think I would make an awful friend or roommate."

"And if you had told me years ago, I would still be around and still be thinking you're the best friend anyone could wish for." I dove in for another hug and held her until she let go.

"Thanks," she said, wiping her tears again. "I needed that."

"You can tell me anything; I'll never judge you."

"I know. That's why I love you," Becky said, giving me the most heartfelt smile.

I'm glad we had that talk. The guilt must have been eating her up all these years. Then I wondered if some of her behaviors that I had often questioned were her way of coping with that guilt. The excessive drinking, going through boys like they were nothing…maybe hoping for the one who would help her forget.

It was close to midnight and tomorrow would be my first day back at work. I had promised Max I would spend the night, so after Becky headed for her room, I headed to Max's place.

Chapter 6
Becky

I felt better getting that off my chest, but I hadn't told Jenna the whole truth. I failed to mention my roommate had killed someone else in that accident. She wouldn't judge me, but I needed to come to terms with my own guilt.

After giving offers to several excited authors, I headed out to the mall. I needed to mail my parents' gifts and get something especially nice for Jenna, Nicole, and Kate. There was still a week and a half left until Christmas, but the closer it got, the crazier the mall would be: limited parking spaces, long lines, and swarms of people with bad, grumpy manners.

Everywhere I looked, red and green Christmas decorations adorned the walls and doors of every store. Parents braved a seemingly endless line with their children to take a picture with Mr. Fake Santa Claus, who looked rigid and bored. As the Christmas music resonated throughout the mall, it filled my heart with a giddy feeling, and I couldn't help but sing along.

Entering Nordstrom, the bright colors caught my eye. A table held neatly folded cashmere scarves lined up in rows, and more hung on a rack adjacent to the table. This was going to be easy. I excitedly thumbed through the layers. They were simple, solid colors, but elegant. Buying a gift I knew they would love gave me a huge thrill, and I was beyond happy that I could get the shopping out of the way this quickly.

I bought a purple one for Nicole and red for Kate, but I waffled on Jenna. Then a thought jolted my mind. Not only did I want to make her blush, I wanted to buy something she could use. Oh, I couldn't wait! Holding the shopping bag with two Nordstrom boxes inside, I dashed to Victoria's Secret.

There were so many options for sexy lingerie that it was difficult to pick just one. I finally picked a black negligee with spaghetti straps, low cut to show cleavage, with lace trim on the bottom. It was perfect. Taking it to the mirror, I draped it on my body. Yup, it would drive Max crazy seeing this on Jenna.

I froze when I heard a soft wolf whistle. No single man would dare come in here alone, so what jackass was standing behind me when he was already taken? I hoped his girlfriend smacked him hard.

Still looking in the mirror, I slowly lifted my eyes the length of his body, checking him out. I saw long legs, tight abs, nice biceps, and oh God! Blistering heat flushed from my head to my toes. Mortified, I turned to him as my breath stuck in my throat, unable to meet his eyes. "Umm…Matthew…wh…what are you doing here?" I hardly knew what I was saying. He stepped closer, as if he wanted me to repeat my words, or was he checking to see how red I was.

"Awww," he pouted like a child who had his favorite toy taken away. "I was enjoying myself."

His flirting made me blush even more, so I wanted to return the favor. I stepped forward, closing the space between us, and held my bold stare. "Do you shop here often or is this your regular hang out?"

My question had no effect. Instead, he lifted the corner of his lips and gave me the most delicious, wicked grin. "Only when I get to see one of those draped on a beautiful live model."

Did he just call me beautiful? Damn! My face warmed again, and I noted some curious customers' eyes gazing at us. "Ummm…" I blinked and refocused. "I wasn't buying it for me. I'm buying it for Jenna as a Christmas present."

"Lucky Max."

Despite myself, that made me giggle.

He smirked and his eyes glinted flirtatiously. "If you want, you can go try it on and show it to me. I'll let you know if Max will like it on Jenna."

"What? In your dreams," I said flatly, turning away from him to pick up my pace toward the cashier.

Thankfully, there was no line so I went straight to the register. As the cashier rang me up, she kept looking behind me with a flirtatious smile that begged for attention. Whoever was behind me in line must have been hot for her to gush like that.

After she gave me back my credit card, I reached for the bag, but before I could grab it, someone behind me snatched it instead. As I turned to see who would take my bag, I smacked into his hard chest.

"Whoa…steady. I wasn't going to steal it," he said, wrapping an arm around me to keep me from falling.

I sucked in air as I dissolved into Matthew's embrace. He was the sizzling sun and I was ice, unable to move, melting into his warmth. As my chest heaved, my knees became weak and I saw nothing but his beautiful eyes staring intently back at me, willing me to see nothing but him. Nobody else existed in our own little enclosed world.

It lasted a few brief seconds, but it seemed timeless until he spoke and released me.

"Here, let me take the other bag for you," he said.

My eyes moved from my hand to his as he took possession of my packages. Then his fingers laced through mine tightly as he led me out the door.

Focusing on our intertwined hands, I felt so incredibly good. Wait—what the hell? After the initial shock of what had happened wore off, I yanked my hand away and halted.

Matthew turned to me and gave me a surprised look. "I'm just holding your hand. It isn't an invitation to sleep with me."

I looked at him with the most evil look I could give him. I couldn't believe he'd said that. The pleasant warmth from his hand became icy cold. Did he think we were going out? He didn't even ask me, and I wouldn't go out with him if he did. He was an arrogant jerk who seriously needed a massive scolding. "I can hold my own bags and I didn't give you permission to hold my hand. You must have tuned out when your mother taught about manners because your brother has them for sure," I stammered.

"Geez…you're feisty. Okay. I won't hold your hand, but I'm holding your bags for you. And no, I'm not like Max. I'm spoiled and I get what I want." He started walking away.

Was he trying to tell me he wanted me? "Where are we going?" I followed him, since he was holding my bags hostage.

"It's past noon. I'm hungry, and considering your grumpiness, you must be hungry, too."

He was right. As if to prove his point, my stomach cramped in hunger. After skipping breakfast this morning, I had forgotten to grab anything to eat since then. Knowing he wanted to eat lunch with me made my heart flutter, but at the same time, I didn't like the feeling. Nothing good could come of me having a secret crush on Matthew Knight. In the end, I would be the one who got hurt. Not only that, he was Max's brother. What if things went wrong? This was assuming he wanted to be more than friends, but what the hell was he doing trying to hold my hand?

As I followed Matthew to the food court, I couldn't stop staring at his perfect ass. Jeans never looked better. Looking like a runway model, he strode with his arms swinging behind his back while holding my two bags, his flexed biceps standing out even through his black sweater.

When we turned the corner, my nostrils immediately took in the aroma of all the food the stores had to offer. My stomach rumbled so loudly I was sure he had heard it when he turned to me. That, or was he making sure I still followed him, since I tried to stay as far back as possible.

"What would you like to eat?" he asked when I caught up to him.

I was so famished I didn't care. Instead of answering, I headed to the first place I saw and grabbed a tray. I didn't bother to ask him what he wanted or pay attention to where he headed. After I told the lady I wanted half and half—steamed rice and noodles, with beef and broccoli, orange chicken, and a bottle of water, I slid my tray to the cash register.

"I'll have the same thing she ordered," Matthew said to the lady.

He had apparently followed me there. Before I even had the chance to take out my wallet, he had already paid for the both of us. Blinking, I stared up at him with a glare.

"You didn't have to pay for me," I said lightly, not wanting to sound rude, but uncomfortable that he had. I didn't want to feel like I owed him a lunch in return.

"Of course I did. I made you mad, so I need to apologize to you with my presence," he chuckled.

My cheeks pinched inward, as I tried hard not to laugh. He was cute and he knew it. "You mean you're going to torture me with your presence. Is that how you apologize to people?"

"Maybe not torture, but punish instead." He slid the shopping bag handles through his arms, placed my plate on his tray, and led us to an empty table.

After we settled down, we each opened our own container and watched the steam escape. From the corner of my eye, I watched him slide the cover off the chopsticks, split them perfectly in the middle, and dive into the noodles. He handled his chopsticks like a pro, not an amateur like me.

Next thing I knew, he leaned over me from behind. Pressing his chest on my back, his arms wrapped around me, fingers touching fingers, showing me how to hold the chopsticks correctly. Heat infused and spread to the rest of my body. I couldn't concentrate on his demonstration or his words. All I felt was his body against mine, and I liked that feeling. His warm breath brushed the side of my neck when he spoke and I imagined him as a vampire, sinking his teeth into me. Oh, for heaven's sake…I had to stop thinking of the characters I was reading about.

"There. Isn't that much easier?"

Too afraid to turn to answer his question—if I did, his lips would touch my cheek or my lips, which wouldn't be so bad, but what was I thinking?—I stiffened, nodded, and that was my reply.

"So you like to read?" he asked, sitting across from me again. "Don't forget the middle finger in the center," he reminded, pointing to the chopstick.

"Yes." Shyness kept my answer short, which was unusual for me. I'm never like this around men. I'm usually the one that makes them lightheaded.

We continued to eat in silence for a while. Sometimes stolen glances passed between us. We were like two shy teenagers suffering through puppy love and we didn't know what to say. After Matthew swallowed, he spoke.

"Did you finish your Christmas shopping?"

"Yes," I replied, wondering where he was going with this. "How about you?"

"I think so. If not, there's always gift cards," he laughed.

I smiled at his comment. "Doesn't look like you shopped today. You don't have any shopping bags."

"I was distracted," he said, looking straight at me.

I think I swallowed my chicken without chewing. Not wanting to blush, I quickly asked him a question. "Don't you have to work today?"

"It's Jenna's first day back. Max will be with her, so I took the morning off. I hate shopping right before Christmas, but I can't seem to find anything today."

"I couldn't agree with you more," I mumbled under my breath, consciously aware of his eyes watching how I was using the chopsticks.

"Not bad." He winked.

Watching him wink at me tickled my stomach so much that my chopstick slipped and I lost my grip on the broccoli. Darn! It didn't matter anymore; we were both done with our lunch.

"Well, Becca, it was nice to see you unexpectedly. I

won't tell Jenna or Max what you got them for Christmas. I'm sure Max will enjoy it as much as she will." Standing up, he took both of our white lunch boxes and threw them away before I could.

"Thanks for lunch, Matthew," I said sincerely, standing up to retrieve my bags from him.

"Anytime you want to model Victoria's Secret lingerie and have a little bite afterward, just give me a call."

After I flashed my eyes to his, I dropped them from embarrassment. He did not just say that to me, did he? "Shut up," I said lightly, and slapped him across his arm.

He pretended the slap wounded him, and gave me my bags. "See ya around, Becca."

That time, I loved how my name rolled off his tongue, like a melody he knew all too well. Still standing there as he sauntered away, I looked over my shoulder before I could stop myself. He was actually walking backward, unmistakably checking me out. When his eyes met mine, he winked once more and mouthed, "Nice ass, Victoria's Secret model." Then he turned the corner.

Not only did I giggle like a school girl, I was too afraid to move a muscle. Too afraid he would know he had completely unglued me with his words and unraveled me with his eyes. Those piercing, drop-dead, gorgeous hazel eyes, caressing every inch of me, producing wicked thoughts in my mind that I didn't want to have.

Chapter 7
Jenna

Being back to work after a two week absence made me jittery. Though the employees had no idea what had happened, I was still a nervous wreck. Max had informed everyone by email that I would be working from home on a special project. I wondered if they'd thought otherwise or questioned the meaning of "special project."

Before heading to Max's office, I stopped by the customer service department I used to work in. I told them I would be right upstairs or a phone call away if they needed me. A part of me felt somber to be leaving them. In the short amount of time I had been there, I enjoyed their friendship, especially with Lisa. I promised I'd join them for lunch when I had the chance.

I also convinced Max to promote Lisa to my old position. She was not only professional, but she definitely proved she could hold down the fort while I was away. Max listened to my suggestion and made it happen. Lisa thanked me repeatedly, but I told her she deserved it, and her expertise and knowledge got her the position.

Until late afternoon, Max trained me how to lay the design on formatted pages. Everything was done through the set of layouts on the computer, which made it easier for me. I would be working closely with Matthew and other employees I had yet to meet, since I was still in Max's office.

"You know, Matthew should really be the one to teach me all this stuff," I said. Sitting on his lap, I had my legs tucked under the desk. He practically held me hostage, but I didn't mind.

"Matthew doesn't know everything. I do. I've been here the longest and I've done everything, or almost everything. Not your old position. I don't answer the phones."

"Confident," I spit out.

Max chuckled, making my body shake with him, and then he tilted his head and gave me a peck on my cheek. "I guess I should be glad you didn't say arrogant." He typed a few words to show me how it could look on page ten. "And besides, I like to have you all to myself."

"You have to share me when we come to work, Max."

His arms swung around my waist. "Only when I give my permission."

"Hmmm…"

Max pushed up from his feet and turned me around to the side but I managed to stay on his lap. "Okay, I will share you, but not every part of you." After squeezing my bottom, he slowly glided his hands up to my breasts and teasingly kneaded them. Then, with a naughty, satisfied grin, he buried his face in the open slit of my blouse. He was so good with his tongue and teeth that he managed to open a couple of buttons without any help from his fingers. "I'm not sharing these," he mumbled into my flesh as his wet kisses traveled from one nipple to the other, waiting eagerly for his tongue. My pulse raced and my heart pounded against my rib cage.

"Max," I moaned. When his hardness pressed against me, as his tongue played with my nipple, I moaned louder and tilted my head back. Thank goodness he had locked the door and this room was sound proof. "It's my first day back," I managed to say, losing any rational thought.

Effortlessly, Max lifted me up and before I knew it, I was standing in front of him, cradled in his arms. His aftershave, and the scent that was simply him, drove me wild.

"Let me welcome you on your first day back," he arched his brows playfully. "I just wanted to tease you a little, but now I think it's me who can't handle having you this close; and don't make that sound, Jenna. You're driving me crazy." Brushing my hair with his fingers, he kissed me tenderly. Then he let out a frustrated growl. "Maybe it'll be better when you are working upstairs. I can't think when you're in the same room or even on the same floor."

I scowled at him. "See, I told you Matthew should be the one to train me."

Max's sexy Adam's apple slightly vibrated when he chuckled as his hand glided down to my fingertips. I loved how his fingers twirled, flickered, teased and flirted with mine. He was good with his hands in more ways than one.

"He will tomorrow, when he comes back to work. He took the day off today. I have to go to a dinner meeting tonight. Do you have any plans?"

"I'm going to have dinner with Becky."

"Good. I approve of Becky being your dinner buddy. Will you be staying at our home tonight?"

His seductive eyes seared me; he licked my bottom lip with one long, slow stroke, while one of his hands caressed between my legs and the other squeezed my behind. Blazing, erotic heat shot to every part of my body and my knees buckled, but somehow I managed to mumble one word. "Yes."

Thank goodness I had slacks on, or I would have lifted

my skirt up myself, just to have him inside me. Max started to nip my jaw, sensually heading to my ear. As he teased with his tongue, he dropped words like breadcrumbs. "I...need...easy...access...Jenna. These pants...are no good." He tugged at my pants and made another annoyed sound.

Max retreated a step, staring at me with wanting, lustful eyes that blazed with searing heat. Gawking at me from head to toe, he left me feeling naked under his hypnotic gaze. When he looked at me like that, with possessiveness so powerful, I came completely undone. I'd lost all motor coordination and any coherent thought as I surrendered myself to him wholly. He could have stripped me naked on the spot if he wanted and I wouldn't have minded.

"I'll be thinking of you. See you at home, Ms. Mefferd." Walking backward, he winked and left the room.

Max called his penthouse our home, which I thought was sweet of him to say. Though he'd rather have me move in with him, my mind told me not to, at least not for a while, especially since we had only recently begun dating exclusively. He knew he was moving fast. I didn't mind as long as he understood the reason I didn't reciprocate was not that I didn't want to, but because I thought it would be best for us to take things slow. Nothing would come of acting as if we'd been dating for a couple of years when we hadn't.

Max left me completely sexually frustrated. Can a woman get "blue vagina" like a man got "blue balls?" The throbbing, flaming need between my legs was driving me insane; he had left me feeling unfulfilled on purpose. I thought walking would help drive that feeling away, so I headed to the restroom. What I really needed was a cold shower, even if I didn't think it would help.

Chapter 8
Jenna

I began to take in the new day as I groggily shifted my head on the pillow from side to side, recalling the wonderful dinner Becky and I had together. Fluttering my eyes open, I froze. I felt something…and it was growing. Growing…bigger…*bigger* within the palm of my hand. A soft, sensual groan filled my ears. *Oh my God.*

Before Max woke up, I needed to take my hands off him, but his hand clamped on top of mine, holding me in place. Heat rushed to my face and I was too embarrassed to turn my head to look at him. It wasn't as if I'd never touched him. I was just so shy when it came to taking the initiative.

"Good morning," he moaned, slightly chuckling. "Don't be shy, Jenna. I like your hand there. I think your hand likes it there, too. Your hand is becoming as mischievous as mine. I think they should play together and see how bad they can get…don't you think so?"

I had to admit, I liked my hand there maybe too much, but I couldn't speak. Oh God, oh God. I had to calm down. I buried my face into his chest so I wouldn't have to look at him, not to mention my stinky morning breath.

"Did you have a pleasant dream?" His tone was sincere yet playful.

I nodded, rubbing myself further into his chest for an answer. Finally letting go of my hand, he lifted himself over me. A blaze of heat shuddered down, practically curling my toes. The only barrier between us was a pair of thin silk shorts and my loose pajama top. Just his body over mine obliterated me, and I quivered with want.

"Open your eyes, Jenna. Don't be shy. You're beautiful," he said softly, slipping his hands to my cheeks.

He embarrassed me when he said things like that, but I managed to open my eyes, and gave him an innocent smile. "Good morning," I murmured, trying to keep my breath to myself, if that was possible, while his lips lingered over mine.

Max looked beyond good for so early in the morning, way too sexy. I wanted to run my fingers through his disheveled hair, but I stopped myself.

"Good morning, sunshine." His eyes were drunk with blissfulness and yearning as he stared back at me. He glowed from the sunlight that seeped through the window, perfectly outlining his body, looking like a mirage. Lost in his eyes, I sunk deeply into the mattress.

Purposely rubbing his hardness against me, his lips traced up my neck. "Do you want me inside you?" His hot breath scalded my ear, sending scorching fire straight between my legs and spreading through every fiber of my being.

As my nipples hardened, moaning sounds escaped my mouth. Unexpectedly, Max placed both of his hands around my waist, scooping me up into his arms.

"Where are we going?" I asked, breathlessly.

"To the shower, babe, a nice long, hot shower; and I'm not talking about the temperature. I'm going to wake you up. We need to get ready for work."

Oh shoot! I had forgotten about work. My eyes shot open, wide and alert from the reality of his words. Max must have felt my body tense.

"Don't worry. We have plenty of time to get to work now that you're working with my brother. But don't let him boss you around, or else I'll have some serious ass kicking to do."

Gently, he placed me down so my feet touched the cold marble of the shower floor. Though we stood in the middle, the water spouting out from the shower heads on both sides still didn't touch us.

After he tested the temperature, he stripped us both naked and pulled me into his chest under one spout. The warmth from the water and having Max's strong hands gliding over my back dissolved me. We had showered together many times, but it didn't matter; I was as shy as the first time.

Max poured the shampoo on my hair and started to massage my scalp. I was lost in his soothing touch, but the smell of lavender filling my nose awakened me. Shifting my body, I turned my back to his chest. He tilted my head and rinsed my hair. Then, he poured liquid soap into his hands and started lathering my neck, massaging my shoulders, and trailing down to my breasts. He glided down my stomach, around my butt, slowly sliding down my legs...gently, feather light, causing all sorts of hyper sensations.

The whole time his hands explored my body, my knees wanted to give out. Every muscle felt like jelly, and I couldn't control the urge any longer. Turning around, I slammed my mouth into his, taking in some water. As our tongues swirled and tasted each other, my hands ran over his hard chest, around his broad shoulders, and down his back. He had a body any man would die for and any woman would love to touch. I closed my eyes as I rubbed his erection, making him growl, a masculine sound that made me want him even more.

Max took a fist full of my hair and forced my mouth away from his. "What do you want, Jenna?" he whispered. His eyes were dark and full of lust.

Water dripped down his face like rain onto his hard, defined pecs. I wondered if he might disappear as I stared, mentally framing the incredibly sexy vision in my mind. Finally turning away from his gaze, I pressed my hand on the glass in front of me without answering him. Swaying seductively from side to side, I spread my legs and leaned forward so my ass thrust toward him.

A hot, territorial groan escaped Max's throat, and that alone made me combust. Rubbing his dick against my ass, teasing me, he took his time until I couldn't take it anymore. I turned my head to the side and looked at him. "Max," I managed to say, desperately asking him to be inside me with my yearning eyes.

He gave me a wicked grin and slapped my ass once at the same time he took me. The combination made me gasp so hard and fast, it sent erotic passion straight through to my core and had my head spinning. Gradually penetrating deeper, in and out, he slowly built me to climax. While pressing his chest on my back, he squeezed my nipple with one hand and the other teased the hell out of my clit. He knew exactly what to do to drive me crazy.

My ragged breath fogged up the glass, and my grip on his hand meant I couldn't take it any longer.

"You want it faster, Jenna?" he asked through his gritted teeth as he heaved through water dripping on his body. Nodding wasn't an answer for him. "Say it," he demanded, as he pumped a little faster, but not enough.

Max made it easy for me to build up the courage to ask for what I wanted. He was breaking me out of my shyness, and I loved every bit of it. It was a big step for me. I turned my head just enough for him to see my face, and finally, I demanded it. "Faster, Max."

That put a huge satisfied smile on his face and he didn't hesitate. He swung me around and lifted me up. My legs wrapped around his waist, my back anchored against the marble wall, and his hand on my behind supported my weight. Then he drove into me hard and fast. My center sizzled at first from the sensation, then pleasure exploded deliciously throughout my body so fast I thought I was going to detonate.

He rode me harder and faster, never taking his loving eyes off me, filling me until I couldn't take it anymore. My hands on his back clawed into him, and I knew I was digging too deep when he groaned. Still inside me, he shifted us over so my back slid against the glass.

The glass shook and vibrated from Max's rhythm, the same rhythm as my hammering heart, drumming delicious, pleasurable beats. I swear I thought the glass was going to shatter underneath us. Max sucked my lip as the water fell on our faces, and I sucked his back. We licked, nipped, and tasted each other as if we were starving. Our panting completely fogged up the glass.

While I closed my eyes, I dissolved into him. I let him take me, every single piece of me. Then I blissfully surrendered in his arms.

When Max moved away from me, my feet touched the ground and I watched him come all over me. I didn't mind; I wanted to feel every part of him. The water washed him away, and then Max held me tightly as our chests rapidly rose and fell together.

"That was amazing, Jenna." His breath was heavy in my ears.

I was thinking the same thing. Too exhausted to stand on my own two feet, too breathless to speak, I nodded in agreement as I continued to hold onto him. Then a thought crossed my mind. Max didn't use a condom. In the heat of the moment, I didn't care, nor did I remind him. I wasn't on the pill, but from my calculations, I was pretty sure it would be okay—there shouldn't be a risk of an accidental pregnancy.

Chapter 9
Jenna

"Welcome to my department," Matthew's smile beamed as he embraced me warmly. Wearing a dark gray suit and tie, he looked very sharp and serious. This was the first time I had ever seen him dressed for work.

Looking past him, I saw that all eyes stared as they approached me with welcoming smiles.

"Everyone, this is Jeanella Mefferd. Jenna, this is Pamela, Stephen, Mandy, and..." He said them so quickly, I couldn't remember their names as I shook many hands. After the introductions, they all got back to work.

The huge room was nothing like an ordinary office. Several white boards attached to the back wall held layouts of articles and pictures of models. In the center was a huge circular table for our meetings, I assumed.

"This is your desk." Matthew led me to the desk next to his.

Both were cherry wood, rectangular, and bigger than the other employees'. I didn't want to be treated differently. I hadn't earned that right yet. Running my finger across the table, I noticed not a single scratch marked it. I wondered if it was new. Knowing Max, it must have been. With a computer and all the office necessities on top, my stomach tingled at the thought of being where I'd always wanted to be, working right at the heart of a fashion magazine. Joy filled up my heart beyond what I could've imagined before.

"Jenna." Matthew broke me out of my daze, swinging his rolling chair toward me. "I've sent you some pictures and articles I need you to format for me. Please don't hesitate to ask for my help. I know Max started training you, but he hasn't taught you everything you need to know. After my morning meeting, I'll show you other layouts, and where you can check for references. We all have a specific job to do in this department, but you can ask anyone for help."

"Sure, thanks, Matthew," I replied, placing my workbag down on the floor and sitting down on my plush, leather seat. Turning on the computer, I could not wait to get to work.

"I'm going to take it easy on you for a couple of weeks so you can get the hang of things, okay?"

"Thanks," I smiled, watching him turn to his desk with a nod. Then I clicked the email to open. The first email I saw was from Max.

Hello, Ms. Mefferd,

Hope you have a fantastic day. Matthew will take good care of you and make sure you're comfortable. Don't let him boss you around. I won't be having lunch with you today, but I'm still good for dinner. I've invited Matthew and Becky to join us. I hope that's okay. See you tonight. Always thinking of you. TKLS

Yours,

Max

Yours? This was the first time he'd written that, and I loved it. TKLS made me smile — touching, kissing, licking, and sucking. The words triggered the memories of us in the shower and Max under the running water. Remembering how sexy he looked, I almost orgasmed from the thought of him. I was at work, I reminded myself. Pushing away thoughts of Max, I checked Matthew's email and got right down to business.

Becky

Jenna offered to pick me up from home since the restaurant was close to our apartment. Max wanted to celebrate Jenna's promotion. I thought that was so sweet of him. When he'd called me on my cell phone, my heart pounded out of my chest. I thought something had happened to her; but after he explained, my heart quickly settled, though the pounding lingered longer than I wanted it to.

I wasn't sure what was wrong with me. Perhaps it was reading all those manuscripts where something bad always happened when things started to look good, or maybe almost losing my best friend, again, had me jumpy. I needed some time to get myself together.

When we walked in, the place was already packed. Since Jenna wore a casual dress, I changed out of my jeans and sweater as well. Almost tripping in my heels, I glued my eyes to the floor to see what I had stepped on. I didn't notice Max standing in front of us until I peered up again.

"Hey, Max," I cheered. He still wore his work attire, suit and tie. He must have come straight from the office.

"Becky." He greeted me with a hug. Then he placed his arms around Jenna and kissed her forehead as they proceeded to the table.

I took off my coat, placed it around my chair, and sat

next to Jenna. After we got our drinks, we talked about my job. Like Matthew, Max asked lots of questions.

Just as I finished explaining it all, Max waved. As I looked in the direction of his line of vision, my stomach knotted so tightly, I nearly choked on my beer. With a cool, relaxed stride, Matthew came toward us as the women he passed checked him out. The dim lights above kissed the side of his face, exposing his flawless, gorgeous skin and glowing over parts of his body. My heart throbbed with heated passion I couldn't control. No amount of oxygen satisfied me. His presence always sucked the air out of my lungs.

When his eyes met mine, I broke away, but that didn't stop my heart from hammering in a delicious way. Jenna didn't tell me Matthew was coming. But then again, she didn't plan this dinner so I couldn't really be mad at her. Besides, she didn't even know how I felt about him, and neither did I.

"Hey," Matthew greeted everyone with a nod. Placing his beer bottle on the table, he took off his suit jacket and draped it behind his chair. Either he had been at the bar waiting for us, or he went there first, before looking for us.

"Hi," I said quickly and hid behind the menu so I couldn't see him sitting in front of me. Boy, this was going to be awkward. I had to stop acting like a child, pretending I didn't have this secret crush on him. After gathering myself, I placed the menu down. Thank goodness he had shifted his attention to Jenna.

"Did you tell Max what a great boss I am?" Matthew asked Jenna, grinning at her.

"Of course. Although we were so busy today, you didn't really have a chance to boss me around," Jenna teased. She looked so relaxed and happy. It was great to see her this way. Instead, I was the nervous one.

"See, Becca? I actually do have a job and I actually do work," Matthew murmured, placing his elbows on the table, leaning closer toward me. At the same time, he tapped his shoe against mine to get my attention. Before he could do it again, I moved my leg. "Did Becca tell you I ran into her at the mall at Victoria's Secret?"

Glaring heat touched my cheeks, especially when Jenna whipped her head to me, her face filled with questions and amusement.

"No." She plastered a huge giddy smile on her face. "Why didn't you tell me, *Becca*?"

Great...she noticed Matthew's nickname for me. I arched my brows with a smirk, making her think a little, but leaving the rest to her imagination. Thank goodness for the waitress. After we'd ordered, Max held up his glass of wine, Jenna held her glass of water, and Matthew and I held up our beer bottles.

"To Jenna and her new position. Hope it is all that you want it to be," he said and winked at her.

After a clink from each glass, we sipped our drinks. During dinner, my heart managed to stay calm. Matthew was actually cordial and talkative. The four of us talked about our jobs, family, and Christmas plans. Jenna's parents would arrive in a couple of days. She was excited about that. They planned to stay for a week at a hotel nearby. Due to Jenna's work schedule, they planned to leave right before New Year's Eve.

Jenna told me last week that Max wanted to pay for her parents' plane tickets, but she threatened she would never sleep at his place again if he did. I had a feeling he'd pay for their hotel though. After all, he was the one to convince Jenna not to fly home. He was always concerned for her safety. I'd never experienced that care with the men I dated. It was great to see that happening for Jenna. Max was a truly swoon-worthy, real life "book boyfriend." God...I had to stop thinking about those damn novels with their too-perfect book boyfriends.

Max convinced Jenna to spend the night at his place. He actually didn't have to try hard; he just pouted and she gave in, but only after Matthew offered to take me home, making it a done deal. Though I hesitated, I had to be an adult about it and stop acting like a schoolgirl who couldn't even think around her crush.

After Max and Jenna departed, Matthew said he'd wait for me at the bar while I went to the restroom. Though the restaurant was packed, it wasn't hard to spot him, especially when giggling females surrounded him. Boy...did he work fast. Against all logic, a part of me was jealous. I wanted to throw them off their barstools.

Instead of heading toward him, I sat on the opposite end of the bar. Not wanting to interrupt the barrage of females by his side by telling him I wanted to go home, I decided to stay away for a bit. If he decided to ask one of them out, I didn't want to be in his way. When he spotted me, his body stiffened; then it stiffened even more when a male leaned into me.

Knowing Matthew couldn't hear our conversation, I gave him a taste of his own medicine and hugged my friend's fiancé.

"Hey, Keith." I gave him a warm hug. Keith was tall and lean, but not as tall as Matthew or built as well. He had short, blondish hair, pretty blue eyes, and the cutest dimples.

"Where's Nicole?" I asked, slightly flirting with my body, twirling a strand of my hair around my finger. Keith was clueless about my ploy, but Matthew caught on. His eyes were deadpan as he stared at Keith and me. It made me feel good that he looked jealous. Wow. What was I doing? I had to stop this.

"Nicole went to the restroom. Are you here by yourself?"

"No. Actually, Jenna and Max were here, but they've already left. Max's brother, Matthew is taking me home." When I turned my head toward Matthew, he had already diverted his attention back to his companions. I don't know why, but that pricked my heart a little.

"Becky," Nicole squealed, giving me a tight squeeze. She was in her work attire like Keith. With her hair curled, pencil skirt and a purple sweater, she looked stunning. "Are you here by yourself?"

After explaining again, she told me they had already finished with dinner. They had sat on the opposite side of the restaurant, which explained why we missed each other.

"Do you need a ride home?" Nicole asked, looking at my line of vision. "Keith and I are headed home. Come on. He looks busy anyway." Nicole looped her arms around mine and led me away from where we were standing.

When I felt the phone vibrate in my purse, I took it out.

"Let me get this," I said to Nicole.

Where are you? Are you ready to go home?

Who is this?

Matt

Surprised to get a text from him, I flashed my eyes to him. He was gazing around, searching for me.

Why don't you stay? My friend Nicole is here. She'll take me home.

No. I promised Jenna and Max I would take you home.

I don't need a babysitter. I can go home with anyone I want. You can stay and entertain your friends. I don't want to intrude.

74

Jealous?
What? No!
I was.
What?

"Sorry about that," I said to Nicole, but she was staring at something or someone behind me. When I turned out of curiosity, Matthew gave me that killer smile.

"Hi," he said to Nicole, extending his hand to shake hers, then Keith's. "I'm Matthew, the one who will be taking her home."

"Max's younger brother," I intervened with a roll of my eyes.

"It's nice to meet you," Nicole replied, looking baffled, most likely thinking she had seen him flirting with those other women and now he wanted to take me home.

Turning to Nicole, I hugged her and whispered in her ear. "Don't ask. I'll call you later." After we said our goodbyes, I started to walk out the door while Matthew paced right behind me. I wasn't going to walk beside him and pretend we were a couple. When he settled his hands on my shoulders, evidently not wanting to lose me, I slapped them. I heard a chuckle and then his hands gripped me again. I slapped them again, but he didn't give up. Grrr! Then he wrapped his arms around me from behind so I couldn't move my arms as he led us toward the exit.

"Oh my God! Get off me!" I yelled over the loud music. Feeling like a puppet and unable to escape, I had no choice but to give in. I didn't mind it so much. He felt good holding me.

"Just keeping myself safe, Becca. These women are trying to throw themselves at me. But you don't mind saving me, right?" His warm breath brushed the side of my neck, sending shivers down my spine.

Yeah, I had to admit, feeling his hard body against mine not only made me wither, I liked it way too much. "I don't think it's you that needs saving, rather the ladies, instead."

His chest vibrated against my back from his laugh, and he squeezed me tighter as he led us out.

Chapter 10
Becky

I had to admit, I liked how Matthew was so protective over me, but at the same time, I had to bring myself back to reality and remember he did it out of obligation. After he walked me to the apartment door, totally unnecessary but very gentlemanly, I thought he was going to leave. Instead, he took off his suit jacket, slung it over the sofa and asked to use the bathroom.

"Why can't I use *your* restroom," Matthew asked with a challenging tone when I pointed him to Jenna's.

"I...umm..." Due to his unexpected question, I blurted out the first excuse I could think of. "Because I'm going to use it." I didn't really need to though.

"Then I'll wait here, but hurry. I need to go." He plopped on my bed.

"You can use Jenna's." I closed my bathroom door as I entered.

"No, thanks. I want to use yours." I heard him say.

Seriously? He had to use *my* bathroom. Why?

"Hurry Becca," he sang, whistling a tune.

After I took care of business, I came out to find Matthew sprawled out on my bed. He wasn't trying to look seductive, but the way he lay on his side with his hand tucked underneath his head for support, he looked like one of those GQ models on a steamy photo shoot. If only he had his shirt off.

Snapping out of my thoughts that could get me in trouble, I paced toward my closet to look for a change of comfortable clothes and gestured to Matthew that the bathroom was all his. Instead of heading there, he went to my bookshelves. Hmmm...he wasn't in a hurry to use the restroom anymore. He was just being a pest.

"Is that a picture of your family?" he asked, pointing to a picture frame.

I walked to where he stood. "Yes. That's my mom, dad, and my sister."

His eyes flickered to my face, back to the picture, then to the bookshelf again. "You read all these books?" A sincere tone rang from his question.

Feeling proud and slightly embarrassed, I nodded. "Some of these books are my clients." I pulled one out. "This one is one of my favorites. It's about a nephilim, half-angel and half-human, who falls in love with a human. They love each other so much, but it's forbidden. They go through struggles and tribulations, especially at the hands of evil angels; but his love for her conquers the darkness. It is undeniable, unbreakable, unconditional; a love that stands through time. Anyway, Michael is wonderful," I gushed.

"May I see it?"

Before I could register what he asked, he reached for the book. Because I didn't act fast enough, his hands covered mine. Peering up to his eyes, an electrical sensation ignited through me. As his eyes held mine, not even a breath released; we stood there in silence, staring... searching...connecting.

"Here," I said, breaking away from the hypnotic

moment. Dropping my hand, I headed toward my dresser.

"*Crossroads*, huh?"

"Excuse me?" I twisted to him, and leaned my back against the dresser.

Holding up the book, he read the title aloud. "*Crossroads*."

"Yes," I confirmed.

Matthew's eyes fell back to the cover. "I'm at a crossroads myself." His tone was somber and low, hardly audible, but I heard the pain. I wondered why he had said those words. I wanted to ask him, but I knew he wouldn't share. Even if he did, our friendship might deepen, and I wasn't sure if I wanted go there, so I tried to lighten our conversation.

"Yeah, everyone is at a crossroad at some time in their life, don't you think? And when we have to decide, we have to make sure we don't regret the road we choose since the other road may not be available if we change our minds."

Placing the book back into its slot, Matthew moved toward me. His expression and mood changed drastically. Flexing his muscles, he planted his hands on the dresser on either side of me, creating a cage around me. There was no escape as his eyes pulled me into him and held me captive as he spoke. "True. I wish we never came to crossroads and our journey in life could be a straight line."

"That would be boring. No drama, no love triangle—"

"No make up sex after a fight?" he said quickly, lifting one corner of his lip.

I paused, registering his unexpected words. I stuttered, "Uh… I guess… uh…" Boy, was that a lame reply. Producing that sexy grin again, he shifted his eyes to my hand. I didn't realize it, but I was twisting my hair with my finger. I slowly released it.

"I've always wanted to do that to mine. Obviously, I can't. I'd like to try it on yours." He chuckled lightly. Not waiting for my answer, he twirled a strand of my hair just like I had. It made me sizzle in places I didn't want to. Unexpectedly, with lustful eyes, he ran his fingers through my hair, melting me to the floor. My legs weakened and my breath hitched. Panic! Then, without a word, whatever connection he tried to produce died when he turned to head into the bathroom.

Unable to move, I stood there as the heated feeling continued to linger. Why did I allow him to affect me that way? The sound of the toilet flushing got my feet moving and I headed toward the kitchen to get a glass of water.

"Someone got roses," Matthew said excitedly, sauntering into the dining area. "Did Max send those?"

"They're for me," I replied quickly, then spit water out into the sink, coughing relentlessly. I panicked at the lie, causing the water to go down the wrong way when he asked that question. It wasn't as if he could read my mind.

"You okay there?" With one hand wrapped around my waist, the other patted my back lightly.

I coughed so hard I thought I was going to throw up, but Matthew sweetly helped me through it. Gripping the edge of the sink with both of my hands, I coughed even more.

"Here, drink some water." Matthew handed me the glass of water I had set down on the counter when I started coughing.

Clearing my throat, I spoke, but the sound of my voice came out hoarse. "Thank you."

"You'll live," he said, twisting his lips in amusement, letting out a slight chuckle.

"Yes." I wiped the tears from the corner of my eyes, and then I smiled. It was all I could do since I felt like an idiot.

Matthew leaned against the cabinet and gazed at me with intensity. I wished I could read the meaning behind it. His eyes seemed filled with yearning and pain. They were two totally different emotions, and that baffled me immensely.

"It's getting late and I should be leaving," he mumbled, but he didn't move a muscle. His eyes never moved from me, making me feel like he was devouring me with his thoughts.

"Thanks for driving me home." I didn't know what to do. Should I leave the kitchen first because he wasn't moving?

"He isn't good enough for you," Matthew muttered out of the blue.

What was he talking about? I tilted my head, furrowing my brows, silently asking for further explanation.

"You deserve bigger flowers, Becca. They're too small," he explained. Walking to the living room, he grabbed his suit jacket, and headed to the door while I followed behind. I was surprised and confused by his words. After he opened the door, he locked his eyes on mine looking somewhat sad. "I hope he brings your book boyfriend to shame and gives you everything you deserve. When I walk out this door, I want you to make sure you lock it, okay?"

I nodded. His words tugged my heart, leaving me speechless. He thought I was seeing someone when I wasn't. Should I have said something? Then the door closed, creating a cool draft. I couldn't tell if it was due to his absence or the air that passed through from the hallway. I didn't know why, but I stood there, soaking in his sweet words, trying to calm my pounding heart—it always beat too fast around him—and pondering the thought that he believed I was taken. I wondered if that was a good thing.

Just as I reached for the lock, the door swung opened, smacked my forehead, and I stumbled back several steps. Thinking it was Jenna, I looked up while rubbing my head. "Jenna…" But it wasn't her. "Matthew? What are you doing back here?"

He didn't respond, but his hand pushed mine away from my forehead. "Shit, Becca. Did I do that to you?"

Instead of responding, I asked him the same question again. "What are you doing here?"

"I told you to lock the door. Why didn't you lock the door?" he demanded, checking my forehead for bruises. "Sorry," he said sincerely. What he did next made me lose myself into him. He embraced me tenderly and gently kissed my forehead. It was brief, but it meant something, and when he sighed softly, I could tell it meant something to him, too. In that moment, I felt utterly safe. In that moment, we connected at another level. In that moment, I fell a little bit deeper.

With another kiss on my forehead, he whispered, "Sweet dreams, Becca. And lock the door *now*."

As soon as he left, I locked the door right away. I wasn't about to have him barge through again; and sure enough, the doorknob rattled. He was extremely protective, but I liked it…maybe too much.

Chapter 11
Jenna

After picking up my parents from the airport, I dropped them off at their hotel to get settled in, and I went back to work for a couple of hours before we would meet up again for dinner. I had offered to pick them up, but Dad insisted they take a taxi since it was so close. He also said they were planning to rent a car the next day, but Max had already asked a company driver to take care of their needs.

Max had made reservations at one of the finest restaurants in Los Angeles, and we had agreed that he would drive me there. Glancing over at Max while he focused on the road, I studied him. He looked so deliciously handsome in his dark gray suit; I was trying hard not to think of him naked.

We had talked about him meeting my parents, but he never mentioned how he felt about it. Maybe it's different for men. I'd been nervous meeting *his* family, so I wondered if Max felt the same. He sure didn't look it. Though I didn't let him know, I was nervous enough for us both. There wasn't a doubt that my parents would adore him, but I hoped Max would like them just as much.

My parents had never met anyone I was dating, since all my dates were after I left for college. I hoped they wouldn't ask too many unwanted questions, especially my mom. My dad was the quiet type, so at least I knew he wouldn't be the one initiating the conversation.

Sitting tall, looking straight ahead with both hands on the steering wheel, Max looked all business and ready to attack the world. How I loved this side of him. It gave me the shivers; like no one could touch him and he could make anything happen.

"Don't stare at me, Jenna," Max said lightly. His lips curled playfully.

"I'm not staring, and how do you know?" I giggled. I wasn't good at fibbing.

"Even though I'm looking straight ahead, I can feel your every move. That's how in tune my body is with yours. I always know."

"Oh." It was all I could say as I took in his words, liking what he'd said.

"But I don't mind," he said while his thumb tenderly and seductively stroked mine. The touch was so innocent, loving, yet so sensual, it made me want him right then, as I could already feel his hands on my body. When we reached our destination, Max pulled into valet parking. After getting out of the car, he held my hand and led me to the entrance.

Since we were ten minutes early, we sat in the waiting area near the front. He didn't want to seem rude and sit at our table first, especially since this was a first meeting.

When I spotted my parents walking through the door, I stood up and Max did the same.

"Mom…Dad," I greeted. I hugged Mom first then Dad, then turned to Max. "This is Max."

"It's such a pleasure to meet you, Max," Mom said, shaking his hand. She was smiling from ear to ear. "I've heard so much about you, I feel like I already know you."

"Hello, Max," Dad said, shaking Max's hand.

"How was your trip?" Max asked.

"Just fine," Mom smiled. "Thank you for asking."

"Good," Max said and raised his hand to get the hostess's attention.

My nerves had settled quickly when our dinner talk proved to be nothing but laughter and great conversation. I could tell Mom wanted to ask him more questions than needed, but Max was a good sport, trying to let her see that he was the right person for me in subtle ways.

"Max, do you like children?" Mom asked, clearing her throat, knowing I would get mad at her for asking such a question at their first meeting. Frowning, I gave her the evil eye. If she'd been sitting across from me, I would have nudged her with my foot. Trying to calm my nerves back down again, knowing Mom was rolling on with her questions, I took a sip of my water.

"Children? What are those?" Max blurted.

Oh my God! He did not say that. I almost spit out my drink. Thankfully, I swallowed before he said anything else, but my hand slipped as I placed my cup down, and I spilled my water. My reflexes kicked in, but too late. It happened so fast, some spilled on Max's pants. He didn't realize it was even happening until the glass slammed on the table, and by that time, he couldn't have stopped the water flow unless he was Superman.

"Jenna?" My mom squealed.

"I'm so sorry." I held my napkin out to Max, ready to help and ignoring my mom. I was so embarrassed, I didn't know whether to touch him or just let it be. He was already standing, wiping himself off. Luckily, the cloth napkin had been draped across his lap, so the water barely soaked through his pants. It would dry by the time we went home.

When Mom's smile faded, he sat back down and spoke again. "I was just kidding, Mrs. Mefferd. I love children. They bring pride and joy to families. I want a minivan full of them."

Mom giggled and gave a sigh of relief. Looking at me with glassy eyes she said, "I wish I had more, but I had a hard time conceiving, so Jenna is my miracle."

"Mine, too," Max agreed, looking at me with loving eyes.

It wasn't so much what Max said, but the fact that he said such sweet words in front of my parents that made me adore him even more.

"Max, your driver is wonderful," Dad muttered, breaking our conversation. Thank goodness he did. I didn't know how long Mom would gush about me. "We appreciate your gesture, but we can rent a car. We're staying for several more days."

"There are a lot of one-way streets in downtown LA and it can get confusing. Please enjoy your trip with one less thing to worry about."

"It's very generous of you," Mom added. "We don't know how to thank you."

"You gave me Jenna," Max smiled. "It's more than I can ask for."

Mom's eyes twinkled against the candlelight. Her facial expression showed how much she liked his response.

Our conversation dwindled when our dinner came. Mom raved how moist her salmon was and Dad raved about how delicious and tender his steak was. We enjoyed our meal as we continued our small talk.

Max raised his glass of wine for a toast. "To our first meeting and many more."

Mom and Dad looked surprised. I guess they hadn't

expected that either. It was a nice gesture. After the toast, Mom only took a sip of her wine. Max didn't know she was allergic to alcohol like me. Enjoying the taste, I drank a little bit more than I should have. Before long, I had to excuse myself to go to the restroom. Not wanting to leave Max alone with my parents for too long, I hurried as fast as I could. I was afraid of them grilling him with a bunch of questions they wouldn't ask in front of me.

When I came back, their conversation stopped, like they were keeping a secret from me, but I didn't think twice about it. After all, there was nothing to hide since I had already told Max not to talk about my time in the hospital. My parents were on a cruise at the time and I didn't want them to know the hospital visit was due to a misunderstanding. It would not leave a good impression of Max, especially when they hadn't yet had a chance to get to know him.

After dinner, Max ordered dessert—crème brûlée and chocolate mousse cake. Dad had tried to pay for dinner, but Max had already given the server his credit card before I had returned to the table.

After dessert, we exited the restaurant. Max had already called his driver to come to the front to pick up my parents, instead of them having to walk through the parking lot.

Jeff, Max's driver, stepped out of the limo and opened the rear door for my parents. Mom gave Max a hug first, then me. "He's a keeper," she whispered. "Don't let this one get away."

Pulling away from her hug, I smiled, hoping Max hadn't heard. Dad gave me a hug next after shaking Max's hand. "He has great teeth, kiddo. That says a lot about a person." He chuckled. That was Dad's dentist way of letting me know he approved of Max. After the goodbyes, my parents entered the car.

"Drive safe, Jeff," Max ordered.

"Yes, sir," Jeff confirmed with a nod.

"Thanks, Jeff," I said.

Jeff rolled down the passenger's window, since the heavily tinted window was difficult to see through. After we set the date for our next meeting, I waved as the car took off. I was happy that our first meeting went well and my parents had a great time with Max. It couldn't have been any better.

Chapter 12
Jenna

"Sorry I'm late." Kate heaved an exhausted sigh as she slid into the booth next to Nicole and shoved a shopping bag under the table. Her hair was in a high ponytail and she had no makeup on. Her attire wasn't what she would normally wear to our gathering. She wore jeans and a plain sweater. "Kristen had a fever last night. I'm so exhausted, but knowing we were exchanging Christmas gifts today, I wanted to be here. And besides, I really need this."

"Sorry to hear about Kristen," Nicole said.

"How is she now?" Becky asked.

"Her fever went down after I gave her Tylenol, and the doctor gave her antibiotics today, so she's much better. Hopefully, she'll feel better soon."

None of us knew what it felt like to take care of a sick child, Kate looked so tired and worn, it clearly took a toll on her.

"Sorry," Kate continued. "I can't stay long. She finally took a nap, so Craig is okay to watch her for now, but if she wakes up cranky, he won't be able to handle it."

"That's okay," I sympathized. "We understand."

Nicole raised her hand to catch the waitress's attention. "Sorry, but could we order now? She needs to get home to a sick baby."

"Sure," the waitress said. "I'll tell them to do your order first."

"Thanks so much," Nicole said sweetly.

The waitress left after taking our orders. We all ordered the Thai chicken salad.

"We should use this excuse whenever we're in a hurry," Becky laughed.

"To save time, let's exchange gifts now," Kate suggested, grabbing her bag. Then she paused. "But before we do, I want to hear how it went with Max meeting your parents."

Everyone listened intently, laughing and smiling at the details of our conversations. I told them about how I spilled water on Max and what he said, and how sweet he was to my parents. "And you want to know what he did after we got home?" I asked, feeling heat rise to my face.

As if reliving what Max had done, my body quivered, and I swear energy burst between my legs, and sent a jolt to my clit. Oh my God! It felt so real. Running my hand down my face, I got ready to tell them. I'd never shared such an intimate detail with my friends. In a way I felt like I was exposing him…exposing us.

"So what happened?" Nicole blurted, leaning closer, as if she could get it out of me faster.

"Okay…okay." I swallowed. Then the waitress came with our food. Wow, that was fast. We looked at each other in surprise. Stabbing a chicken slice, Kate stared at me as the waitress left.

"Don't leave us hanging."

"Okay," I giggled again, stalling to reveal the can of worms I opened up. I'd never been open about the topic of sex before. I was the one with open ears most of the time while they did the talking. "After we got home, we went upstairs. Max took off everything but his shirt. Before I could undress, he picked me up and took me into the shower.

"I screamed about getting all wet with my clothes on. Then he said all seductively, 'You spilled the cup of water on me. You want me wet, Jenna?' We were both completely soaked under the running water and his white dress shirt clung to every curve of his muscles. He looked so hot. Then we...well...you know what happened after that."

"Oh my God, you have a better sex life than I do. How did that happen?" Kate swallowed.

"I need a cold drink just thinking about it, but I don't want to think about you and Max," Nicole laughed, placing her cold drink on her cheeks. "I need to cool down."

"I wonder if Matthew is like Max," Becky snorted, but stopped when I looked at her with questioning eyes. "I didn't mean anything by that...you know...cause they're brothers," she explained.

When it looked like I didn't buy her story, she nudged me and I understood that as "no need to explain further."

"Enough about my sex life. Let's exchange gifts so Kate can get home," I suggested, taking a bite of my salad, since I had barely eaten. Pulling out my shopping bag, I handed out their presents. "Let's open mine first."

With the ripping sound, they peeled the thin layers of the wrapping that covered each small box.

"Awww...Jenna. This is so beautiful," Becky raved, putting on the bracelet I got for her.

"This is beautiful," Kate smiled. "Look. It even has our names on each heart charm."

"This is so sweet of you. I totally love it," Nicole squealed.

"I bought one for myself, too. Now we all have

something sentimental that bonds the four of us."

"You're so cute and sweet. That's why we love you," Becky said, giving me a sideways hug.

I couldn't have been happier. They loved the engraved bracelets I got for them. Then Becky handed hers out. She got a scarf for everyone, but she said she left mine at home. No big deal, but I wondered what she was up to. We always opened our gifts together before Christmas. Kate bought each of us a cashmere sweater from Banana Republic. Mine was red, Nicole's was purple, and Becky's was black.

Nicole bought us each a Swarovski clear heart, hand-made necklace. She explained one of her co-workers made jewelry during the holidays. Not only was it beautiful, it sparkled like a real diamond. When it caught the candlelight, it gave off the hues of the surrounding colors.

After dinner, we hugged tightly, wishing each other the best Christmas. Secretly, I slipped an envelope attached to a small box in Kate's purse. It was a baby's first Christmas card and baby's first Christmas ornament I bought at Things to Remember. Since Becky and I drove in separate cars, I told her that I would meet her at home.

"You have a minute?" Becky asked, as we entered our apartment.

"Sure, let me call Max to let him know I'm home." After I took off my coat and placed it on the sofa, I took my phone out of my purse and leaned against the dining table.

"What's wrong?" Becky asked.

I didn't know she was watching me. "It's Luke. He's stopped texting me *every* day, but it's still annoying."

"Does Max know?" Becky sauntered to the Christmas

tree and lit it up, then picked up a box.

The Christmas tree brightened up the room. I couldn't help but smile at the sight. The meaning of Christmas filled my heart and peace flowed through me. It reminded me to be forgiving and to have more patience, especially with people like Luke.

"No, I don't want him to worry or do something crazy. I'd figured Luke would eventually get the message. Why is it when you're not available, you're wanted more? I don't get it." I let out a short laugh. "He had his chance."

"Maybe you should change your phone number," Becky suggested, handing me a gift box. "This is for you. I didn't want you to open it in front of Nicole and Kate because I knew how embarrassed you'd be. Plus, I don't think it's appropriate to display this in front of people at a restaurant."

I narrowed my eyes at her. "What did you get me?"

"It's not a big deal. Well…maybe for some of us," she laughed and sat on the sofa.

"Seriously, you were embarrassed for me to open this in public?" My tone rose. "What is it?" Curious, I placed the box on the dining table, ripped the wrapping off, and opened the box in record time. "Oh my God!" I lifted the black lingerie out of the box.

"Max is going to love you in it." She beamed a mischievous smile.

Now I understood why I had to open this gift at home. As blood rushed to my face, I quickly placed it back in the box. "Thank you. It's beautiful and sexy and I'll wear it after Christmas." Sitting on the sofa next to her, I gave her a tight squeeze.

"You're welcome," she said as I let go. "You don't have to wait until after Christmas, you know."

"Okay, I'll wear it on Christmas Eve."

"Confession time. Have you ever worn one before?" Becky asked.

My lips curled into an innocent smile. "Nope."

"Wait till you put it on. It will change you," Becky laughed a good, hearty laugh, finding humor in this situation.

How would it change me? Becky's expression said she wouldn't tell, but somehow, I knew she was right.

Max

"Mr. Knight, welcome," Shawn greeted in his strong French accent. The store manager extended his hand and offered a firm handshake. His jewelry was pricey, but knowing he sold only the best quality diamonds was worth it. Not only that, he accommodated his clients by making appointments while the store remained closed to the general public.

His store wasn't very big, but being in the heart of Rodeo Drive, he catered to many famous people and wealthy businessmen.

"It's been a while."

"Yes, it has." Releasing his hand, I went to the first glass case. I knew exactly what I wanted.

"What can I get for you?"

"I'm not sure." I said, so he wouldn't know I definitely planned to purchase a piece or two today.

"This is a gift for your special lady, yes?"

"Yes." I couldn't help but smile when I thought of Jenna. Everything about her made me feel alive, though it was hard to put it into words. She brought joy, laughter, and dreams of the future into my life the way no other woman had ever done before. What could I say? She captured me, locked the door, and threw away the key.

"Ah, I know that smile. It is the smile that says you are in love. Are we looking for a diamond ring, sir?"

"No, not yet. She'd probably freak out." I snorted and wondered why I thought that was funny. No, not funny at all. When the time came for me to propose, I would hate for her to react that way. It would break my heart. It was the reason I hadn't done it yet. I'm usually the kick back and relax type of guy, but when you know you've found the one, you don't let go.

"Oh." Shawn looked surprised. "Then this must be a Christmas gift." Shawn walked to the other side, opened a case, placed a few items on a black velvet tray, and headed back to me. "How about these, sir?"

The diamonds sparkled magnificently, catching the colors nearby. "They're beautiful, but they're too small."

Shawn went back to the same case. Instead of waiting, I followed behind him. "How about these, Mr. Knight?"

"They're too big." Jenna wasn't the flashy type, and I could picture her wearing it only for me and not for her. "But these..." I pointed. "These are perfect. I'll take the matching set."

"Very nice. Simple and elegant. I'll ring you up right over here."

Shawn took the words out of my mouth. That perfectly described Jenna...she was classy and elegant in every way. "Please have it sent to my office and make sure it's handed to my secretary."

"Of course, Mr. Knight. As always, it has been a pleasure doing business with you."

"Same here," I nodded.

On my way out, a lady walked through the door with

keys in her hand. She had to have been one of the employees, since the door was locked from the outside. When she gave me a warm, yet seductive smile, I finally remembered her. I'd seen her at one of Crystal's parties.

"Maxwell Knight. It's been a while. How have you been?" She stopped in front of me, blocking my exit. First thing I noticed was her makeup; she had too much on. I didn't understand why an attractive woman felt the need to put on that much makeup.

"I've been very well, thank you. And you?" I tried to sound businesslike. I didn't want to give her the impression that I was flirting with her, as I had done at our last encounter. In fact, after Jenna, I considered all women off limits. No matter how beautiful they looked, or what they tried to offer, I wasn't interested at all. I had become a new man.

Darcy started to gently stroke my arm, giving me a heated look. "You know, Crystal and I aren't friends anymore," she announced in her most seductive tone.

I had to laugh at her comment. A good friend would never flirt with their friend's ex, although Darcy and Crystal were never really friends anyway. They were too busy competing with each other. I looked over my shoulder to see if Shawn was listening, but he had slipped into the back room without a word. That left me vulnerable to whatever Darcy had in mind, but I wasn't worried. I had control of the situation.

Darcy continued, "We could have dinner if you'd like, then go to my place afterward."

"I wasn't aware Crystal had any friends. In fact, I didn't think she was even capable of being a friend." I ignored her comment and answered her other statement, trying to save her the embarrassment of rejection.

"You're so funny," she giggled, while wrapping her arms around me. When she pressed her breasts to my chest, it was time to peel her off me. I thought she would get the message when I didn't flirt back, but she didn't.

Lifting both of her hands off me, I placed them down to her side gently. "It was good to see you, Darcy." That was all I said. I didn't even give her time to respond as I scooted around her and bolted out the door.

Chapter 13
Becky

I had made up my mind not to visit my parents for Christmas, since I had been there not too long before, but seeing Jenna's parents in the living room really made me miss mine. Our conversations never centered on our parents, but I knew she was close to hers. However, this was the first time I would be meeting them in person.

It was easy to see who Jenna got her looks from; she looked just like her mom. Jenna's mother was beautiful. Even at her age, she could easily pass for Jenna's sister. She had dark brown hair to her shoulders, smooth skin, and only a thin line of a wrinkle on her forehead.

Jenna's dad was good-looking as well. His salt and pepper hair suited his age. He didn't say much, but I could tell he was all eyes and ears into our conversation.

Max was a sweetheart. He had dinner catered with prime rib, shrimp, and lobster, plus side dishes—mashed potatoes, salad, and green beans. Jenna didn't want him to go out of his way, but since Max told her he'd already ordered, she had no choice. I was happy he had, because I wasn't in the mood to cook. Besides, I was too insecure about my cooking. Of course, Jenna would help, but our dinner wouldn't have turned out nearly this nice.

Sitting comfortably in the living room, we chatted

about our jobs. I never asked Jenna about the details of her work, but it sounded not only challenging, but interesting as well. As I listened intently to Jenna's dad, the sound of the doorbell startled me. Who could that be? All the guests had arrived. It was supposed to be Jenna's parents, Max, Jenna and me.

"Come in," Max said. "Good, you got my text to bring dessert."

"Hello, Matthew. Welcome."

My pulse shot up. Jenna didn't tell me Matthew was coming. But then again, she didn't know I had a crush on him. I only hoped he would behave tonight and keep his distance from me.

When Jenna's parents stood up to greet Matthew, I did the same. Instead of reaching out his hand to shake as he did with Jenna's parents, he pulled me into a quick hug, and then let go. With a mischievous grin, the kind of grin that screamed trouble, he greeted me. "Hello, Becca. It's nice to see you again."

Surprised from the hug, I gave him a quick smile and turned my back to him without a word. I flashed my eyes to Jenna to see if she caught that he called me by that silly name again or noticed the playfulness behind his demeanor, but she was too busy taking out the desserts Matthew had brought—cheesecake and tiramisu.

Since dinner was all set, presented on our finest dishes, we each took a plate, and helped ourselves to some food. While Max poured the wine, Jenna passed out the napkins. It was our place, but Max was helping, so I got to relax. I liked this arrangement.

Jenna's parents sat on the sofa and Max carried two dining chairs over to the coffee table. The only area open was the smaller sofa on the other side. Hoping Jenna would sit next to me, I gestured with my head, but stopped when Matthew headed toward me with a sway that made me drool.

I sat down and set my eyes on the food on my plate. My eyes shifted when the cushion sank, and his arm brushed against mine. There was plenty of room for the both of us. Knowing he sat close to me on purpose, I refused to look at him. Obviously, he was trying to get my attention.

"Jenna tells me you've done some traveling and now you're back to work," Jenna's mom asked Matthew. Thank goodness for her. She kept the conversation going.

"Yes. Have you traveled much?" he asked, putting his plate on his lap to give her his absolute attention, but his damn feet were touching mine.

"We plan to go next year."

"I can email you the places I've been to."

"I would love that," Jenna's mom said. "Thank you."

"No problem. It will be my pleasure." He smiled.

"Jenna tells me that you're single," she mentioned, placing her glass down on the table after taking a sip.

"Mom," Jenna scolded. Looking embarrassed, she gave her mom the look that pleaded for her to stop asking questions.

"Leave the poor boy alone. He doesn't want to have to answer countless questions," Jenna's dad commented.

"That's okay, Mr. Mefferd. Mrs. Mefferd, I don't mind, but if you really want to know, I'm interested in someone, but I'm not sure if she realizes it. You know how dating goes." Grinning after he answered, he shoved a piece of prime rib in his mouth.

Jenna and Max shifted their eyes in unison to Matthew, then to me. Were they as surprised as I was? For that matter, why were they looking at me as if I had the answer?

"If things don't go well, and if you're interested in meeting someone, just let me know. I have a few friends I would love to set you up with. Such a handsome man as yourself would be a great catch."

"*Mom!*" Jenna looked like she wanted to hide. No, she looked like she wanted to die.

Mr. Mefferd coughed. "The shrimp tastes delicious," he said, purposely changing the subject, while nudging his wife.

"Yes, it does, dear," Mrs. Mefferd agreed, snickering lightly. "Thank you again for dinner, Max."

"It's my pleasure," Max replied with a warm smile.

"You'll have to let us take you out on our last night. We insist," Mr. Mefferd said.

Max didn't say a word; instead, he beamed a smile toward Jenna. Looking at the two of them, I could see how much love they had for each other. Jenna did the right thing by giving a guy like Max a chance. He wasn't the stereotypical, good-looking, rich man that wanted to take advantage of his status. He was genuinely a great guy who wanted to find the right woman. Jenna was perfect for him. They were lucky to have found each other.

"You didn't get any beans. You should try some," Matthew suggested.

"No, thanks," I said politely, looking at them on his plate.

"Here."

How could I refuse with his fork headed toward my mouth? Matthew caught me off guard when his eyes set on mine. With every bit of willpower in me, I desperately tried not to look him in the eye. Fail. Heat emanated not only from his proximity, but also from his charming, sexy smile. After I took a bite, I thanked him and looked away.

Friends...we are just friends...act casual. I said these words repeatedly in my head, but it became extremely difficult when he crossed his legs and placed his arm along the sofa behind me, making us look like a couple. Smooth move. I was so aware of his presence, his smell, and the heated electricity that tingled every part of me. My body stiffened even more when his fingers lightly touched my shoulders.

Max and Jenna mirrored each other's amused expression when they finally diverted their attention from the conversation with Jenna's parents and turned to look at us. Needing to stop them from getting any strange ideas, I stood up, grabbed their empty plates, and asked them if they wanted dessert.

As I headed to the kitchen, footsteps followed me. Looking over my shoulder, I saw Matthew holding the rest of the plates I hadn't picked up. A part of me wanted to smile because he was following me, but the other part of me was nervous.

"Let me help you with the dishes, Becca," he said sweetly, taking the plates from my hands after he placed the stack he had in the sink.

"You're the guest. I wouldn't feel comfortable letting you wash the dishes." I turned on the water, squirted soap onto the sponge and started to scrub.

"I've cooked here before and besides, we're friends, so I'm not really a guest," he said, rinsing the plate I just scrubbed.

"Seriously, it's not much and I can do it myself." Grabbing more scrubbed dishes to rinse, I nudged Matthew with my hip to make him move over. He pulled the spout from the faucet with one hand and wrapped his other arm around my waist, pulling my body against his. After he peered at me with a playfully dangerous look, he leaned in to whisper, his lips brushing against my ear. "If you don't let me help you, I'm going to make you extremely wet. You'll be so soaked, it will drive you crazy. Believe me, either you'll be begging me for more or begging me to stop; it's your choice." Then he let go.

Blistering heat sizzled throughout my body. Was he talking dirty to me or was I really off on the interpretation? Swallowing a big lump of air, I surrendered and moved aside; I had no choice. He had completely captivated me, leaving me weak in the knees and absolutely speechless.

"See? We're two friends washing dishes together. Not so bad, is it?" He bumped his hip into mine as he rinsed the fork in his hand.

Friends, I repeated the word in my mind as a reminder. Trying to hold in my smile, I gave him a playfully evil eye. "Watch it, I have a soapy sponge here," I threatened.

Matthew twitched his brows and bit his bottom lip, looking at me with a lustful gaze. "I know something we could do with that sponge, but you'd have to be naked."

Shit! He did it to me again. My skin flamed, but not from anger. Yup, I was going to have to keep my mouth shut and hope to make it the rest of the night without wanting to get naked for him.

Thank goodness, Max and Jenna stepped into the kitchen.

"Where's our dessert?" Max asked, sporting a huge smile, while gazing at the both of us. His eyes were full of suspicion.

Then I remembered why I'd come into the kitchen in the first place. "Sorry, I thought I would do the dishes first."

"Why don't you get the dessert while Becca and I finish

the dishes," Matthew suggested.

Max raised his brows. "Hmmm. I'm not going to ask. Just don't get her too wet."

Matthew's lips curled into a smirk and winked at me. "I believe I already have."

Not only could I not look at either of them, but my face was redder than it had ever been before, and I wanted to pull out the spout and drench myself in cold water.

Chapter 14
Becky

After coffee and dessert, Max and Matthew said good night and left together with Jenna's parents. Jenna and I sat on the sofa and kicked our feet up. Leaning back, I flicked at the bracelet Jenna got me for Christmas, listening as the charms made a clinking sound. "I love how they sound," I snorted.

"Me, too," Jenna said, mimicking my motion. "So..." She dropped her hand and intently focused on me, "Anything new?"

"Not much," I replied, continuing to shake the charms.

"I'm not talking about your daily routine."

I knew what she meant, but I wanted to give her a hard time. And besides, there was nothing going on. Still, I didn't want to give her any reason to think otherwise.

"You know what I mean. Don't try to steer away from the subject. You know what I'm talking about." Jenna narrowed her eyes at me, as if that could get me to answer faster. Truthfully?

"I have no idea."

"Matthew. Sound familiar?"

Just hearing his name got my full attention, even knowing she would spit his name out. Placing my hand on Jenna's, I stated matter-of-factly, "We're just friends." I didn't want this to be awkward for her, plus I didn't want her to tell Max all the details of what had happened between Matthew and me, so I left it at that. This also reinforced why it was best if Matthew and I just remained friends. That was the way he thought of me anyway.

"Did you get him anything for Christmas?" Jenna asked softly, sounding unsure if she should ask.

"Of course not. I hardly know him. I only gave your parents a little gift because you are my best friend and it was the first time meeting them."

"Thank you. That was so sweet of you." Jenna stood up. "Stay here." She went into her room and came back holding a wrapped box.

"That's not for me, is it?" I asked worriedly. Jenna's parents had already given me a gift certificate to Nordstrom.

Handing it to me she said, "It's from Matthew. He told me to give it to you after he left. It was difficult to hide it from you. First, I hid it in the kitchen and then I brought it to my room when you weren't looking."

"Sneaky," I said, referring to her. "But I didn't get him anything."

"You can always take him out to eat. After all, that's what friends do."

A mischievous note sneaked into Jenna's tone, or was it just me freaking out?

"Well I think this was one of the best Christmases ever. I got to spend it with my three favorite people and my parents." Jenna reached down to give me a hug. "Merry Christmas, Becky."

"Merry Christmas, Jenna." I hugged her back.

"Anyway," she started heading to her room. "I'm meeting Max and his parents for Christmas dinner tomorrow night. Matthew will be there too, of course. Do you want to come?"

"No!" That came out short and quick. "I mean no, thanks. I have things to do." I quickly diverted the subject. "Are your parents going too?"

"Max asked me if I wanted to invite them, but I thought it would be too soon."

"Yeah. I understand." I looked at Matthew's gift, wondering what he got me. A book?

Jenna swung her door open. I stopped her with a question. "Did you get your gift from Max?"

"Yesss," she replied, sounding more than a little happy. "He got me a diamond pendant and matching earrings. Now I don't have to borrow yours."

"That's one expensive gift. He did great. I approve, but you can borrow my fake ones any time."

"It really was sweet of him, but I think it's too much."

"Nah, he's got tons of money. He should shower you with tons of gifts."

"Becky, you know I'm not comfortable with that, especially when I can't give him equally in return."

"So what did you end up getting him?" Recalling the conversation Jenna and I had about what to get Max for Christmas. What do you give to a person who has everything?

"I got him an engraved picture frame with a picture of us, some dress shirts and ties. I know, I know…lame, but it was so hard to shop for him."

"I can imagine," I muttered. "I think he would love anything you give him, even if you tied yourself with a pretty bow and walked in naked."

"Becky," she squealed.

I loved making her blush. It was the cutest thing to see with her angelic appearance. With the right makeup, she could look like a sexy vixen, but she could never act like one. She was too innocent and sweet.

"I'm just saying. He would love that lingerie I bought for you. It's just as much his gift as it is yours," I reminded.

"Good night, *Becca*." She giggled and shut the door behind her.

Shaking my head, I let out a breath. I'd known sooner or later, she would tease me about that. Deciding to open the card first, I pulled it out of the envelope.

Becca,

I can't believe you don't have one!

Hope this comes in handy when you're reading all those manuscripts.

Don't read on the computer. It's bad for your eyes.

You owe me lunch or a trip to Victoria's Secret.

Your friend who actually works.

I guessed it was an e-reader and I was right. His gift and words touched my heart deeply. On Christmas Eve, he showed me how sweet and caring he could be, but that wasn't the first time. Some lucky girl would get to see that side of him often, if she was his. Tonight he stole a bit more of my heart, though I had not wanted to give it to him.

Jenna

Max and I had been texting back and forth, trying to figure out if Becky and Matthew had something going on. When I had asked her about it on Christmas Eve, she claimed they were just friends. Matthew was smooth and charming, just like Max. I only hoped he wouldn't do anything to hurt Becky or ruin their friendship.

We had a wonderful Christmas at Max's parents' house. His parents and Matthew were a joy to be around. Carlos, their Italian chef, cooked up a delicious meal as usual, and we ate till we were stuffed. After dinner, we exchanged Christmas presents. Max and I left before midnight to head home.

"What are you thinking about, Max?" I asked, as we lay shoulder to shoulder on the bed, too tired to even get undressed. Holding up my arm, he caressed my skin gently while moving idly back and forth, causing a tingling sensation.

Max had opened the curtain, providing us with romantic lighting. Though it was dark, the city lights reflected inside his bedroom just enough to see each other clearly.

Releasing my arm, he turned toward me. "I'm thinking about how lucky I am. I never believed true love existed until I met you." His hands slowly laced through my hair as he continued. "I didn't think it was possible to love anyone so much. You come first, Jenna. Every morning I wake up happy, knowing I get to hear your voice. I look forward to the moments I get to hold you in my arms. Sometimes I feel I don't deserve you, but you make me want to be a better man. I'm going to show you I can be worthy of your love, worthy of those lips." He sensually caressed my bottom lip with his thumb. "Worthy of your smile," he moaned as he glided his thumb to my upper lip, then ever so slowly down to the middle of my chest. My heart thumped mercilessly from his feather-light touch, anticipating what he would do. "Worthy of this gorgeous body that commands me to do whatever it wants and needs." Then his hand softly stroked my cheek. "I'm going to show you I can be worthy of you every single day."

Feeling his words fill my heart, I replied while caressing his face. "Love changes you in ways you didn't expect, molds you to be a better person, and opens your heart to something wonderful. You are my something wonderful, Max. You have given me all that and so much more. I can't possibly put it into words."

"Jenna," My name rolled off his tongue, sounding so hot and sexy. His eyes grew wicked, full of want and need. I knew that look. I could almost feel his hands all over me, my body surrendering to him. I practically felt him inside me, exploding with pleasure. "I'm going to show you how worthy I can be."

That was all it took for me to become completely unraveled. 'Take me now!' I silently pleaded.

Sliding one arm around my back, he pulled me closer. Max softly kissed my lips, taking his time as his hand explored from my neck, over my breast, down my side, and to my thigh. Lifting the hem of my dress, he tugged it upward and started to unbutton it as he continued to tease me with his tongue, licking, tasting, and savoring my exposed skin.

"I love this red dress on you, babe. It reminds me of the red dress you wore during the New York fashion show, not to mention the buttons in front give me easy access," he mumbled as he moved his lips further down. "I like easy access," he moaned pleasurably.

I barely heard him as I drowned in pleasure. Cool air wafted over me; he had completely unbuttoned the dress. "Babe, you have on another sexy layer."

I opened my eyes and recoiled beneath him. I had forgotten I was wearing Becky's gift. Shyly I said, "Compliments of Becky." Then my finger went straight to my mouth as my face flushed with warmth. Before I realized what I had done, Max grabbed my finger and started to suck on it, sending sizzling heat down my arm.

"You're seducing me, and you have no idea that you are doing it. Thank Becky for me. You are so beautiful and crazy sexy. I'm going to make you want to wear one of these every night."

There were no words after that. Max crushed me with his mouth. He sucked my tongue so hard, I thought he was going to swallow me up. As he pulled my straps down slowly, he kissed and nipped at my exposed flesh. So sensual, it was driving me senseless. Slowing things down even more, he kissed my shoulder, and then lowered his lips to the base of my breast.

Anticipating what he would do next, I quivered and arched my back for him, letting him know I was ready as my nipples hardened. He swirled his tongue around my breast, teasing me, making me moan. Then finally, the wetness of his tongue brushed over my nipples and I arched my back even more. The electrifying sensation shot between my legs so fast, I burned and ached for him.

Pulling the lingerie aside, he kissed a path down my stomach, lower and lower till I thought I'd explode when his tongue licked, flicked and stroked my clit. A whimpering sound escaped my mouth when he devoured me even more. When his finger teased my opening with fast quick strokes, I wanted to scream; I was pretty sure I was drenched and beyond ready for him.

"Max," I panted, spreading my legs further, letting him know I needed him. Tugging his sweater, I pulled him toward me and opened my mouth to take in his lips. With my other hand, I tried to pull off his sweater. Seeing I was getting nowhere, Max lifted himself up and did what I couldn't do. The reflected light cast perfect shadows on his beautiful, toned body. I couldn't help myself as I ran my hands across the hardness of his chest.

Max seized both of my hands and pinned them down on either side of my head. Releasing the pressure slightly, his mouth cupped my breast and sucked until I screamed inside with intense pleasure. The building ache of wanting him was overpowering. "Max," I sighed under my breath.

"You want me inside?" he taunted, hovering over me, wearing that confident smirk. He knew he had the power to seduce me, to fulfill me, to dissolve me, to take me completely.

"Yes." I squirmed.

Max slowly moved off the bed and casually took off the rest of his clothes. Turning to me, he shifted my body to a ready position. After he got me completely naked, he put on a condom and anchored his body on top of mine. Brushing the hair from my face, he glided his finger over the diamond pendant necklace he had gotten me for Christmas.

"Merry Christmas, babe," he said, looking lovingly into my eyes. Again, the city lights shone dimly, reflecting in his eyes. I could see the sincerity of what he said next. "I love you, Jenna. You are my forever."

Then he was in me, making me gasp and suck in air. He rocked to the rhythm of our bodies pressed together as our eyes locked. Max took it slow at first, teasing me with an irresistible smile. When he started to pump faster, I had no control and my eyes naturally closed as I took in all of him. He filled me up with his love, his passion, his need. I was expanding, bursting.

Max was full of energy. It seemed endless as he pounded into me again and again. Cradling me, he went deeper and faster, until the room started to spin. His deep groan filled my ears, telling me he was at the point of no return. We were both high in the state of ecstasy, both bursting to the core, climbing higher with no limits. Wanting to explode, my moaning grew louder.

"No one can hear you, babe. Scream louder for me," Max said in between heavy breaths. Pushing me further up on the bed, he bent from his knees, lifting my butt with both of his hands. Half my body was on the bed; the other half lifted in the air.

As the mattress bounced and the bed frame rattled, he rocked my world. Tears started to stream down from the corners of my eyes and I had no idea why. Feeling drained, but wanting more, my fingers dug into the sheets as my pulse intensified. Then my hands reached for his hard, defined chest, but I was unable to grip it. My hands didn't belong to me anymore, neither did my body, heart or soul. Every part of me belonged to Max.

Taking all of what he gave me, I let myself go. When Max pulled out, my body shuddered from withdrawal. Panting, Max held me to his chest and kissed my lips. "Merry Christmas, Jenna. I think I may be worthy tonight," he chuckled softly as his naked body vibrated against mine.

"Merry Christmas, Max. You are more than worthy," I replied out of breath, snuggling to mold my body to his, as we shared a sweet moment of laughter together.

Chapter 15
Becky

I was slowly getting used to having the apartment to myself. I was usually the one traveling to book conventions or not coming home for whatever reasons. Though I missed Jenna, the peace and quiet was appealing.

It was the first time I had spent Christmas alone, but I didn't mind. We had celebrated the day before so it wasn't a big deal that I was alone on Christmas day. Unable to sleep last night, I decided to watch *"It's a Wonderful Life."* They play it every single year and somehow, I end up watching it every single year.

Leaning over to my nightstand, I looked at my phone; I had gotten texts from my friends, all wishing me a Merry Christmas. They must have sent them late last night. Though Christmas was over, I wished them all the same back.

I was just about to kick back with a book in bed when there was a knock at the door. Putting my robe on, I looked in the mirror and quickly fingered through my hair to look presentable. Oh well, it must be a delivery.

"Coming," I yelled when another knock sounded, louder that time. So impatient! Looking through the peephole, I couldn't believe my eyes. Knowing I would be looking, Matthew showed me all of his white teeth.

Opening the door half way and hiding behind it as

much as I could, I tried to greet him without coming off rude. "Yes?"

"You're still in bed," he exclaimed, scouring his eyes over me. "I should've come earlier."

"Max isn't here. Earlier?"

"Open the door, Becca or I'll let myself in. We have things to do. I know where Max is." As Matthew took a step toward me, I had no choice but to back away.

"We?" I crossed my arms and stood next to my bedroom door while Matthew leaned against the dining table. "I don't recall 'we' made any plans; and don't you have to work?"

"When you work for yourself, you can set your own time. Kind of like you. Besides, we're a little slow since it's the day after Christmas, so we gave everyone the day off."

"That's nice," I said sincerely, nodding and wondering why he'd come.

Matthew cleared his throat and did a once over on me with his eyes. "Are you going to stand there and undress for me or are you going to get some clothes on?" He curled his lips into a cocky smirk, and then sat on the chair to wait.

"What?" I stammered. Since he kept making me flush with embarrassment from his comments and actions, I decided to return the favor. Not knowing how this would play out, I built up the courage and swayed my hips as I sashayed my way toward him. I pretended to be one of the characters I just read about. It was easier to be bold when role playing. "Maybe I'll undress for you," I said in my most seductive tone.

Matthew looked completely surprised; his eyes growing wider with every step I took. My sexy stride toward him appeared to fill him with a look of passion. Still keeping my eyes locked onto his as my tongue sensually glided across my bottom lip, I pulled the tie allowing my robe to fall open slightly, but not all the way, as I stood in front of him.

Looking like I was ready to give him a lap dance, I lifted my legs one at a time to straddle him. Wrapping my arms around his shoulders, I let my hair fall on his face. When I heard an intake of breath from him, I imagined his dick inside me.

My mouth found the side of his neck, and brushed against it with a delicate stroke of my lips. He stiffened and his breath hitched when I moved my hips, writhing as if he was inside me and I made the most pleasurable moaning sound. Holy shit! I had turned myself on.

"Becca, you don't want to do that," he snarled through his teeth with a low, gruff sound. He may have been right, but I was having too much fun. I didn't want to stop.

Taking a fistful of his hair with both of my hands, I turned his face to expose the side of his neck. I wanted him to think I was going to run my tongue there, but instead I nipped the tip of his ear and growled slowly, "Is this what you wanted? Do you want more or shall I stop?"

Recalling the incident in the kitchen when he pulled out the waterspout and talked dirty to me, I wanted to reciprocate. Before he could answer, I continued. "I'm going to ride you so hard and fast, your dick will melt in my pussy. I'll be so wet for you, it will drive you crazy. You'll be begging me for more or you'll be begging me to stop. Your choice."

Matthew let out a deep breath, but didn't say a word. For the first time, he was speechless. His hands lifted, then dropped several times, seemingly fighting what he wanted to do. Before the teasing got out of hand, I pulled back and stood up, but I wasn't finished. I let the robe slowly slide off, only to reveal a tank top and cotton shorts. I even had the words Victoria's Secret written across my ass.

I could see the amused, yet disappointed look in his eyes, but he let out a hearty laugh when I walked away from him. Looking over my shoulder, I watched as Matthew swept his hair back, released a heavy, sharp sigh, and glanced at me. His legs sprawled out in front, his arms dangled lazily, and he looked totally drained. I was pretty sure I left him with a case of blue balls. Who was blushing now? Too bad he didn't know how much he turned me on and how much I wanted to continue.

Even after my little performance, Matthew wanted to take me out, so I agreed. Seeing he was wearing a pair of jeans and a T-shirt, I dressed for a warm day. After I changed, I went to the bathroom and quickly smeared sunscreen on my face, then brushed mascara on my eyelashes. Thank goodness, I didn't need a lot of makeup to look decent. While I brushed my teeth, I heard footsteps inside my room.

"Hey," I said, trying to convey my message with a mouth full of toothpaste.

"You're taking too long," he said with a mischievous grin.

"So wait in the living room," I mumbled, taking my toothbrush out of mouth and pointed in that direction.

"I've waited in here before. I even laid on your bed," he gestured, then threw himself on the mattress.

Shaking my head, I went back in to spit. Before he could snoop some more, I rushed out, only to find him holding up a pair of my panties. Oh my God! Intense heat rushed to my face. I had done laundry last night and somehow must have missed those.

"Give me that," I ran over and tried to snatch it out of

his hand, but Matthew was faster. He swung around to the other side.

"I found these next to your bed. How did you know G-string panties were my favorite?" Matthew swung them around with his index finger, biting on his lower lip.

"Give them back," I said aloud, swinging my arm. Matthew raised his hand before I could get to the panties.

"Say pleeeeease."

I stopped jumping and gave him an evil eye as I came up with a devious plan. I pushed him, and we ended up toppled on my bed. It would have been just him, but he pulled me down with him. "Matthew!" I screamed, and tried to release myself from his hold, but there was no escaping. He started to tickle me and my body wiggled and jerked as his fingers dug.

"Stop!" I laughed as we rolled around on the bed, but Matthew didn't stop. "Please, stop." I was laughing so hard that it hurt.

He stopped and I found myself on top of him again. We stared into each other's eyes without words; our chests collided with the rhythm of our heavy breathing. Something entered his gaze that was difficult to define; an unspoken message of both surprise and confusion. When his eyes shifted to my lips, he dragged in a breath and released it ever so slowly, and a long, soft puff of air brushed against mine. That was all it took to have me spiraling out of control. I was on fire...burning...yearning...needing him.

As the urge of wanting to open my mouth for him intensified, I closed my eyes and pulled away before I did something I would regret. The unwelcome possibility of rejection crossed my mind.

"Are you going to take me out or what? I'm hungry," I

said pushing away. Standing up, I walked away, trying to cool off.

"Hold on," he mumbled, still flat on the bed. His hand covered his face. "I need a minute."

If he felt the same way as I did, then I knew why, and I couldn't help my private smile of satisfaction.

"Where are we going?" I asked.

Matthew glanced at me before shifting his eyes on the road ahead. His hands were on the steering wheel, but his lips curled into a smirk. "I told you I would show you what fun meant."

What was he talking about? I remembered him mentioning that during our encounter at Starbucks, but it had come out all flirty at the time. What was he up to?

"Why do you look so concerned?" Matthew gave a quick sideways glance again. "Don't worry; I'm taking you to the Santa Monica pier." He paused, grinning with a purpose, the smile that said 'I'm going to tease you.' "Oh wait a minute. You thought my idea of having fun was something kinky, didn't you? Get your mind out of the gutter, Becca."

"What?" I stammered. "I... I wasn't... I didn't mean...stop putting words into my mouth," I laughed out loud, but my mind stayed in the gutter with him. "Oh my God!" I started to smack his shoulder lightly.

"You're so lucky I'm driving right now." Matthew laughed while he raised his hand to block me, then he grabbed ahold of my hand. He held it so tightly, I couldn't let go. It actually felt nice to have my hand held that way, sending warmth and comfort to my core.

"You won," I said, expecting he would let go if I

surrendered.

"Okay," he repeated, but kept my hand in his.

Stunned that he hadn't let go, I looked at him. His expression was stoic and he remained silent. My decision? I let it be.

Feeling nervous that he held my hand so long, I looked out the window to distract myself. One of the best parts of living in Los Angeles was the weather. The sun always let you know it was there, even during the winter. Today, it shone brightly, breaking through the puffy, thick, dreamy clouds. I hadn't realized we reached our destination until Matthew finally let go of my hand.

After he parked, we got out and walked side by side down the boardwalk. Since it was a Monday, it wasn't as crowded as it would have been during the weekend. The weather was perfect, not too cold and not too hot. The cool breeze gave me the shivers.

"Are you hungry?" Matthew asked.

I'd skipped breakfast to sleep in, so I was starving. "I could eat."

"Good, me too. Feel like anything in particular?"

"I'm good with anything."

Following Matthew, we walked into a restaurant I'd never tried before. We agreed to share a bucket full of steamed seafood, and he ordered us each a beer. Casually looking around, I noted that people ate with their fingers; there were no utensils. I'm glad I was observant or I would have felt like a dork asking for some. I also noticed everyone wearing plastic bibs.

After the waitress brought our food, we put the bibs on and dug in. Both of us reached in at the same time and our hands collided. "I was going to be a gentleman and put some on your plate," he said. Reaching into the bucket, he did just as he'd said.

"Thank you," I smiled, taking a bite of the delicious shrimp dipped in warm garlic-butter sauce.

"I'm going to assume that you've never been here before," Matthew said in between chewing a small potato.

"How did you know?" My face turned red, though I had nothing to be embarrassed about.

"I didn't. I guessed and you just answered." He grinned. "So when do I get to meet your boyfriend? The one who gave you those puny flowers."

The beer I'd just sipped sprayed out of my mouth like rain. Choking, I coughed and couldn't stop. Shit. It was the second time I did that with him. How embarrassing.

Matthew swung around and started to pat my back. "Water, please," he hollered. "Here, drink."

After taking a few sips between coughing, I finally settled and Matthew sat back down. I had forgotten he thought I had a boyfriend. So we were just two friends having lunch together, and there was nothing wrong with that. So why did I feel a twinge of disappointment?

"How long have you dated this guy?" Matthew started with his questions. I hoped he had forgotten, but he was persistent.

I was usually pretty good at making things up if I needed to, but with Matthew, I had a difficult time lying to his face. Not knowing what to do, I stalled by taking my time peeling the shell of my crab. "Not that long," I finally said, unable to make eye contact.

"I'm going to assume he's okay with our friendship since you're here."

That made me look up. "Oh…yeah…sure." That was a dumb thing to say, but I didn't know how to answer.

"Here, let me. Looks like you're having a hard time

with that."

I looked up again and saw Matthew's fingers in front of my mouth. He had peeled the shell off his crab and offered to feed me. Without thinking, I opened my mouth and bit down on nothing but air. I glared at him as I heard him snicker.

"Sorry. I couldn't help myself. Here."

Slowly, I opened my mouth again and allowed Matthew to place the whole piece of crabmeat in. "Thanks," I said, still chewing. It was not ladylike, but what did I care at that point?

When the bill came, I reached for it, but he grabbed hold of the other end. We tugged back and forth, but I didn't stand a chance. With his strength, it was out of my hands.

"Matthew, let me pay it. You bought lunch last time," I insisted.

"That was nothing, and besides, I'm the one who asked you out. You can pay next time," he winked.

Then I remembered my Christmas present. "You have to let me pay for it since I didn't get you anything for Christmas. I don't mean to sound ungrateful, but you shouldn't have. I mean…I'm thankful, but it wasn't necessary."

"It was necessary. I can't believe you read novels on your laptop. And by the way, I was hurt you didn't get me a present," he pouted like a little boy, resting his hands over his heart. He looked so adorable. I wanted to bite his bottom lip when he stuck it out.

After blinking away the thought, I tried again to steal the bill from him, but to no avail.

"Not here, Becca." He shook his finger and his head, making a tsk, tsk sound. "You already threw yourself at me in your bedroom. Don't get kinky with me here. I don't mind, but I'm sure others will."

Secretly laughing at his words, I scowled at him. "Fine."

Chapter 16
Becky

After lunch, Matthew showed me what he meant by having a great time. We went on a Ferris wheel, a ride that dropped you down twenty floors, bumper cars, and even a dragon swing. We didn't do much talking, but we sure laughed a lot. Since it wasn't crowded, we went on each ride several times. We acted like children who couldn't get enough.

Afterward, he bought a bag of cotton candy. "When I was a kid," Matthew started to say, taking a handful of it, "I dipped a cotton ball into a bowl of sugar and tried to eat it."

"You did?" I laughed out loud, taking a bite. That first bite tasted unbelievable; it melted on my tongue, shrinking so fast in my mouth that I wanted another one.

"Of course, it didn't taste the same," Matthew chuckled. "Why would you call this cotton candy if it wasn't made out of cotton, right? Little did I know cotton came in edible and *non*-edible kinds."

I reached over and took another piece. "Were you a bad boy? I mean, did you do mischievous things?"

"Let's just say, I was very curious, but Max always covered for me. And I still am," he smirked and wrinkled his nose.

I scowled at him. "I'm sure you are. That was sweet of

Max. I was the same with my sister, only I was the curious one."

"You don't say?" Matthew grinned, licking and sucking the sugar off his two fingers from the piece he just finished.

Matthew made eating cotton candy look sexy. My gaze lingered on his lips, and I wanted to be one of those fingers.

"Ice cream," he said, breaking me out of my trance. "What flavor do you like?"

"Any flavor is fine," I replied. I wasn't really in the mood for ice cream, but figured what the heck. I didn't have to finish it. Matthew speedily took off and I waited where he left me.

When Matthew brought back only one, I figured he didn't want one, but it turned out he wanted to share. Share? We weren't dating.

"I just want a couple of bites, if you don't mind. I need to be back before six. I have a dinner engagement."

"Sure. You take some first," I offered, as a feeling of disappointment settled through me. Of course, he has plans, and as curious as I was, I swore not to ask. I didn't want to hear he was taking some girl out to dinner.

Unable to take my eyes off his lips again, I watched him open his mouth and let his tongue indulge one side of the ice cream cone. OMG. Quivering from the way he licked and slurped, while his drop-dead gorgeous eyes were glued to mine, it felt as though he was licking me instead of the cone.

"Thanks, that was good," he commented, wiping the remains with the back of his hand.

If this were a date, I would have cleaned his face with my tongue.

"Here, you should take it away from me before I become too selfish and eat the whole thing."

125

"Thanks." I took a bite. I realized I had overlapped the part he bit. In a silly, 'teenager thinking' way, I just made out with him and he tasted sweet and yummy.

Instead of heading to the parking lot, Matthew took a detour to the park next to the pier. An older couple snuggled on the bench as we walked up. It was the sweetest thing to see. Shortly after, a group of women jogged past us, checking Matthew out as they went by. I had to raise my brows at him since he knew they were gawking at him. He waved at them, getting giggles and smiles in return. I closed the gap between us when a couple walking their German shepherd headed our way.

"Not a fan of dogs?" he asked, guiding me behind his back as if to protect me.

"No. I like dogs, just not the big ones. You never know."

"I understand. I don't like them either. When I was about eight years old, Max and I were playing catch in the front yard. A homeless German shepherd came into our yard barking and snarling with drool dripping from its mouth. It was ready to attack. Max stood in front of me as we slowly backed away toward our front door. We only had a pair of baseball gloves to protect us. I can still remember that day, how scared I was. I thought it would kill both of us. Luckily, our nanny came out armed with a bat and a piece of ham that she threw as far as she could. As much as Max and I fought, I knew that day he truly cared about me."

"Wow. I never had an experience like that. I think I just saw too many incidents on the news regarding dog attacks."

Matthew started walking backward "Never fear, my Becca. Super Matt is here," he chuckled, making me laugh, too. "Is your sister older or younger?"

"She's younger; she's in her senior year in college. My dad is an insurance broker and my mom is a teacher." I said more than I had intended, but it was easy with Matthew. He was a great listener.

"So when do I get to meet your sister? She's kind of hot; she looks a lot like you, but in a different way."

"No way," I blurted before I could stop myself.

"And why not? Are you trying to keep me all to yourself?" Matthew continued to walk backward.

"Yes...*no*...I mean..." This was not coming out right. "You're bad for her." I didn't mean to say that either. Was I jealous?

"Bad? You barely even know me."

"I know your kind. You flirt with anything that doesn't have a penis. You make a girl feel special, sleep with her, then crush her heart."

"Do you think that is what I'm trying to do to you?" His playful tone changed and he watched me so closely that he unknowingly headed straight for a tree. I thought he would turn around, but he didn't.

"Watch out, Matthew." Simultaneously, we grabbed each other. With his body backed against the tree and nowhere to go, our bodies collided. Gazing into his eyes, too close for comfort, I whispered, "Are you hurt?"

He didn't answer, but his eyes continued to search mine. There was something comforting, yet terrifying about the way he connected with me. His hurt look surprised me.

"You must've dated some assholes, Becca," he continued. "Sure, I'll admit I flirt a lot, but it's my way of coping. You don't know what I've been through the past two years. I was completely dead inside. I watched as the girl I wanted to spend the rest of my life with died in the same hospital Jenna was in. For two fucking years, I blamed myself and swore I would never fall for anyone again. But you know what? Your heart has a mind of its own. I found out you don't have a choice. Your heart makes those choices for you and no matter how hard you fight it, you can't. Then you're totally screwed."

My mouth dropped and my heart ached for him. I had no idea about what he'd been through, and I accused him of being an ass. Wishing I could take back what I said, I closed my eyes and whispered softly, "I'm so sorry."

Matthew continued to look at me, but with a softer expression this time. I was waiting for him to curse at me, but instead he laced his fingers through my hair, searching my eyes again. Then his gaze shifted to my lips. His breathing grew faster and intense, fighting what he wanted to do. I wanted him to kiss me so badly, but it didn't happen. After all, he thought I was seeing someone, and being the gentleman he was, I knew he wouldn't proceed. Sliding his hand around my back, he held me tenderly.

"I'm sorry. I didn't mean to dump all that on you," he said gently. "I don't want to ruin what we have. I enjoy your company so much, Becca. You make me forget the pain. You make me forget her," he sighed softly against the tip of my ear. His tone held so much sadness. Tears blurred my eyes. I felt the depth of his pain shooting through every part of my being, especially into my heart.

Matthew held me longer than I had expected. When he finally released me, he was back to himself. Grabbing my hand, he started sprinting. "Come on, Becca. Let's see how fast you can run."

"Matthew!" I yelled. Unable to release his tight grip, I had no choice but to run with him, but it made the awkward situation better, and it felt good to run like that.

Yup, he was smooth.

Chapter 17
Jenna

A couple of days after Christmas, Max and I met my parents for dinner. My parents paid for dinner this time around. Like the last time, we had a fabulous time getting to know each other better. Max and my dad talked about sports, and of course, my mom probed with more questions. We also had dinner the next night since they were leaving the following morning. Max's driver and I took them to the airport, and then I went straight to work.

There were two more days until New Year's Eve. I could already feel the excitement. For the first time in a while, I'd have someone to kiss at midnight—my Max. I couldn't wait. Not to mention spending a fun filled night with my closest friends.

Gazing quickly around the room, I noticed everyone was busy at their desks. Matthew went to a meeting with Max regarding another department, so I was holding down the fort. There wasn't much to worry about, since we were all working on the same project and Matthew had delegated the jobs before he left.

Looking at my project on the screen, I started typing about the upcoming London Fashion Show, and all sorts of thoughts fluttered through me. I wondered if I would be invited to go. Since Matthew was back, would he be going instead of Max?

Heavily focused on the layout screen, I jumped when my phone buzzed on my desk. I kept it on vibrate, so it rattled. It was from Max.

Good morning, Ms. Mefferd. Missed you last night. My bed was cold and it felt so big without you.

Sorry! Can't have me every night. You would get bored with me.

Never!!! You're too sexy, gorgeous, and soft. Not to mention, you've stolen my heart, so it goes wherever you go.

Awww...gushing...blushing. You're so sweet, Max.

Want me to make you blush even more?

Aren't you at your meeting?

We took a break, but gotta go soon. Come over tonight. I promise you'll be blushing all night.

I'm coming, Max!

That sounded dirty. You just made me hot all over. Need to take a cold shower. Love you, babe. Oh, by the way, I've ordered a sandwich for you from Café Express along with a special dessert. It's in my office. Looks like we're extending our meeting into lunch. I'll miss my lunch buddy. TKLS

Thank you! You're too good to me. See you tonight. XO

"TKLS," I repeated, smiling, recalling what it meant. Yup! I needed a cold shower, too. Rereading his text, I remembered that Max had easily said the word "love" before, but I had a difficult time saying it back. I cared about him deeply, but I wasn't ready to say the "L" word yet. I wasn't sure if it was just easy for him to say or if he meant it. Did he truly know what it meant? Did I?

Another text appeared. It was from Luke. *Texting you to let you know that I'm thinking of you. When you're ready to meet with me, let me know. I'll be waiting. Sooner or later, he'll screw up and I'll be there to catch you when you fall.*

Becky was right. I should change my phone number, but too many important connections had this number. Feeling extremely aggravated, I told my staff I was heading to the break room to get a cup of coffee. 'When he screws up…' Luke, you're the one who screwed up. Actually, I was glad he did or else I wouldn't have given Max a chance.

Speedily walking down the hall, my footsteps tapped a rhythm. In order to stop hearing the sound from my heels, I slowed my pace. I was about to enter the break room when I heard laughter and voices.

Leaning my back against the wall, my heart went into overdrive, thumping erratically. As I homed in on a conversation, I kept my eyes alert in case anyone else walked by. I wouldn't want to be caught being nosy. Though it felt childish, I couldn't help myself, especially when I realized the conversation was about Max.

That is so sad.

I know.

It's not right what she's doing. She's either taking all she can or trying to make him suffer.

I'm just glad she doesn't work here anymore. She was a total bitch. I have no idea what he saw in her.

I agree, but I'm glad he's going out with a nice girl now. I heard Jenna is a genuine, sweet person.

I hope she doesn't break his heart, but if she does, I will be more than happy to take her place.

The ladies giggled; I didn't recognize their voices. As I stood there, I debated whether to go inside or leave, but knowing they were talking about me, I wanted to stay a little longer. They hadn't said anything negative and with any luck, they weren't spreading any rumors. I wanted to be sure what they were saying wouldn't get me fired up, so I stood there frozen and listened.

You wouldn't stand a chance.

True, but I can dream.

What do you think will happen?

I don't know. I'm sure he didn't do the things she's accusing him of.

Hell! I'd love to do the things he's been accused of with him.

I bet she kept him satisfied. Maybe that was the reason he kept their relationship that long.

Maybe it was her? Maybe she manipulated him so he thought he needed her.

Some men think with their dick. That's why they cheat.

Maybe, but how do you know?

I'm good at judging people. You shouldn't believe the rumors. There are always two sides to the story.

Well have you heard the other rumor? The one about how she did the same thing to another man?

I don't know how she has the guts to do the things she's done. I bet she's done this to a bunch of men and they all paid her off.

Hearing enough of the conversation, and not sure what they meant by 'what do you think will happen' I backed away slowly, so as not to make a sound. Max had assured me Crystal had taken the money. Perhaps they were hearing old rumors. I dismissed it. I had planned to leave since I was not the confrontational type, but angry heat burned my face. The fact that they were talking about Max that way fired me up even more. I wanted to walk in on them and let them know how I felt, but I couldn't. Instead, I came up with a better plan.

When I had backed far enough away, I started walking my normal speed and let my heels click to warn them. Sure enough, their voices stopped. Our bodies almost collided as the two women I didn't recognize exited.

"I'm so sorry!" one squealed, looking at me. She almost spilled her coffee on me. Thank goodness I jumped back just in time. The girl with blonde hair ran back in to get some paper towels and started to wipe the floor. "Are you okay?" she asked.

"I'm fine. It's my fault," I replied. "I should have been more careful. I'm fairly new. Which department do you work for?"

"Oh, we used to work in customer service a while back, but we were moved to the sales department," the brunette answered.

"Actually, we asked to be transferred when Crystal was our boss," the blonde happily explained.

"Crystal?" I pretended not to know as I studied their expressions.

"If you've never heard of Crystal, then you must have started *very* recently," the brunette said, looking amused.

"I started working here a couple of months ago. My name is Jeanella Mefferd." I extended my hand. Each took it without hesitation, both with a warm smile.

"It's nice to meet you. My name is Kendra and this is Susan."

Susan, the blonde, shook my hand. "Some people call me Susie."

This was a perfect opportunity to drop the bomb on them. With a cunning smile, I released my hand and said, "Some people call me Jenna."

Both of their mouths dropped and their eyes widened as their lips trembled into nervous smiles. They both turned pink with embarrassment and tore their eyes off me.

"Uh…well…see you around. We're late for a meeting," Kendra said abruptly, tugging Susan down the hall.

"Uh, yeah. We're really late," Susan mumbled.

I figured either they thought I might have been eavesdropping on their conversation, or they felt guilty for talking about me. Either way, I could understand their situation. Had I been in their shoes, I would have blushed, too. However, I wouldn't be talking like that at work. It served them right, and it almost felt good embarrassing them.

A few questions popped up in my mind again, questions I had dismissed before. Due to my insecurities, I began to wonder if I was right to bring them up again. It didn't do any good seeing that text from Luke — 'Sooner or later, he'll screw up.' Neither did overhearing the nonsense from those ladies who had no idea what was going on. No matter how many times I told myself Max was different, my self-doubt undermined me.

After making a cup of coffee, since that was why I went there in the first place, I made a quick stop at Max's office to pick up my sandwich and a heart-shaped Rice Krispie treat. Then I headed back to my department, this time with my heels clicking as loud as they wanted.

Chapter 18
Becky

After my confusing day with Matthew, I tried not to think about what it all meant. Obviously, Matthew had some issues he needed to deal with and if I could be a friend, albeit a flirting friend, I certainly didn't mind that. He was great company and fun to hang out with. Knowing for sure we could only be friends, it would be easier to remember our limitations and move on.

It had been about four days since I had seen Matthew, but to my surprise, he texted me a couple of times. They were short and to the point, asking me how I was, but that was it. It was definitely friend-to-friend texting.

As I finished making dinner, Jenna walked through the door. I was confused since Jenna always spent Friday nights at Max's place.

"Hey, Jenna. This is a wonderful surprise," I said, waving my spatula. You want some curry?"

"You made your special curry?" Jenna looked happy.

"Yup. Almost done."

"I would love some. Let me go change and I'll be right back." She was gone for just a few minutes. It didn't take her long to change and put her hair up.

"No Max tonight?"

"I told him I'd like to stay home and spend some time

with you, since I'm seeing him tomorrow night. What can I help you with?"

"Awww, that's so sweet, but one day, you'll get married and you'll have to leave me. I might as well get used to it."

Jenna started to scoop rice on the plates. "How do you know I'll be getting married first? Besides, Max isn't…I mean…we've never even discussed marriage. It's way too soon."

Jenna swung two plates around to me. With a ladle, I dumped two scoops of curry on each plate. "You just never know. Max has been moving fast. That's bound to be the next step."

"Could we not talk about this subject?" Jenna asked softly. She looked so drained.

"What's wrong?"

"Could you bring the water?" she requested, ignoring my question as she headed to the dining table.

Already seated, she had a slight smile on her face and she looked ready to eat. "Nothing's wrong, Becky. I just don't see the point of discussing something that won't happen in the near future."

After I put the glasses of water down, I sat down and took a bite. Studying Jenna from across the table, she looked agitated. "Come on, Jenna, something is up. I can see it in your face. Did you and Max have a fight?"

Jenna took a sip of water, closed her eyes, and then peered up at me. "No, honestly, we didn't have a fight," she shook her head.

"Jenna, I'm like your other half, though recently my spot has been taken over by Max." I got a small smile out of her. "I know when something is bothering you, even when you think you're fine."

With one elbow on the table, she let out a soft sigh and looked over at me as if to gather her thoughts. After she swallowed some more curry, she started letting go of her worries.

She told me about Luke's latest text, an incident with some women at work, and even how she was worried she might not be good enough, sexually, for Max.

"I think you're overthinking. You're letting Luke and some break-room conversation get to your head."

Jenna nodded. "I know, I know. I feel awful for thinking this, but I have a bad feeling that Max is keeping something from me."

"From what I can see, whatever Max does, he does in your best interest. I don't think he's hiding anything from you, but rather protecting you...if what you're imagining could be true."

Twirling her spoon around, she looked like she was a world away. "Earth to Jenna...Jenna...Jenna!" My tone got louder every time I called her name. She looked up, finally coming out of her daze.

"Do guys like to experiment? I mean...you know...like play with sex toys or role play?" Jenna's cheeks flushed when she asked me that question.

We rarely talked about sex, since she was uncomfortable with it, so the question surprised me. "To tell you the truth, most of the guys I've slept with were selfish in bed. However, I did have a long-term relationship with this one guy and we played around with some toys."

"You did?" She sounded astounded. "Do you think...could you show me?"

I laughed aloud. "I'll show you a few things you can buy on the Internet."

Jenna giggled, blushed, and covered her eyes with her

hand. "I don't want to buy yet. I just want to look. I mean…I don't really want to look, but…" She shoved a spoonful of curry in her mouth on purpose so she couldn't continue and I did the same.

"Jenna, look at me." She did, blushing even more. "Hey, it's okay. You'd be surprised how many people buy these things. It will open your eyes."

"Really?"

Jenna was the sweetest, most naïve friend anyone could have. I loved her innocent virtue and her big heart. I couldn't wait to show her the things that would rock Max's world even more. Though he'd probably already experienced it, if Jenna initiated something steamy, it would drive him crazy.

"Do you have a dress for tomorrow night?" I asked, changing the subject to a more comfortable one, so her cheeks could turn back to their normal color.

"I was just going to wear something from my closet. I don't have time to go shopping."

"No, no, no," I shook my head and my index finger, knowing what kind of dresses she had. "I have something you can wear. Not only will it drive Max crazy, seeing other guys undress you with their eyes will send him over the edge."

"Becky, you know what type of dress I like to wear."

"Exactly, but it's New Year's Eve. Dress to impress. Be a little daring. It's not like you're doing something terrible."

"Okay," she agreed. "And by the way, please don't tell Nicole and Kate about our little conversation."

I nodded, "You know I would never share without your permission."

"I know. Thanks for being such an amazing friend. What would I ever do without you?"

"I don't know, Jenna, but I hope you never find out," I said in a playful tone. "By the way, did you get Nicole's text about where to meet tomorrow night?"

"Yup, do you think you can drive us there so I can go home with Max?"

"Actually, I knew you would go home with Max so I asked Nicole to pick us up since it's on the way. Besides, I want to be able to drink as much as I want and not worry about how I'm getting home."

"Sure. That's fine," she agreed.

Chapter 19
Jenna

Shaking my head, I frowned at Becky. "I'm not even going to try that dress on. It looks too skimpy. I might as well be topless."

"Max would love that," Becky teased. "Come on. Just try it. If you don't like it, take it off."

"You always tell me that and somehow I end up wearing what you chose."

"'Cause I'm always right." She handed me the black dress and gave me a little shove into her bathroom.

I felt like a neon sign that screamed, "Look at me!" However, with my hair and makeup already done, my mirror self had transformed into a diva. Although I was still a little uncomfortable with so much cleavage showing, I had to admit I looked pretty good. "So what do you think?" I shrugged my shoulders as I came out of the bathroom.

Becky's eyes glistened, as she looked me over from head to toe. "Oh my God. Well, I am proud of myself. I'm right again. You know, you have that innocent, angelic face, but with the right makeup and a hot dress, you look gorgeous.

"Thanks," I said shyly.

"Okay." Becky dropped her phone on her bed and opened her closet door. "Now I'd better get dressed while you go get your shawl. I just got a text from Nicole saying she's almost here." Walking into her bathroom, she looked over her shoulder at me. "I can't wait for Max to see you. We're going to have an awesome time."

The traffic was horrendous, not to mention the parking. Thankfully, Nicole's fiancé opted to valet park. He was all sorts of handy today. One of his good friends owned the club, Stellars, so even though it was grand opening night, he reserved a table for us. It was good to have friends with connections. Max texted to let me know he was already at the table with Matthew. We just had to get through the line to show them our IDs.

As soon as we entered, excitement filled the air as we passed several intimidating bouncers. The music pounded against my chest and I wanted be on the dance floor already, but first things first. I was starving, and I knew Becky was too, since we both had a light lunch. Peering up, I noted there were two levels. They designed it so the people on the first floor could see the people on the second level. The second story had a big gap in the center, protected by bars for safety.

It was dark, but the neon lights and the surrounding white lights that dangled from corner to corner kept guests from bumping into each other. It would have taken some time to search for Max on my own in the huge room. Thankfully, he had texted me again to let me know he would wait for us at the bar instead of at the table. However, the bar was ginormous!

I had never seen a bar that size before. Off to the side, people checked in their coats, which we decided to do as well. Becky took out her credit card and her driver's license before she handed hers over. She didn't bring a purse. She said she didn't want to bother bringing one since she wasn't driving. There were only two places to hide her cards, and I wondered where they were going this time.

Tugging Becky along as she held onto Nicole, we searched for Max. Carefully avoiding others, we weaved through the crowd of people. They all looked like they had a head start drinking. Someone suddenly bumped into me from the side.

"Watch it!" she said. Turning my head, I spotted the person who smacked into me. She was tall and blonde, in a tight red dress. She looked familiar, but I couldn't place her.

About midpoint on the bar, I spotted Max. He was all dressed up in a crisp shirt, sleeves rolled up half way. He propped one leg up on the rail as he leaned forward on the bar, holding a drink. My heart skipped and flipped, just like the first time I saw him; then we set our eyes on each other. He was dangerously good-looking, too good to be true in every way, and I was the lucky one who got to say—he's mine.

Instead of approaching him, I waited while he chatted with the lady beside him. Actually, she was talking to him, but I could tell Max was being polite, trying not to lead her on by his posture. He leaned away as she leaned toward him. It was time to rescue my man, and time to tell the lady to back off. Becky nudged me, letting me know she saw the same thing. "Wait right here," I told Becky.

"Max." I placed my hand on his back.

Max swung around, all smiles, and embraced me. "Babe, you finally made it. You look beautiful." He looked so relieved. When he released me, his eyes twinkled and his face radiated bliss. It was comforting to know I could make him look this happy. I was also quite relieved to see that the lady he had been chatting with disappeared into the crowd. After he hugged Becky and Nicole and shook hands with Keith, he led the way to our table.

Holding Max's hand, I followed as we weaved through tables and people. Finally, we ended up in a cozy corner with a big reserved sign. It was a big, kidney-shaped table with a plush, black, cushioned booth seat. We all fit easily. The volume of the music was lower in this area, too. When Matthew spotted us, he excused himself from the crowd of women who surrounded him and came to our table. Then, we spotted Kate and Craig. Everyone was there.

After the introductions and greetings, we ordered our dinners. As we ate, we laughed and talked about our jobs, Kate and Craig's daughter, and Nicole and Keith's wedding. It was the first time we were all together having a great time and getting to know each other. Occasionally, it seemed as though Matthew and Becky held their own private conversation. They got along very well, compared to the first time they met, but surprisingly they acted like old friends. I wondered what had changed and what Becky was keeping from me.

Still feeling self-conscious because of Becky's revealing dress, I looked at my friends' attire. I was the only one with a shawl draped over my shoulders. Becky's dress showed more cleavage than mine. Kate wore a dark gray spaghetti strap dress, but didn't show much cleavage, and Nicole wore a snake print tube dress, which was way too much for me to handle. I felt like I was looking at a sexy serpent. I'd never wear a dress like that, but to each her own.

Every so often, Becky gestured for me to take off my shawl. I would reply by shaking my head and giving her a "you can't make me" smile. By the time we'd finished our dinner, two hours had passed. Since we had the table all night, we kicked back and relaxed with the cocktails the waitress brought back from the bar. I knew my limitations, so I only took a few small sips of my drink. It totally sucked to be allergic to alcohol.

The dance floor was packed, as was the second floor. Nicole and Kate had already joined the fun. Matthew went to the restroom and never came back, so I figured he went off with a girl. Not wanting to leave Becky here by herself, Max and I stayed behind.

"Well, I see an old friend from college. You two go have fun and I'll meet you back at the table before the count down." Becky took a last sip of her drink and scooted out. Just before she was out of my sight, she yanked on my black shawl, exposing me. She dropped the shawl on top of Max and left giggling. Oh, she was going to get it.

Pulling the shawl off his lap, Max reached for me. Backing up as far as he could into the booth, he bit and sucked my lip. His naughty hands glided all over my body as he engulfed me, unashamed of groping me in public; but then again, we were in the far back corner, with a lot more privacy than any of the other tables.

"I've wanted to do this since you first came in. Seeing what you're wearing under that shawl, I can't help myself. I missed you last night," he said between pressing his lips to mine.

"I missed you too, Max," I breathed heavily, feeling his lips travel down to my breast. The lower he went, the faster my pulse raced. Tugging the dress to one side, Max's tongue found my nipple and I exploded. He didn't stop there, as one of his hands slipped up my dress to rub between my legs. If we were home, I would've been begging him to take my clothes off.

Max pulled back as my urges raged out of control. "I

think we need to stop now," he panted. "I'm practically molesting you." Max fixed my dress and kissed my forehead, making sure I was still in one piece, and sitting properly. "If your friends weren't here to ring in the New Year with you, I would've picked you up and taken you home. Now I need a drink."

Dazed, I watched Max gulp down a full glass of ice water. The waitress left several glasses just in case, so I took one and gulped it down too.

"Let's go dance, babe. If we stay here, I won't be able to keep my hands to myself, and you already know how my hands can be."

"Let's go," I said, following him to the dance floor.

Chapter 20
Becky

I lied so Max and Jenna would go dance without feeling guilty, but when I spotted Aaron from college, I was more than happy to greet him. Not that I expected Matthew to hang around with me since we were just friends, but I wondered where he went. He had to be with someone at the bar or dancing. I didn't care anymore. It was New Year's Eve and I was going to party the night away.

"Aaron." I wrapped my arms around him, raising my voice over the loud music. He and his group of friends looked way too happy. It had been several years since I last saw him, but he still looked good. He had shorter hair this time around and he was dressed to impress, so he looked mighty fine.

"Becky...Becky...Becky...Where have you been hiding?" Aaron squeezed me tighter, making me feel his hard chest. He probably could crush me with his hug. Not to mention, he reeked of alcohol.

"I've been around." Aaron's smile was contagious.

"You look great." He turned to his buddies, "This is Becky. And boy can she..." he stopped, giving me an impish grin. "Did you come alone?"

"I came with Jenna, Nicole, and Kate. Do you remember them?"

"I remember Jenna. She was your roommate, right? After Amber."

"Yeah." Aaron bringing up her name turned me somber. "I could use a drink," I said, looking toward the bar.

"How about shots, the way we used to?" Aaron suggested. "If I win, you owe me a dance and a kiss."

"I don't think so. I need to get back to meet my friends before midnight."

"You still have an hour," he winked, begging me with a flirtatious grin. "For old time's sake."

I was about to say no again, when I spotted Matthew surrounded by a bunch of other women, laughing and having a great time by the bar. One of them rubbed Matthew's thigh. He looked like he was enjoying himself. I didn't know why a spark of anger ignited in me, but I agreed to do shots with Aaron.

"Here you go." Aaron placed a shot on the bar in front of me, as his friends surrounded us. I closed my eyes and chugged it down. The burning sensation wasn't pleasant. I had forgotten that feeling. It had been a while since I had done shots. Slamming the glass back on the bar, holding a bold stare and cringing, I yelled over the loud music, "One. Your turn."

Aaron chuckled, doing the same. "One. Looks like you're out of practice."

"Maybe. But if memory serves, I've whipped your ass every time." Squirming and wondering what the hell I had gotten myself into, I swallowed again, banging the shot glass in front of him. "Two."

Wondering if Matthew was still there, I glanced in his direction, but quickly turned away when I thought he might catch me looking. Oh God, why was I trying to get his freakin' attention? I hated that.

Obviously, he had no feelings for me or he would have been by my side instead of flirting with every woman in the place. Why did he have to say I made him forget about his late fiancée? I totally sympathized with him regarding her death, but he made it sound like he thought I was special. Something I didn't need to hear.

Aaron's friends were loud. Matthew had to have seen us. A couple of the girls around him looked our way, I was almost sure of it. Whatever.

"Three," I challenged, wiping the side of my mouth with the back of my hand. Hearing Aaron's friends cheering me on got me all pumped up, and Matthew slowly faded out of my thoughts.

"Maybe you still got it, Becky, but we shall see. You look a little out of it there," Aaron teased. "I can't wait to get my kiss and — "

Aaron stopped talking, looking over my shoulder. Feeling the warm sensation on my arm, I turned to see the person who had put it there. Matthew's smile gave me fluttering tingles in my stomach, which pissed me off.

"Do you mind? I'm having fun." I nudged his hand off me.

Matthew glanced at the shot glasses, then back to me. At first, he narrowed his eyes at me disapprovingly, but then they became playful. "You like to do shots? You like to swallow?"

I twitched my brows. "Only ones that squirt in my mouth." I could not believe I'd said that, and from the expression on his face, neither could Matthew. His eyes sparkled with amusement, trying not to give me a grin, letting me know how much he liked my answer. I just couldn't help myself. A perverted question deserved a perverted answer.

Matthew swung my stool around. Putting his hands on my shoulders, he leaned into me, catching me by surprise. I thought he was going to kiss me, but he sniffed me instead. Looking squarely into my eyes he said, "I think you've had enough."

I knew he was right, but he had no business telling me what to do. That pissed me off even more. "I'm fine. I can handle my liquor. And besides, I didn't drive here, so I can get as drunk as I want." I smirked. If he could hang out with a group of girls, then I could hang out with the guys.

"You came with Jenna. And if you didn't drive, how were you planning to get home?" Matthew looked concerned.

"That's none of your business. Why don't you go back to your friends?" I sounded angry, like a jealous girlfriend, but my buzz gave me the courage to do so. I could always use that as an excuse.

Matthew gave me a sideways glance, looked over my head, and curled his lips into a satisfied grin. What was he thinking? "You had a clear view of me. You were jealous?"

"I was not," I stammered. "What are you talking about?" Before he could get me to admit it, I got off the stool and grabbed Aaron by his shirt. "Come on, Aaron, I owe you a dance."

Aaron was more than pleased to follow me to the dance floor. When we got there, I didn't even bother to look where Matthew went. Feeling the bass pumping through my chest, I shook my hips. Aaron's arms rubbed all over my back and he gave me no room to breathe. Body against body, I raised my hand as he bumped and grinded against me. I even let him put his hands on my ass. We were practically having sex on the dance floor. Next thing I knew, Aaron was off me and someone was dragging me away.

"What the hell, Matthew!" I yelled.

"What would your boyfriend say?" He clenched his jaw and his eyes pierced into mine with anger. "And where the hell is he?"

I laughed out loud. I had forgotten about my fake boyfriend. Was that the reason why he ignored me? He thought my boyfriend would eventually show up.

"What's so funny?" he demanded to know. He was mad. I had never seen him like this before.

"Nothing," I shook my head.

"Your friends are looking for you. Max texted me several times. I'm taking you back to the table now."

Aaron had already given up on me and moved on to the next girl. We dated in college, but after a few dates, I knew he was not only a chick magnet, but he would eventually break my heart. I told him I thought we should just be friends. That was one wise decision.

Matthew climbed the stairs behind me. Sure enough, the gang had gathered off to the side.

"Where have you been?" Jenna pulled me next to her. "It's almost midnight."

Shit! I'd almost forgotten why we were here in the first place. Not letting me answer, Jenna asked another.

"Are you buzzed?"

"Sort of," I smiled, placing my head on her shoulder.

"Are you having fun?"

Before I could answer, Nicole placed one of the dunce hats on my head and gave me a small blow horn. "Cute," I said.

"You're welcome. New Year's Eve would not be the same without them." One by one, Nicole handed two things to everyone. When she got to Matthew, he'd put the hat on his head. He looked so adorable that it took every ounce of strength to stop me from smiling.

In fact, he looked damn hot tonight. With black trousers and a dark gray dress shirt that fit perfectly across his muscular chest, he looked dashing and edible. I couldn't stop thinking about how aroused I felt when I pretended to give him a lap dance.

Matthew glared at me. He was still upset about something, but I didn't care. Kate and Craig passed out wine glasses filled with champagne. Then everyone in the building started counting down...10...9...8...7...6...we started counting too as we surrounded each other.

"3...2...1 Happy New Year!" we all shouted. My friends each had someone to kiss, except for me. Looking at my glass, I swallowed it with one gulp. When a hard body brushed up against mine, I automatically knew it was Matthew. That simple touch produced all sorts of tingles I didn't want to feel, and I was drowning into him, unable to come up for air.

"Happy New Year, Becca," he whispered in my ear, holding me longer than I had expected. Pulling back slightly, he pressed his warm lips to my cheek. I got a taste of what was going to keep me up that night. That one tender kiss didn't feel like a friend-to-friend kiss. Breathing him in, I didn't want him to let go, but I had no choice. Jenna grabbed the two of us before I could gather my willpower and push him off me.

After we all made our rounds of hugs, Kate and Craig headed home. Shortly after, Nicole and Keith took off, too. I knew the look when Jenna pouted as she gazed my way.

"Sorry, but Max wants to leave. He offered to take you home, but Matthew volunteered. At least we know you'll be in good hands."

"He did what?" I sneered, but then toned it down when Jenna looked bewildered. "I can ask my friend Aaron." Glancing toward Matthew, it looked like he was having an intense conversation with Max.

"Aaron from college? Aaron West?"

I shrugged, looking guilty. Jenna had loathed him.

"He's just a friend."

"I think it's better if Matthew takes you home, but I trust you to make the right decision. I can't tell how buzzed you are. You can discuss this with Matthew. He was pretty adamant about taking you home. By the way, when did you start getting along so well?"

"Long story. You should get going. Looks like Max is either upset or tired."

"Okay, but please text me when you get home." Jenna and I exchanged hugs. Without wasting any time, Matthew walked over and said he was going to take me home, but I had other plans.

Chapter 21
Jenna

I asked Max to get my coat from the coat check and I would meet him out front after I took care of business in the restroom. Knowing my alcohol tolerance, I only drank a little, but it was enough for me to want to go. Thankfully, the line was short.

I had made a mental note to go on the pill after the unprotected sex in the shower. We couldn't do that again. Getting pregnant was the last thing I wanted, especially since I wasn't ready to be a mom. Knowing my period was going to start soon, I wore a thin liner. When I saw I started spotting, I was beyond relieved. At least I didn't have to hold my breath in anticipation any longer. I wasn't worried about it...too much. I was almost positive I hadn't been ovulating, but I was a couple of days late. It scared me.

After a quick glance at myself in the mirror to make sure I looked presentable, I headed out the door when someone tapped me from behind.

"Excuse me, are you Jenna?"

She looked familiar: tall, blonde and beautiful. Her dress was revealing and the color of it reminded me of...yes...she was the rude woman who had bumped into me earlier, but there was something else. One of the models I had seen at the New York Fashion Show, perhaps?

Peering up, I smiled and nodded. "Yes, I'm Jenna. Can I help you?"

Her expression changed to something I had not expected. Her stoic face became aggressive and she leaned into me like a bully. "If I were you, I would leave Max right now before things get ugly. He'll eventually run back to me. He always did. Just fair warning, we don't want your precious heart to get broken again."

My pulse shot up as I stood frozen, not believing what I heard. Not believing that I had run into Crystal again. I only had a quick glance at her that time I saw her at Max's penthouse, but how could I have forgotten that face? The right thing to do was to walk out, so I started heading toward the exit when she spoke again.

"Max didn't tell you, did he?"

That caught my attention. "Tell me what?" My tone grew hostile as anger and curiosity boiled inside me. I told myself I should walk away, that I shouldn't listen to her nonsense, but I couldn't help myself.

"We're getting back together. He's just trying to find the right time to let you go. I suggest you break up with him first. That way it will be easier for him. I see what he saw in you…sweet and innocent, but you were just a shiny new toy he wanted to play with. And now he's bored with you."

In seconds, I was back at the penthouse when I first saw her and remembering the hurtful words she had said. Even the break room conversation popped up, 'what do you think will happen,' and all sorts of thoughts fluttered through my mind. I had to speak to Max.

"Excuse me. I have to go," I said and turned. Why was I being polite?

She grabbed my arm. "He's not satisfied. No one can

satisfy Max the way I do. You'll see. Run while you can."

I'm not the violent type but I wanted to slap her face to get her off me. Yanking my arm free, I swiftly walked out of there. With every step toward Max, my heart pounded harder and faster against my chest. With every step, my anger grew. I had my suspicions ever since the lunchroom encounter, but I dismissed it, thinking it was just rumors, but now I knew for sure he was hiding something from me.

"Jenna." Someone grabbed my arm, pulling me to the side of the bar. I thought it was Max and didn't resist. "How have you been? You look great?"

"Ethan? I'm great. How about you? You haven't changed a bit." Ethan was one of the first friends I had met in college. Our friendship took a turn when he wanted more from me. It had been a while since I last saw him. Though he looked like he hadn't aged much, he plumped up a bit and looked like he was losing some hair.

"What are you up to?" he asked, wrapping his arms around another woman.

That was a relief. He wasn't going to hit on me. "I'm working for *Knight Fashion Magazine*."

His eyes grew wide. "Really. I used to work for their competitor, Rave. This is my wife, Kim."

"Hello, Kim. It's nice to meet you." We shook hands. She had a pretty smile. "Ethan is a lucky man."

Kim smiled. "We're both lucky to have each other. It wasn't all smooth at the beginning, but we pulled through."

Okay, I sure didn't need to know *that* much information, but whatever the problem was, I was happy for them. "Ethan. I need to go find someone."

"Wait. Don't tell me you're the Jenna dating Maxwell Knight?"

"How did you know?"

He stood silent with a blank stare for a moment. I began to worry. Then Ethan flashed me a short grin. "He was my nemesis." He chuckled lightly. "Let's have lunch when you get a chance. Here's my business card."

"Thanks." I retrieved the card from his hand. "That would be great. It was nice meeting you, Kim. Hope to see you at lunch too someday." With that, I took off again, heading straight for the front exit.

"Thank you," I said to the bouncer who politely opened the door for me. I didn't even look at him as I rushed out. Hugging my shawl in the dreadful cold, I shivered as I looked for Max.

Strangely, tons of people crowded around the door. What were they doing? My answer came when a bunch of blinding lights started flashing before my eyes, accompanied by the clicking of cameras. This had to be a case of mistaken identity. They must have thought I was someone else, but when people began shouting my name and threw dozens of questions at me, I became immobilized.

"Miss Mefferd, what do you think about the lawsuit?" one shouted.

"How do you feel about Max's past?"

"Were you the reason Max broke up with Crystal?"

Backing up with my eyes covered, trying to get back into the club, I shouted for Max. When the music blasted louder, I knew the door had swung open.

"Jenna!" Max called.

More flashes and questions drowned out whatever he had said. "Get the fuck away from her!" Max yelled. He said it several more times before he was able to get to me. Covering me with his body, we went back into the club. He told the bouncer not to let any of them in. Then he tipped the other bouncers nearby, asking them to escort us out to the car.

Max held me as we followed behind them. As we weaved through the crowds, I looked for Becky, but I couldn't find her. Perhaps Matthew had taken her home, but it was hard to find anyone when we moved fast and away from the massive crowd.

When we got to the exit on the other side, the bouncers told us to wait for their return. It was my chance to pull away from him. "Max, I'm not going home with you."

Max looked hurt and frustrated. "Jenna, don't do this." Max reached for me, but I backed away. "Jenna, let me explain."

"I already know you kept something from me. What else are you hiding? How am I supposed to trust you?" Tears started to pool in my eyes. I wasn't good at fighting back, but I was so hurt, the words just flowed out. Unable to think clearly, and with Crystal's words echoing in my head, I asked a dumb question. "Are you seeing Crystal?"

"What? Who told you this?"

"That's not an answer Max," I said sternly.

"Jenna..."

The bouncers came back in. "It's clear, but we'll have to hurry. Your car is with the valet right in front. The doors are open, ready for you."

"Thanks," Max said, reaching for me again.

I shook my head with my arms crossed.

"Jenna, I'm not letting you go. Either you come with me willingly, or I'll carry you out. You're coming with me one way or another. Your choice."

He wasn't bluffing. Instead of letting Max protect me, I stepped in front of the bouncer. Max scowled, but he knew at least I would go home with him, and that was enough.

Becky

There was no way I was going to let Matthew take me home. Besides, I wanted to party some more. It was going to be difficult to dodge him when he wouldn't stop following me wherever I went.

"Look, Matthew. I'm glad you want to be a good friend and take me home, but Aaron is more than capable."

Matthew glanced over to Aaron, and looked back at me. His eyes drilled through me with anger. "You take a good look at him? Do you see how drunk he is?" He turned the bar stool around so I could see, then he swung me back to him. Matthew was right; Aaron's coordination wasn't all there on the dance floor. "There is no way in hell I'm going to let you get in the car with him. In fact, I'm going to tell one of the bouncers to make sure he doesn't put his sorry ass in his car. If you want to call someone else that's fine, but I'm going to wait until that happens before I leave."

"I don't need a babysitter."

"Apparently you do. And just where is this so called boyfriend of yours? Why isn't he here? Did you two get into a fight?"

"Lots of questions. I don't want to answer them." I waved my hand. Feeling tired, I yawned as I covered my mouth.

For some strange reason seeing me yawn made him grin. Matthew tried his best not to show his amused smile, but he failed. I could tell he had an ulterior motive.

"Well, that's my signal. You're tired. Let's go," Matthew said.

"I've already told you that you're not taking me home," I pouted.

"Oh, yes I am." Without warning, Matthew lifted me up, swinging my body over his shoulder.

"Put me down," I shouted as I smacked his hard ass, finding myself enjoying it.

Matthew's shoulders' shook as if he were chuckling, but I wasn't sure. It was hard to hear much in there. Walking toward the exit, he gave me a good smack on the ass too.

Dropping me next to the hostess so I could retrieve my coat, he looked squarely into my eyes and said, "Every smack you give me, I'll return even harder. You don't want to do that, Becca. You've already got me turned on, and I promise you, I'll make you want to cheat on your boyfriend. I'm that good."

I dropped my jaw and mentally took off my clothes for him, yet again. With just words, he made my panties wet. Holy shit!

"Thanks," Matthew said to the lady who handed me my coat. Matthew broke me out of my trance by putting his arms around me from behind. I was certain the lady heard what he said from the way she smiled at him, and I'm pretty certain she mentally took off her clothes for him too.

"Let's go, Becca. I'm taking you home," his words were too close to my ear, making me quiver as I thought about what he said. He made me so completely weak in the knees I had no fight left in me. I hated that he had that kind of power over me.

Chapter 22
Jenna

I backed away, keeping my distance from Max. Once his lips touched any part of me, there was no way I could control myself. I had no willpower when it came to Max. My body automatically succumbed to his voice, his wink, his sexy grin, his touch, and simply him. Releasing a deep breath, Max went to the bar to pour himself a drink.

"Please sit. You're making me nervous." Max sat on the sofa, tapping the seat next to him.

"No," I said with conviction.

"You're acting like a child, you know that?" he chuckled.

He made my anger worse. "No, I'm not," I huffed.

Max's eyes darkened, heated and dangerous looking. "If you don't sit down and listen, I'm going to take you right here, right now and make you wish you were this bratty all the time."

That came out too playful and I didn't want that. Well, not yet anyway. Plopping myself on the sofa, I waited for him to take another sip.

With his feet apart, elbows on his thighs, he looked at me tenderly. "Babe, Crystal didn't take the money. She is going ahead with the lawsuit. Matthew told me he handed her the check with both of our lawyers present, but she never cashed it. My lawyer called several days ago, and I didn't want to ruin our New Year's Eve party. You have to believe me. I was going to tell you when the time was right."

Max took another sip. "I'm sorry. I didn't want you to be in the middle of this; and I'm so sorry about what happened with the paparazzi. Crystal must have leaked the news. It's the only explanation. My parents are not even aware of it. I was going to tell them after I told you."

Max was telling the truth; I could see it in his eyes. I knew how to read his eyes so well. Pushing away my pride, I decided to sit next to him and comfort him. "I'm sorry too, but you have to see it from my side as well."

Nodding, Max took my hand and gingerly stroked it while he spoke. "Who told you? How did you find out?"

"I ran into Crystal at the restroom."

Max arched his brows, looking stunned. "She was there? I wouldn't be surprised if she's stalking us. Don't believe anything she says. She manipulates and lies to get her way."

"I know," I agreed.

"I'm going to hire a couple of security guards. I want them to watch your apartment, but not right in front; and two will be hired for our place. Don't worry. Crystal is not the violent type. I'm doing this in case the paparazzi decide to follow you home." Max's hands slipped through my hair, pulling me in for a kiss. I let him kiss me, but I couldn't kiss back. I wasn't mad at him, but the situation frustrated me. Before I could show affection in return, I needed to calm down.

"Let's go to bed. It's late," Max said, holding my hand, and I obliged. New Year's Eve didn't turn out as I'd planned, but we were safe, healthy, and together, and that was all that mattered.

Max

As tired as I was, I couldn't sleep. Closing my eyes and trying to take deep breaths didn't help, so I turned toward Jenna. She slept soundly, looking like an angel. As I lay and watched her, I thought about how hot she looked in that black dress.

She didn't flaunt herself the way most girls would have done. In fact, if Becky hadn't pulled the shawl off her, I would've eventually. When we finally had alone time, I couldn't help myself. I kissed her like there was no tomorrow, especially when I saw what the dress really looked like on her. I wouldn't have been all over her the way I had been if anyone could see us, but having the secluded area to ourselves made it that much easier.

Matt and I were offered two tickets each to go to a party many celebrities attended every year. It would have been the perfect opportunity to introduce Jenna to some of my good friends, but I didn't tell her about it, knowing she wanted to be with her friends. I had my reasons, but I had no idea why Matt decided to come along.

Becky and Matt looked pretty cozy during dinner. Knowing my brother and his record with women lately, I didn't know if it was a good idea for him to hang out with Becky, unless they were really just friends. Nevertheless, the way he'd been acting around her, my gut feeling told me he wanted more. I hoped neither of them would get hurt in the end. If something bad happened between them, it would become extremely awkward for all of us. Perhaps I needed to have a talk with him.

This whole incident made me wonder if I should have

taken Jenna elsewhere, but I was relieved to get the topic of Crystal and the lawsuit out of the way. I didn't know how she would react. I also didn't want to ruin New Year's Eve for either of us by causing a fight, though I didn't know if there would be one.

If we ended up going to court, Crystal was sure to try to embarrass me by bringing up the games we had played. I worried that Jenna would look at me differently. As much as I'd like to think Jenna loved me as much as I loved her, she had never said it to me. I know the word "love" is a huge thing to say to someone you're dating, but I meant it. It's the reason why I could say it so easily. I'd never felt like that before, nor had I ever said it to anyone else I dated before; not even to Crystal, who happened to be my longest relationship. Why the fuck had I gone out with her?

Being successful, lonely, and especially young, I had all the time to play. That's when Crystal entered my life. She was beautiful, available, and knew how to please a man in more ways than one. I blame it on stupidity and wanting to experiment. After all, I was single and finding the perfect woman to have a future with seemed impossible...until Jenna came along. I knew when I laid eyes on her, she was my one in a million and I would do anything for her.

I continued to watch the beauty beside me, and she consumed me with her presence. As I watched her chest rise and fall with the rhythm of my own, I lightly brushed her arm to feel her warmth; to know she was really there, and I uttered the words I wanted her to hear and feel. "I love you, Jenna."

I don't know how long I watched her, but the peace I felt from doing so made my eyelids heavy, making me sleepy. "See you in my dreams, babe," I mumbled as I fell into darkness.

Chapter 23
Becky

Matthew practically dragged me to his car as I tried to escape his hold. He kept insisting he wasn't going to let me go home with someone who was drunk or someone he didn't know. He said he would never forgive himself if anything ever happened to me. Naturally, I thought of my former roommate and his dead fiancée.

"Thanks a lot for caring," I sneered, trying to slam the door of my apartment as I walked inside, but he blocked it. Stomping to my bedroom like a child, I looked over my shoulder. "Why are you still here? I'm home! Thanks to you. You can leave now." I should have been thankful that he cared enough to bring me home, but I resented him instead. Flashes of Amber crossed my mind. Maybe I should have been that aggressive with her...no, not maybe, I should have been. Then guilt took over my mind.

Matthew plopped on the sofa with his legs crossed, stretching both of his arms along the top. You could see the results of his workouts. He had nicely chiseled arms, and I wanted to touch them.

"I'm not leaving until you apologize for acting like a spoiled brat."

"Then you might as well sleep here forever. I'm not apologizing." Leaning against the wall, I crossed my arms.

Matthew wasn't paying attention to me anymore. His thoughts were miles away. He pointed at the beautiful roses Max had recently given Jenna, for the hundredth time. His realization took me completely by surprise. "You don't have a boyfriend, do you?"

"I do," I said softy, but I knew my tone deceived me.

Matthew stood up. "I can't believe you did that."

The expression on his face not only made me feel guilty, but also ashamed.

"Why?" he continued to ask with his fist tight. He clenched his jaw until a vein protruded from the side of his neck.

I had no reason for my response, other than it had built up from emotions I couldn't control. I walked directly in front of him. "I hate you," I sneered in his face, standing on my tippy toes. I wanted to be face to face with him, so he could hear the intensity of my words.

He leaned closer with a fiery, yet amused expression in his eyes. Not what I had in mind. I stepped back from his lips, which were now too dangerously close. "Yeah, I hate you more," he replied nonchalantly, with a cool tone as if what I had said didn't faze him at all.

"Good. At least we have that in common," I declared.

"Oh, we have more things in common than you realize." His demeanor was playful. Holding a wicked grin, he leaned in closer.

Tantalizing heat shot through every nerve in my body and that stance alone made me feel like his hands moved all over me. Damn! Then his eyes fell down to my lips, causing me to become weak all over. I didn't like it at all. I didn't like how he made me want to dive into his arms. I wanted him to leave. If I were rude, perhaps he would go.

"You're egotistical, rude, crazy, and so not perfect." I

poked his chest. Oh God! Wrong move on my part. Touching him made me want him even more.

"You're not perfect either." He raised his voice.

The muscles on his arms tensed as he stepped toward me again, causing me to back against the wall. Thump...shit!

"But you're perfect for me," he continued. His tone softened unexpectedly.

What did he just say to me? Frazzled, I started to stutter. "I...I...but...you're crazy," I said softly, matching his tenor.

I twitched when his hands banged the wall on either side of my face as his muscles flexed. Though his proximity unnerved me, I was utterly melting into him. No! I needed self-control.

"You're crazier," he retorted. His eyes shifted down to my lips again.

Please don't stare too long. I knew I wouldn't be able to handle it, but his insult triggered my anger again. When I didn't have any sophisticated words to say, I spit out the first thing that came to my mind. "You're an ass," I seethed.

"I can be worse." His eyes sparked with amusement. It was not the effect I hoped for.

"I want you to leave," I demanded.

"But I don't want to."

"I didn't give you a choice."

"Make me." His brows lifted in challenge.

"You're impossible."

"You're incredible."

"Shut up. Don't say those words to me. Get out," I shouted this time.

"I don't want to be out. I want to be inside you." His voice was just as loud as mine.

Holy shit! The gap between my legs fired up. "I won't ever give you the pleasure." I calmed down, giving him a look of conviction.

"Then I'll dream about it."

Confusion filled my mind.

"I dream about it all the time." He brushed the words against the tip of my ear, sending erotic, sensuous heat all over me. His hands, still on the wall, gripped tightly into fists, as if he was fighting what he wanted to do. "Your lips on mine, your naked body under mine, me inside you, giving you pleasure and feeling you all night long. Listening to you scream my name until you come."

In my mind, my panties dropped. I was only rude to him because I didn't want to feel the things he made me feel. He had issues, and I didn't know if I could be there for him, or if he would be too much for me to handle. Plus, the fact that he was Max's brother made everything worse, but after what he just said, I couldn't control myself anymore. It was the hottest thing anyone had ever said to me.

My rational thought had disappeared as his hot breath caressed my neck. Oh, he was good and he knew exactly what he was doing to me. My chest rose and fell with gasps as my breasts gravitated toward his chest. "What are you waiting for? Make your dreams come true."

"I want to kiss you so badly right now." His eyes begged for my permission as he licked and bit his lower lip, making me want to do the same thing to him.

I drilled my eyes into his with a look of wanting. "Then kiss me," I whispered.

He didn't wait any longer. Cupping my face, he slithered his tongue inside my mouth, and slammed me into the wall. The sensation went straight between my legs. The arms I had been holding against the wall for support twisted around the nape of his neck. Gliding my hands along the curve of his muscles I had wanted to touch since the day I first saw him was beyond satisfying.

"Becca," he managed to say between his kisses as his hand explored my breast, around my waist, down to my ass, cupping it there as his hardness pressed into me. "I want you so much," he growled.

The sounds he made pulled me over the edge and I moaned with him. Thank God, Jenna was at Max's place. Wanting more of him, I started to pull his shirt up so he would get the message, but instead, he loosened his grip on me. His kisses trailed to my cheek, my jaw line...kissing and nipping...down to my neck. Then he backed away breathlessly, looking at me as if he decided he had made a mistake.

"Sorry...I...I shouldn't have done that." He raked his fingers through his hair, looking confused. Then he ran out the door.

What just happened? He left.

He

Just

Freakin'

Left.

Unbelievable. What the hell! Leaning my back against the wall for support, I slid down to the floor and placed both of my hands over my face. I will not cry! I will not cry! I will not cry! In my humiliation, the stern talk I gave myself didn't work, and the uncontrollable sting of the pain in my heart twisted deeper. Then the tears came. Why do I let assholes into my heart? There was only one answer. I was an asshole magnet. I always was.

Chapter 24
Becky

The door crashed open. My heart leapt out of my chest. In fear for my life, thinking it was a burglar, I tried to bolt to my room, but I was still stuck to the floor.

"Why is the door still unlocked?" Matthew hollered as he walked in. His eyes froze on me for a second, but then he swiftly came toward me looking concerned. "Are you okay?"

He tried to lift me up, but I slapped his hands away. "Why did you come back?" I ranted, burning my gaze into him with venom. Somehow, we stood face to face. How the hell was I standing and how did he do that without me even knowing? Damn his beautiful eyes that I always get lost in.

"Were you crying?" his eyes and his attitude became soft. He lifted his hand to wipe my tears.

"Don't touch me." I smacked his hand away and shoved him, but he didn't budge. Since he didn't even attempt to give me space, I pushed him harder and when that didn't work, I started to get a little more aggressive and drummed on his chest.

Matthew gripped both of my arms and pinned them high above my head on the wall. "Had enough?" he asked in a calm tone.

"No," I spat. "I don't want you here. Leave." I turned and twisted to release myself from his grasp, but it didn't work.

"No." His expression was stern.

"Then I'll scream," I threatened, hoping he would let go.

"I can make you scream all night." His tone came off too playful.

How is it possible he can make me almost orgasm with a few words? "Go away."

"Not until I know you're okay."

"I'll be fine when you leave. Why did you come back?"

"Because I didn't want you to think I don't like you." His hand was strong enough to hold both of my wrists in place while the other hand slid down my back, making me forget what he had just said.

"What?" I snorted. He was the one who left. "Well, you shouldn't have bothered, 'cause I don't like you."

"That's okay. I have plenty of like for the both of us."

"You're insane." I blinked.

"You're insanier."

"That's not a word."

"I don't care." he shrugged. "But *you* on the other hand should care, because you lied to me about having a boyfriend and you're a thief." His hand slowly slid down to my waist, then to my back again.

"How am I a thief?"

"Cause you stole a tiny piece of my heart when I didn't want to give it to you."

"Then that's your fault. You were a willing victim. I'm not giving you any piece of mine."

"I'm not asking for it." His hand wrung the back of my dress, causing me to gasp.

"Good."

"Good," he repeated, releasing my hand. "Now I'm going to kiss you; but if you don't want—"

I broke free from his hand and grabbed a fistful of his hair. "Shut up. You talk too much." Then I crushed my lips on his in hunger, madness, and hurt. I saw how it would end, but I didn't care. I wanted him, even just for one night. He gave me that tiny piece of his heart, and that was more than I'd ever had before. Though he didn't know it, I already had given him mine. Now who was the unwilling victim?

Matthew pulled back, pulled his shirt over his head, and not an ounce of shyness marked his face. I had already seen it once before, but good Lord have mercy. The view of his chest drove me crazy. Still drilling his eyes on me, he pulled my dress and my bra down at the same time, leaving me exposed. While I was so busy spitting my words at him, he'd already unhooked my bra.

Matthew took in the view with a satisfied, lustful grin. I stood there as boldly as he did, though I was uncomfortable as never before. I didn't have to stand there too long; he molded his lips to mine while one of his hands kneaded my breast. His warm touch drove me wild and I caught fire between my legs. Were we really doing this?

Kissing, nipping my face then my neck, he somehow brought us to my room and kicked the door closed behind us. Still keeping his gaze on me, he lowered me gently to my bed, kicked off his shoes, and then unbuttoned and pulled off his pants. He was masculine and beautiful.

He reached down and pulled out a condom from his jeans pocket, and placed it on. "You never know." He twitched his brow.

"Don't worry, I'm on the pill," I said.

"Just in case," he muttered. With his tongue, he began working his magic; stroking, licking, and tasting my clit. I couldn't take it anymore, but just before I moved to pull him up by a fistful of his hair, he ran his tongue from my belly button to my nipple. Showing me no mercy, he sucked hard.

Arching my back in raw pleasure, I dug my fingers into the sheets and lost control. It got worse when he began to rub his erection on the perfect spot. My head and vision spun, so I closed my eyes and took in his pleasure. When his kisses trailed upward to my neck, then to my cheek, he pressed his warm body onto mine and rocked back and forth as if he was inside me.

He was teasing the hell out of me and enjoying it. "Are you sure you want this?" he asked softly, nibbling my ear while one of his hands aroused my hardened nipple. "I can stop if you want me, too."

I didn't want him to stop. I was blistering underneath my G-string. Why hadn't he taken it off? I took his mouth onto mine and swirled my tongue all over inside. "Don't stop," I panted, between kissing. "Please, don't stop."

Before I knew what he'd done, he pulled down my G-string with his teeth, and then started to penetrate me.

"You're so wet, Becky," he growled, as he pushed in further.

When he finally entered, I gasped in pleasure. Oh God! He felt so good. He cupped my face, looking deeply into my eyes. His soft eyes turned darker, then greedier as he pumped faster and harder...reaching deeper. Loud moans escaped my mouth. I didn't realize I was screaming until I covered my own mouth.

He was right. He could make me scream, and that made me squirm even more underneath him. As he pumped and ground into me faster, he twisted my nipple, causing pleasure and pain. He filled me up to the point I thought my insides were going to burst out of my body. I wanted him to stop; I couldn't take more exploding as I climaxed repeatedly.

Then he pulled me onto my side and he kept going. As I ran out of breath and energy, he continued from all different positions. Sometimes, he slowed down and teased me until I begged for more. When he finally reached his limit, I was exhausted beyond words.

Unexpectedly, he pulled me onto him and tenderly embraced me. I stiffened at first, but relaxed when he kissed my forehead. He didn't say anything. In fact, I had expected him to get up as if nothing happened and walk out the door, but he didn't.

"You were amazing," he finally whispered. "I'm glad I came back. I want to give you more, but I..." He didn't finish his words.

I didn't know what to think of what he said. Too exhausted to care, all I wanted to do was sleep. Trying to break away from Matthew's hold wasn't easy. Every time I shifted to pull away from him, he held me tighter. Drained from the passion we shared, I allowed my eyelids to close. I knew by the end of the night I would be alone in my bed, though a part of me hoped he would stay. But that was wishful thinking.

Chapter 25
Becky

I woke up to the delicious aroma of eggs and ham, making my stomach churn with hunger. Finding myself naked in bed startled me, and then I remembered last night. *Matthew*. Sitting up, I buried my face in my palms. What had we done? Getting out of my bed, I dressed and headed toward the kitchen, wondering if I would find Matthew or Jenna, but I remembered Jenna was at Max's place.

"Good morning," Matthew said cheerfully with a spatula in his hand. He turned to look as I entered the kitchen. His blissful smile faded to a nervous one, but that didn't stop him from giving me a kiss on the forehead. "I hope you don't mind. I thought I would make us breakfast."

"Umm...sure," I said, taking out the plates. After I gave them to him, I reached for the refrigerator handle when he stopped me.

"I got your coffee from Starbucks. It's on the dining table."

"Uh...thanks," I mumbled, looking dumbfounded.

"Go have a seat, I'll be right there."

Nodding, I left the kitchen. As we sat there eating, I thought about talking to him about last night, but he cleared his throat.

"Becca, do you remember what happened last night?"

Was he serious? "Yes," I nodded, looking at the eggs I'd stabbed with my fork, and feeling my cheeks burn.

Matthew put his fork down and lightly sighed. "I enjoy being with you, Becca, more than you could possibly know. It's just that...I don't know where this is going. All I know is that when I'm with you, I feel free, like I can be myself. It has been a long time since I felt that way. When I'm with you, everything is right. And when we kissed, that was incredible, but..."

Hearing Matthew's words made me giddy like a schoolgirl, but then I heard the word "but."

"I can't give you what you want right now. Maybe—"

"Matthew, it's okay." I placed my hand on his thigh, accidently so close to his crotch that he angled his brows playfully, which reminded me of how he made me feel last night. My clit twitched from the memory. Touching him produced naughty thoughts, so I took my hand away. "Look, I'm a big girl. I'm not one of those girls who believes that once we have sex, we're supposed to get married or even hook up. I've had one-night stands before."

Matthew's brows arched in curiosity. "How many?"

"None of your business. And don't tell me this was your first."

That seemed to end that topic of discussion. "Okay. Sorry. It's just that we're friends and I don't want it to be weird between us. I want to, but I'm not ready to—"

I cut him off. I didn't want to hear excuses or make him feel obligated to explain what had happened between us. After all, we were two consenting adults. I don't know what made me ask the next question, but a part of me wanted to know how his girlfriend had passed away.

"What happened to her?" I thought he was going to

brush me off, but instead, his eyes stared somewhere else in time and he started talking.

"Being the youngest child, and with my parents working all the time, I was somewhat spoiled. I was irresponsible and did what I wanted to do. I knew how to work my parents to get what I wanted by using the guilt trip on them. I met Tessa during my senior year in college. She changed me. She made me become a better person. I think Max was relieved and he thanked her for that," Matthew lightly chuckled and continued.

"Tessa and I had been together for more than a year. I loved her so much that I knew I wanted to marry her someday. We were too young to get married, but she practically gave me an ultimatum. In fear of losing her, I proposed. Then we started fighting about the date of our wedding. I wanted to wait until after I graduated from business school, but she didn't," Matthew paused, as if gathering his thoughts. With a deep intake of breath, he continued.

"It was raining hard that day. We had a fight at her apartment. She ran out the door and I let her go. Later that day, I got a phone call from her roommate, letting me know Tessa was in the hospital. She had been in a car accident, just like Jenna." He paused, but I remained silent knowing Matthew had more to say. His face was full of torment. "She left this world with misunderstandings that needed to be resolved. I will never have the chance to fix that. Our argument was the last memory I have of her."

Poor Matthew! I gasped and covered my mouth with my hand. My heart thumped faster with every word pouring from his lips. He had relived that moment with Jenna. "I'm sorry, Matthew," I mumbled through my hand. I knew where this would end.

"She was brain dead when I got to the hospital. Her parents and I didn't want to let her go. We watched. We waited. We hoped God would answer our prayers and she would come out of it. I rarely prayed before, but I prayed that day. I prayed for a miracle, but God denied me. He shattered my world. I was so angry and hurt I cursed him. I lost myself in that hospital. I lost my love, my heart, and whatever was left of my soul, because someone with so much anger and hate can only go to hell."

Tears streamed down my face as I listened. I felt his anger, his passion, and loss, because I'd been there. I had been through it with my roommate and almost with Jenna. I knew what that kind of pain does to a person. It eats you alive and spits you back out with the feeling of emptiness and all you want to do is die too. No matter how rich or poor you are; money can't buy happiness or a shield from the cruelties of life. It doesn't discriminate. Pain knows no boundaries.

"I'm so sorry," I whispered, in fear if I had said it any louder, I would sob uncontrollably in front of him.

"Becca." Matthew pulled me into him, wiping the tears off my face with the brush of this thumb. "My sweet, Becca. I didn't mean to make you cry. Don't cry, sweetheart." Surprisingly, Matthew kissed the lingering tears away. "I knew you weren't as mean as the spitfire you were last night. You were just trying to get into my pants."

I appreciated his attempt to lighten the mood, and I would have given him a good comeback, but I couldn't. Holding me tightly, swaying back and forth, he muttered, "What are we going to do from here?"

I didn't answer, not knowing if he really wanted an answer, so I said nothing. Did he even know what he wanted?

Since I didn't answer, he held me tighter—all of me. "Thanks for being my friend. You make me happy. You make me forget. You make me forget her."

I pushed aside my own regret and loss. Matthew was still suffering and for some reason, he needed me. I would be his comfort, his rock, even if that's all I had to offer him. I couldn't deny him, even knowing I would be the one left with a broken heart. I was okay with it. Hell, I was even used to it.

Chapter 26
Jenna

The rumors had spread like an untamed wildfire. Max's dad called and told us not to come to work. It was all over the media—Internet, television news, radio stations, and even the pictures of Max protecting me at the nightclub were in the newspaper. The headline read "Max Moves on to Next Victim." My poor Max!

What made the situation even worse was the phone call from my parents. I tried to tame it down as best as I could, but with the media being cruel to Max, it was impossible to hide anything. I reassured them that Max was innocent and that it would be over soon. I hoped I was right.

I jerked my head in the direction of a flutter and thump. Max had angrily thrown the newspaper across the room with a deep, frustrated growl. I wasn't sure what to do or say to help him through this. Though I was a victim too, Max and his company were at stake. The best thing I thought I could do was stay out of the way and pretend everything was fine.

"Sorry, babe." He looked apologetic. After dragging both of his hands through his hair in frustration, he sat next to me and looked at my computer screen. "What are you working on?"

"I'm getting a head start on our February issue.

February is one of my favorite months."

"Because of Valentine's Day?"

"No. Well, maybe it will be this time around, since I have you, but it's the month of the London Fashion Show."

Max's eyes were tender, as he began stroking my cheek. "Would you like to go?"

My eyes grew wide with excitement. "Yes, I would love to."

"I'll take you there with the company, but we won't be working," he winked. "And we don't have to go to the after party if you don't want to."

"Do we have to decide now?"

"No. We still have time." Max fell into a daze and looked at me with a smile. "I haven't seen your finger in your mouth. You know how I love to take it out and suck it."

"Shall I do it for you now?" I flirted.

"I would love to see," he said in a playful tone. His cell phone rang, and he looked to see who it was. "Give me a sec. It's my lawyer." Max stood up and headed toward the window.

It was a clear, sunny day. Looking out, you could see the beauty of the city. When you looked at the whole scene, everything was perfect, so peaceful, in contrast to what was going on in Max's head. His expression said it all. Looking concerned, he turned to me after the conversation ended. "Babe, I need to meet with my lawyer in his office right now."

"Okay," I nodded, trying to stay calm.

"He wants you to come with me."

I don't know why lawyers frightened me, just as I don't know why I worry when I see a cop's car beside mine when I'm driving. I was a worrier by nature, and though I told myself I would remain strong, the fact that the lawyer wanted to see me made me uneasy.

Max

"Thomas." I shook his hand. He wore a dark gray suit, white dress shirt and a floral tie; lavender mixed with black. "Thomas, this is Jenna. Jenna Mefferd. Jenna, this is Thomas Shaw"

"It's nice to meet you, Mr. Shaw," Jenna said, taking his hand.

"Please, have a seat."

Thomas went around the large wooden table while I pulled out a chair for Jenna. She always smiled with appreciation at every small gesture from me. Crossing her legs, she leaned toward me and almost placed her head on my shoulder, but stopped. I wanted to give her a quick kiss to reassure her that everything was fine, but I refrained. Instead, I held her hand and rested it on my thigh.

Thomas opened a file and placed his elbows on the table. He took a glance at Jenna before he started to speak. "I'm going to cut to the chase. We have a good case against her, but things are going to leak out. She is accusing you of sexual harassment, which you already know, but she actually goes into more detail." Thomas cleared his throat, glancing at Jenna again. "A *lot* of details."

Jenna shifted in her seat, but still kept her hand in mine. Acid rose in my throat. I wanted to know what the "details" were, but I didn't want Jenna to hear.

"Babe, why don't you wait in the waiting room? I need a minute with Thomas."

Jenna nodded and stood up, but stopped when Thomas spoke. "Are you sure you wouldn't want her to hear it from you, instead of from the outside source? That way you can explain...I mean...tell her what information is true or false. This is going to get out one way or another and it might be best if you two talked it out."

Jenna turned to me and gave me a questioning look. I didn't want her to hear what Thomas had to say. It would change the way she looked at me, possibly our whole relationship, but I had no choice. He was right. It was better she knew now so she wouldn't be surprised, like when she found out about the lawsuit from Crystal. That was a freakin' nightmare. "Jenna, have a seat," I said reluctantly.

After she nodded, she sat back down, but a worried expression lingered behind her faint smile. Instead of leaning into me like before, her back was straight against the chair. Holding her hand again, I prepared myself for what Thomas was about to expose and prayed to God it wouldn't be as bad as I thought it would be.

Thomas gave me that look that said 'prepare yourself' and started speaking. "Crystal is suing you and your company for two million dollars."

I sank into my chair and tried not to make a sound or any movement to show Jenna how upset I was, but I wanted to throw a chair out the window. Jenna, on the other hand, made a tiny gasping sound.

"She is accusing you of forcing her into sexual activities at work and at home. If she refused, she was told her job was in jeopardy."

"I did no such thing!" I shouted. Blood rushed to my face as I burned inside with anger.

"Calm down, Max," Thomas said quickly. "I know you didn't, but I have to read what you are being accused of, so we can discuss our plan."

Closing my eyes to calm down, and then opening them

again, I agreed with a heavy sigh. If this one accusation got me this angry, the rest would make me explode. I had to settle down for Jenna's sake. She shuddered when I raised my voice and I didn't like that I made her feel afraid.

"Max, let him finish," Jenna said softly. That's all it took for me to find peace again. Her smile and her tender, angelic voice automatically made me surrender to her request. She was my anchor, my strength, and I would do anything for her.

"All right." I kissed her hand as I held it, and placed it down on my lap again. "Go on, Thomas."

"It gets worse. She said you mentally and physically tortured her, using whips, handcuffs, other sex toys, and even blindfolding her. She's claiming you mentally abused her by calling her names, and embarrassing her in front of her co-workers. She alleges she is no longer able to hold down a job, for fear any boss would do the same. She claims you threatened that if she did not comply, not only would she not get a recommendation from the company, but you would make sure she would never be hired anywhere else again."

"This is absurd. I should sue her for causing me grief," I shook my head with a small laugh. "Unbelievable. This woman did not think things through. All of this is false." Almost all. I told Thomas we used sex toys, but they were her idea. She had purchased them. As Thomas continued down his list, I wanted desperately to take Jenna out of the room; I saw the disturbed expression on her face. She had heard enough.

She couldn't even look at me when I called her name. She looked anywhere else but my eyes. Maybe I was overreacting, but I doubted it. I read Jenna like a book. That's how in tune we were. My gut told me things were going to change between us, and I wanted to hold her in my arms and never let her go.

"I think we've had enough for today, Thomas," I said sternly.

"Max, I just have a couple more."

Looking at Jenna, she already looked drained from information overload, not to mention the shock of hearing all the cruel things I had supposedly done. Hopefully, she knew me well enough to know I wouldn't do those things. I desperately wanted to know what she was thinking.

"Thomas, I thank you for doing your job, but I really think you and I should meet again tomorrow. I'm taking Jenna home. She and I need to talk this out." Without his consent, I stood up and tugged Jenna out of her daze, helping her out of her seat.

"Max," Thomas started again.

"No, Thomas. I mean it," I said firmly. If he tried to talk me into staying, it wasn't going to be a polite conversation. I reached for the door.

"There is something else."

"What is it?" I huffed, feeling irate.

"I think it's best if you and Jenna saw less of each other during work hours. Try not to be the source of any rumors. People are bound to talk, and we don't need anyone making assumptions. The prosecutor will call Jenna to testify. I also need to set a date to meet with Jenna alone to help her get ready. This is my professional opinion as your lawyer. If you want to win this case, these are my suggestions."

Thomas meant well, but I didn't like anything he said. What happened next was something I could not have expected or prepared myself for. For the first time, Jenna's hand slipped away from mine and she walked out the door without waiting for me to open it for her. It felt as though she was saying goodbye. A dagger twisted in my heart, and all I could do was hope I misinterpreted her reaction.

Chapter 27
Jenna

Taking my hand away from Max's hold, I pushed the door and walked through. Max always opened doors for me, but I wanted to be in control. It wasn't that I didn't want him with me. I was just deep in thought and only wanted to get out of there as fast as I could.

We didn't talk much during the drive back to my apartment. In fact, it was the first time he failed to make me smile. When we got to the front of my apartment building, two men that looked like secret service stood their ground. Max had hired them to ensure the paparazzi stayed away. With a nod to them, we headed up to my place. As soon as we got to my door, Max stood in front, preventing me from entering.

"Jenna. Talk to me, please" he said softly.

Any other day, I would have jumped into his arms right then and there. He looked so alluring and tempting, the way he leaned against the door in a natural pose, but I had to remain strong. Smiling, I gazed into those welcoming eyes that looked so sad. "Max, I'm fine. We should do what Mr. Shaw suggested. I can even work from home."

"Babe..." He leaned into me, but thoughts of what Crystal threatened to tell the whole world made me sick.

My poor Max. His reputation and the company his family worked so hard for would crumble, just because of one crazy, vindictive bitch. It wasn't fair.

When I finally looked at him again, he continued. "Get some rest. I know this is a lot for you to deal with. I didn't want you to hear all those things about my past with Crystal. I was young and naïve. I certainly didn't want to give you all this stress. I wouldn't have brought you into my life if I had known this would —"

"Shhh." I whispered as I placed my finger on his lips. "It's okay. I'm stronger than you think."

Max slipped my finger inside his mouth, teasing it with his tongue. "I've wanted to do this for so long, but you haven't been biting your finger," he mumbled in between suckling it.

If he continued, I would have no choice but to surrender and yank him inside with me. My self-control was non-existent around him. Pulling my finger away, I mouthed, "Max." As tears welled up in my eyes, I gave him a quick peck on the lips and somehow managed to unlock the door.

"We'll get through this. I love you, Jenna," he said, turning me around, placing his forehead against mine.

I took a moment to take in his words, the words I only partially believed. What if we couldn't get through this? I told myself I wouldn't make a big deal of it, but I asked, "Why didn't you tell me?" My words came out soft, but he could tell how upset I was.

"I was going to tell you about the lawsuit after the New Year's party. But instead, you ran into Crystal, of all people," Max sighed heavily.

"Not just that. Why didn't you tell me about the things you did with her before we met with your attorney? You should have told me."

"I'm sorry. Yes, you're right, but I really wasn't thinking. I was worried about the lawsuit, but I still should have spoken to you before I brought you to Thomas. That will never happen again. More importantly, I promise you, I did *not* do all those things Crystal has accused me of. You believe me, don't you?"

"I want to, but part of me doesn't." The admission slipped out. My anger got the best of me, and besides, I was hurting. The look on his face told me I had hurt him too, but what I was about to say would hurt him even more.

"You told me I could trust you, but you kept things from me. It's because…you…don't…trust…*me*. I have some thinking to do. I'll talk to you later." The words came out fast. I entered my apartment and shut the door behind me even faster.

The tears streamed down my face as I leaned back against the door. Everything was happening so fast. So much had happened in the short time we'd been together that I needed a minute to de-stress. Max and I would get through this if we truly loved each other. Looking through the peephole, I could see Max's hands planted on either side of the door and his head was down. I felt his pain, but it couldn't possibly be the same degree as mine.

Seeing him hurt like that made me miserable, and I was almost certain he had heard me crying. My resolve weakened, and I was about to open the door when he started to walk away. Max walked away! The Max I thought I knew would've broken the door down to get to me. That made my heartache deeper. Tears ran even more as I slid down the door. Letting it all out, I sobbed until there was nothing left of me.

Max

As soon as I walked through the door of my home after leaving Jenna's place, the air seemed colder. Though I'd been here alone many times before, it felt so empty without her, especially tonight. I'm not sure what part of our fight, if I could call it that, got me more worked up: me not telling her everything beforehand, her shutting the door on me, or her saying I didn't trust her. Which was worse, I didn't know.

I headed for the bar, poured myself a drink, and then sat on the sofa. All the "should haves" popped into my mind. I tried to protect her, but I ended up hurting her instead. I guess between our age difference and Jenna being as innocent as they come, I felt a great need to protect her. That was just the way I was.

After taking a sip of whiskey, feeling it burn down my throat, I took out my cell phone. I had missed calls from Matt, Dad, and Thomas. That was it. I re-read Jenna's last flirty text, where she told me she would have something fun for me. Though my dirty mind thought of a few things, I couldn't imagine her having the same thoughts.

Jenna was the most innocent woman I'd ever dated and if I had it my way, she'd be the last, but we couldn't get there if we didn't get through this. I had expected her to call me to say goodnight at least. She called every night, since she went to bed first, but as I sat and stared at the phone, it never rang.

I knew she was upset with me, but I didn't know how much. I tried to put myself in her shoes, wanting to understand her, but all that went through my head was 'Jenna didn't call.' Sure, I guess I could call her instead, but why? She practically slammed the door in my face, shutting me out, not willing to listen any further. She didn't let me explain.

Maybe she was better off without me. She didn't deserve all the trouble that surrounded my life, though I wasn't sure I was capable of letting her go. Because I loved her so much, I would sacrifice my want for her happiness. I would do anything for her. Hell, if I had known she would walk into my life, I would never have dated Crystal.

Crystal passed the time, not to mention the things she would do to me. I thought we were consenting adults with a mutual understanding that the relationship wasn't long term. Who knew she would turn out to be a psycho bitch, out to ruin me?

Looking at my phone, I checked again in case I had missed Jenna's call, but that would have been impossible since I had it in my hand. Wishful thinking. Drowning in my sorrow, I hoped I was overreacting, but 'Jenna didn't call' echoed though my head again as I swallowed the last sip of my drink. Was she telling me she was letting me go?

I didn't know what more I could do to prove to her how much I loved her and that I would stay faithful to us. My past was my past and I wanted to keep it there. Some things she didn't need to know because they didn't concern her. I decided the ball was in her court. Actually, it was always in her court. Maybe she just needed time to think things through.

I was probably too much of an alpha male, but I wouldn't have pursued her if she wasn't interested. I saw it in her eyes and the way her body responded to me. She wanted me as much as I wanted her. Maybe I needed to back away and give her time and space to breathe. Too much has happened since the day she met me. But giving her time could mean she would leave me. Oh hell, I didn't know what to do. But if she left me, I would stop breathing.

Maybe it was because I was tired, or the effect of the whiskey, or too much thinking, but my body felt heavy with an overwhelming feeling of loss and sadness. Rubbing my face into the palms of my hands, I let out a long sigh of frustration. Too tired to walk up the stairs, I spread my legs, tilted my head back and sunk into my sofa so the dream world would take me away. At least there, Jenna would be in my arms and we would be together. But she didn't call…

Chapter 28
Becky

I came back from the market to find Jenna at home. Strange. Heading toward the kitchen, I noticed her door was closed. After I put everything away, I decided to knock on the door.

"Come in," she said softly.

Swinging the door open, I started to jabber about the two big buff men by the front entrance, but I cut my sentence short when I saw her face. She didn't need to say a word. I knew that look all too well. Something was definitely wrong. If Max had hurt her, I would kill him with my bare hands. "Jenna, what happened?" I sat on the edge of the bed.

After she closed her eyes, as if to gather her thoughts, she spoke. I tried not to drop my mouth open as the words spilled out of her. Holy shit! It sounded like something in a novel. Jenna told me about how she ran into Crystal at the club, the lawsuit, the paparazzi, the security men watching our apartment, how Max kept things from her, and about what the lawyer suggested. What words of advice do you give to your friend when you have no idea what to say? I was totally dumbfounded by it all. "Wow, Jenna." That was the most idiotic thing to say, but I couldn't think of anything else.

"I know," she agreed. "I can't believe all these things are happening. What happened to 'meet a wonderful guy, date, get married, and have children?'"

"You don't think Max is the one?"

"I thought he could be. I care for him so much that it feels like my world is falling apart. Who knows how long this lawsuit will last? Who knows how we will feel about each other after this?"

"What do you mean? Max loves you. I can say it without a doubt."

"He kept things from me. He should've told me."

"Jenna, I'm going to stop you right there. What guy is going to discuss what he did with other women? Quite frankly, I'm glad he didn't tell you. Knowing you, you would've freaked out and wouldn't have given him the time of day. Am I right?"

"It doesn't matter. It should have come from him and not his lawyer. He should have known better."

"Something else is bothering you."

Jenna didn't reply. Instead, she moved on to another subject, blowing my mind. "Apparently, Max likes to use handcuffs, whips, and stuff like you talked about."

I didn't need to know this about Max, but okay. Jenna needed to talk about it so I would try to forget afterward. "He actually used them with you?" I sounded surprised. I think I even raised my voice.

"No." Jenna shook her head. "Max and Crystal. I think it was why he stayed with her. I'm sure he cared about her at the beginning, but I think in the end, that's how she controlled him."

It was cute how carefully Jenna chose her words, always looking for the positive side of people. "Well, hun, sometimes a woman like her knows how to control young, naïve men. To tell you the truth, any guy in his right mind would want to experiment if the lady was willing."

Jenna bit her bottom lip, her gaze drifting. "What if he needs more? What if I'm not enough? What if he gets bored with me? I'm as plain as they come. You of all people know that."

And there was the answer to the question she ignored earlier. "Don't sell yourself short, and don't think that far ahead. It will drive you crazy. Yes, I do know you. You happen to have the most beautiful heart I know. Max could never be bored with you. It was one of the reasons why he never stopped asking you out. He knew he'd found someone special. You guys have something wonderful. Don't walk away from that."

"I know," Jenna murmured. I hope she agreed with me and didn't say it for my sake. Jenna always assumed the worst in fear of having her heart broken. When her ex-boyfriend cheated on her, her world fell apart.

Draping my arm around her shoulder, I pulled her in for a hug. "You know what? When a guy has sex or makes love, or whatever you want to call it, with the woman he loves, it's a lot more intense and enjoyable for him. So just know that you rock Max's world."

Jenna let out a small laugh. "I'll keep that in mind."

"I don't mean to change the subject, but did you get the text from Nicole? We need to go for our first fitting next Saturday. I think we need another ladies' night out."

"Sounds good. I did get the text, but with everything that happened today, I didn't get a chance to respond."

"Don't worry. I told her we would be there."

"Thanks, Becca." Jenna raised her brows in a confused look. It made me think of Matthew. "Becky. Sorry. I don't know what possessed me to call you that."

"That's okay," I let out short laugh. "Let's get on your computer."

"To do what?"

I curled my lips into a wicked smile. "To look at toys."

"What?"

"So you can rock Matthew's world even more."

Before I could get up, she gripped my wrist. "You just said Matthew instead of Max. What's going on with you two?"

I wanted to tell her what Matthew had told me about his deceased fiancée, but it was something between him and me. I thought I should keep it to myself in case somehow it got out that I told Jenna, Jenna told Max, Max told Matthew that I told Jenna. Yup, that sounded confusing even in my own mind.

"Nothing," I finally said.

She gave me a look with one eye closed, as if she could see if I was telling the truth.

"Don't give me that look," I said, almost laughing. I couldn't stop smiling. Matthew and I had a one-night stand, but I didn't want to tell Jenna about it yet. I didn't want her to think badly of him, or judge what we did. Our friendship was complicated. Hell, I didn't even know what we were to each other.

After I tugged Jenna out of the bed, she headed to her computer. My back pocket buzzed with a text. It was from Matthew.

Sorry. I have to cancel dinner. I have something important to take care of for Max.

Matthew had texted me yesterday, asking me out. I texted back.

No worries. Take care of Max.

It had to be something about the lawsuit. Had Jenna not

told me about it, I would have thought he decided to have dinner with a real date. That would have hurt a little.

"Are you going to sit next to me or are you too busy thinking about Matthew, *Becca?*"

Scowling at her, I strode toward her. "I was not thinking about Matthew." Her joke indicated she was feeling better.

"Uh huh. Sure."

"Shut up." I nudged her shoulder with mine after I squeezed in to the other half of the chair.

Jenna

I'd always called Max before I went to bed, so not doing it felt so odd. I don't know why I didn't, only that I was so furious with him. I wanted to punish him. It was silly and immature, but when you're that angry, you don't care how much it might hurt the other person. I didn't even know if it mattered to him. After all, he could have called too. Then again, I did tell him I needed time to think, but that didn't mean to stay away.

Tossing and turning in bed, I thought about what my friend, Ethan, had said when I had run into him at Stellars. He had given me a funny look when I told him I was dating Maxwell Knight. I guess that shouldn't surprise me, since the world seemed to know about the lawsuit. When I thought about that reality, I felt so bad for Max. Still, right now, I needed to blow off some steam.

If he tried to sweet-talk me, there was a real possibility I would go flying back into his arms. As if there wasn't enough to deal with, if Luke called me one more time, I was going to tell him off. It's something I would normally never do, but the anger inside me gave me the fuel I needed to act out of character.

Chapter 29
Matthew

Throughout the day, I couldn't stop thinking of Becca. I just couldn't get her out of my mind. Trying not to text or call her proved to be difficult. She was becoming the drug I needed to make me smile. It wouldn't be so bad if she wasn't Jenna's best friend. If things ever got ugly, Jenna would never speak to me and that would make life difficult, since I was convinced she'd be my sister-in-law someday.

Oh, what the hell. Becca knew I couldn't give her more than friendship. Not seeing the harm in having dinner with a friend, I texted her.

What are you doing, Becca?

Working!

What are you wearing?

What? Lol!

There was a short pause and another text popped up soon after.

Naked.

I'm coming over.

No!!! I'm just kidding. I'm really working! Play with yourself.

I like to play with myself, but I'd rather play with you.

That sounded too flirty and I regretted sending it. It was so easy to be me with her. Before I could delete it, another text popped up. She was fast.

I can play dirty, but I gotta work.

I missed her even more.

Go out to dinner with me.

Nope! Gotta work. Lots to read.

Come on. I'm giving you my sexy pout and if you were here, you wouldn't be able to say no. So either I come to you and let you see my sexy pout while you're naked or you come meet me for dinner. Your choice.

There was a pause.

Okay. Where and what time?

I don't remember how many times I told myself we were just friends, but every time I saw her, she stole a little more of my heart. It wasn't just that she was super hot; there was more to her. It was so easy to open up with her. The more time I spent with her, the more the memories and pain of Tessa started to fade. Being with her healed me.

Sitting at the table, I sipped my beer as I waited for Becca. Heels clicked softly across the room, and I knew it was her. At first, I stared at the amazing vision. With her hair tied behind her and wearing light makeup, she wore tight jeans, a loose black sweater and killer black boots. She looked good enough to eat coming toward me with that smile, cute as a button, but sexy as hell. She was like an angel and a devil sent to undo me.

My libido told me to take her to the nearest restroom, strip her naked, and have my way with her. Taking a deep breath and controlling my urge, I repeatedly reminded myself: only a friend. I needed to behave. Friend...my friend...Jenna's best friend.

"Hey," I greeted. Standing up, I embraced her as if she were a delicate flower. Taking a whiff of her perfume, I became dizzy as I fell under her spell. Pulling out the chair for her, I went back to mine.

"Thanks for asking me out to dinner. I would've been

stuck at home all day. Sometimes I forget to take a break. I have so much to read. But at least I can say I love my job, and not many people can say that."

"I would stay home all day and read about potential book girlfriends if I was an agent myself." I winked, trying not to offend her. "Better yet, I think you and I would get naked, read a book and act out the parts," I croaked a laugh.

She gave me a wicked scowl with one eye narrowed at me. Clearly, I wasn't doing a good job trying to be just a friend. I quickly changed the subject. "You must be starving." Gliding the menu across the table to her I asked, "What would you like to eat?"

"Want to do family style? My friends and I always do that when we eat Chinese food."

"Sure. You pick one and I'll pick three."

"Hey." Becca laughed, enjoying the humor.

"Just checking to make sure you're listening because I think the menu is getting more attention than me."

"You're so full of it," Becca snorted.

"Watch out firecracker, I can give you more than you're asking for."

"I bet you can."

Her sexy, flirty tone caught me off guard.

After waving the waitress over, we placed our order.

"Do you get to see your family often?" I asked, taking a sip from my water glass.

"No. Only like four or maybe six times a year. I always try to stop by to see them during book conventions and holidays. This year was unusual. I didn't go to them during Christmas because I had just been there a couple of weeks before.

"I see. Well, I'm glad you stayed."

Becca's brow lifted. What did I say to make her look a little upset? Was it too much to say I had a good time with her?

After a while, our food came. Using the serving spoon, I placed some on her plate first, and then mine, as I asked her another question. "Have you lived in San Francisco all of your life?"

"Thanks," she said, watching me spoon the rest of the food on her plate. "Yes. I lived there growing up, except when I came here for college. How about you?"

"Yes, I've lived here pretty much all my life except when I traveled alone around Europe."

"I see." She nodded, understanding my reasons. Taking nibbles of food, I watched Becca struggle with her chopsticks like before. It was the cutest thing. Wanting to help her, I got out of my seat and sat on the chair next to hers. When I draped my arms around her, her body stiffened. I loved how I made her nervous.

"It's like this." I explained as my fingers rubbed against hers. She felt so soft and she smelled so sweet. Her presence intoxicated me. Uncontrollably, my face sank deeper into her hair. As her hair parted, I wanted only to indulge myself by nuzzling into the side of her exposed neck. Oh God, help me now before I do it.

"I think I got it now," Becca chuckled, breaking me out of her spell. Then she turned and froze. My lips were a breath away from hers. Remembering how she tasted the night we had sex, I was so tempted to succumb to my desire, but I had to restrain myself. I don't know how much time had passed, but neither of us spoke as we stared at each other.

Becca's eyes shifted to my lips and I almost lost it. I wanted to clear the table with one swipe of my arm, taking her right then and there. I didn't care who was watching. The thought made me feel guilty. For the first time, it wasn't just about sex. I'd started to care for Becca in ways I never thought I could again. Tessa's face appeared in my mind, a sign I wasn't ready to let her go.

"Would you like some more water?" the waitress asked.

Her interruption felt like she had dumped ice water over my head. It would have been a good idea to help me cool down from this heated feeling.

"Uh...we're fine," Becca said, glancing from her glass to mine, noting how full they were.

Sliding back, I let go of the hold I had on Becca and took some deep breaths. Being friends was harder than I thought it would be. I didn't know how much longer I could handle it, and I didn't know how to let Tessa go either.

Chapter 30
Jenna

It had been several days since Max and I last spoke. They were the longest days of my life. My reason was stubbornness, but what was his reason? I told him I needed some time to think, but I didn't really mean it.

Having a relationship was fairly new to me. I'd dated a handful of guys, but I'd never fully opened up ever since what happened with my ex. Mostly because I had thought he was the one. He told me he loved me. How can you tell someone you love them and then break their heart into pieces? It destroyed my self-esteem and trust in relationships. Even though part of me believed Max, a small part said I couldn't.

In order to move on with Max, I would have to put the past behind me, but the memory of that pain stayed with me. I wanted him to hurt as much as I was hurting. I wanted him to feel my pain. That's why my pride wouldn't let me call him. The Max I knew would've called already. Why didn't he call? Maybe he finally realized I wasn't experienced enough, and he needed someone more mature to handle situations like this.

"Ms. Mefferd."

"Ms. Mefferd," the voice said a tad louder, breaking me out of my trance.

I peered up at Mr. Shaw. His green eyes looked concerned. He had called me yesterday and asked me to come in after work. "Yes, Mr. Shaw. I'm sorry. What was the question again?"

"Ms. Mefferd, let me stress again. I asked you to come here to get you ready in case they call you to testify regarding Max's character. I'm going to fire away with questions and you may not like what I ask or how I ask it, but you must answer them truthfully. You need to be prepared. They will get nasty. Unless we find some miracle witness against Crystal, in the end it will be her word against Max's. Are you ready?"

"Yes." I nodded, but I wasn't. Something about being in a lawyer's office made my pulse race.

"Where did you and Max meet?"

"At Café Express."

"How long ago?"

"About five months ago."

"Do you work for his company?"

"Yes."

"And what do you do there?"

"I work in the publishing department."

"Isn't it true that you were promoted from the Customer Relations Department to the Publishing Department?"

"Yes."

"Was that before or after Maxwell Knight forced you to sleep with him?"

"Excuse me?"

"Was that before or after you slept with him?"

"After, but we were —"

"It was after. So you slept with him with the promise of a bigger and better position?"

"No!" I said loudly. "He didn't promise anything."

"He didn't promise, but he promoted you in exchange for participating in sexual activities with him."

"That's not true," I said aloud again, feeling irate. I knew Mr. Shaw pressured me so I could get used to being bombarded with ugly questions, but I was fuming inside. I had to learn how to block it out.

"Ms. Mefferd. What kind of car do you drive?"

"A BMW."

"More specific please."

"It's black. The windows are tinted. It has four tires."

Mr. Shaw's lips quivered with suppressed laughter, but then he got serious again. "Are you trying to mock my question?"

"No, I wouldn't. You said to be specific."

"What model and style?"

"I think it's a BMW 760."

"You think? Or you don't want to say?"

"I just drive the car. I don't care what kind it is. Why does it matter what kind of car I drive?" I huffed, getting frustrated, and a headache began throbbing at my temples.

"That's an expensive gift, Ms. Mefferd. The Knight Company maintains the registration, but did you know Ms. Tate received the same gift?"

Blood drained out of my face, and I would swear I was going into shock. The newfound information paralyzed me. The fact that Max had given Crystal the same gift was a huge blow. For the first time, I wondered if Max was playing me too, and I hated that the thought even crossed my mind.

"How do you feel?" Mr. Shaw asked with a softer tone. This time his shoulders and his stiff body relaxed. As for me, I was the opposite.

"Exhausted and frustrated," I sighed.

"Crystal's lawyers will come at you fast and hard and even put words in your mouth like I just did. I know their law firm. They are ruthless and their main goal is to suck every penny they can get from their opposition. This was nothing compared to how they will be. I wanted to give you a taste of what is to come."

"I didn't do so well, did I?" After running my fingers through my hair, I massaged my temples.

"Sorry. I know this is difficult, but I need you to come again tomorrow. We don't have much time. The trial will begin in a few weeks. I'm doing my own investigation, and I have asked Max to give me a list of potential character witnesses. Since you and Max are currently dating, you are probably the most important key to our winning. If you know or hear any information that could be vital for this case, please let me know."

"Sure, anything I can do to help." He had no idea Max and I weren't on speaking terms, and now, knowing he had given Crystal the same car he had given me didn't make the situation any better. Max probably gave the best to any woman he dated. That was the way he was. However, that made me worry more. Who's to say I wasn't one of the flings he would soon get over, moving on to someone else?

Becky

I could tell Jenna had suspicions about Matthew and me, but there was nothing to share. He wasn't ready to move on, and though I would be there for him, I wasn't going to let him take over my heart or my schedule. Who was I kidding? Any time he texted or called to ask me out, I would put everything aside and take off.

I guess I held onto hope that I could be the one to break through his wall, but at the same time, I prepared for the worst. I had to remind myself that we were just friends, but I thought about the night we spent together constantly. The way he kneaded my breasts, the way his hands gripped my ass. That thought alone practically made me climax; he was that good. The lingering sensation tingled throughout my veins, making my body infuse with heat.

"Oh shit!" I yelled, slamming on the breaks. Driving while thinking about sex with Matthew was not a good combination. "Sorry." I raised my hand to the car to the right of me after I almost veered into his lane.

Besides that one hot night, Matthew and I always had a great time together, sharing our deepest fears and dreams. Actually, he shared and I listened. I still didn't feel comfortable letting him know all of me, so I did what I do best…I listened.

Looking for Matthew since he'd texted me he was already seated, I walked past the hostess after I'd explained I had a friend waiting for me. As I excitedly searched from table to table, I saw Matthew with his arms around a woman. They looked awfully cozy as they chatted and laughed. He knew I was on my way, so why would he hold her like that?

My heart ached as if he had cheated on me. I told myself I wouldn't let him get too close, but my own words betrayed me. As I stared, the piercing pain intensified. Watching him give her a kiss on her cheek disgusted me, and an ugly knot gathered in the pit of my stomach.

Why did I do that to myself? It's like I got some sick pleasure from feeling pain, being used. Because that's how I felt. Sure, use Becca when you feel horny, or use Becca when you feel lonely. I should have known better. There was no hope. All his words were lies, probably to get me in bed. As hatred boiled through me, I knew I needed to leave before I made a scene.

I turned to leave. If only my legs would have moved faster, Matthew wouldn't have seen me.

"Becca," he called, as if it was no big deal.

I had to make a choice, so instead of acting mature and going to his table, I started walking away, hoping he would let me be. Too late. His hand gripped my arm.

"Becca."

From the force of his pull, I reluctantly turned. "Hey, where are you going? I'm sitting back there."

I wanted to say something mean or tell him off, but I couldn't. I also didn't let him explain, because why? Even if his explanation was, 'we're just friends', there was something more to this…to us. No matter how much time I had invested in whatever we had, he would leave me with the broken heart.

I was freakin' jealous, and I wanted to be the one in his arms. If he hurt me that much, it was already too late. These situations never worked out for me at the end. From there on out, I could no longer be the friend he needed me to be.

"Matthew, I'm sorry, but you know what? I just got an emergency text from one of my clients and I need to take care of it," I lied, faking a smile. I desperately tried to stop my heart from breaking. My heart drummed an aching beat while shattering into millions of pieces. "I'll call you later." As I dashed out of there, tears blocked my vision. It had been a while since I felt that kind of heartache. It was another reminder to stay away.

Chapter 31
Jenna

"How do you like this one?" Nicole asked, holding up a long, strapless dress.

"It's a nice shade of lavender," I replied, leaning back in my chair as I watched Becky tilt her head, examining it.

"Do you have other choices?" Kate asked, looking unsure.

Nicole laughed. "Okay, this is like the fifth dress I showed you guys and we can't seem to come to an agreement. Ladies, go to that rack and pick one out. Meanwhile, you want to see my wedding dress?" Nicole couldn't contain her excitement. Her smile outshone the room. That was the way a bride should smile and feel about her wedding and the man she was about to marry.

"Go put it on," I exclaimed, trying my best to hide my own sorrow. I moved and felt as if I were dead inside. At least being surrounded by my friends and sharing in the excitement of Nicole's wedding did help.

"Let's see it on you," Becky said excitedly.

Nicole headed to the dressing room while we gathered around the rack. Becky and Kate took out several dresses and placed them off to the side. They chatted about what they liked and disliked about them, but as for me, I was in my own world as I stared at the dresses without any opinion.

I couldn't be happier for Nicole. She and Keith had been through the breakups, the heartaches, and made it through stronger than ever. From Nicole's point of view, Keith didn't want the happily ever after, but knowing he might never be with Nicole again, he agreed to move forward. I hoped it would last forever.

As Becky and Kate decided on two dresses, something white caught the corner of my eye. I turned my head to see Nicole standing by the dressing room with the sales clerk. My heart skipped a beat as she took my breath away.

Nicole looked absolutely stunning and I couldn't peel my eyes off of her. Her strapless, A-line dress was simple, with pearls and crystals adorning the waistline. A long veil flowed down her back from the matching headband.

Speechless, tears flooded my eyes to see one of my best friends who would soon be a beautiful bride. She would call Keith her own and he would call her, his; and forever they would be united as one. It was a pivotal moment in a person's life, and I felt blessed to be a part of it.

A little ache pricked my heart as I thought about Max. I often thought about our future and the type of dress I would wear. It was foolish of me to think so far ahead when I wanted to slow things down, but a girl can dream.

"Oh, Nicole," Kate squealed. "You look absolutely gorgeous." She clasped her hands as her eyes glistened with tears, standing there admiring the bride to be.

"Wow," Becky said softy. "I'll marry you right now." We all laughed. "Wait 'til Keith sees you walk down the aisle. He'll want to drop his pants for you right there and then. I wouldn't be surprised if he ripped that dress off you before the night ends."

"You really think so?" Nicole giggled. "I mean not

about Keith wanting to rip my dress off, but do you think this dress is the one?"

"It's perfect," I said, and it was perfect on her, but more so, because it was the same style I would wear.

"Let me try on a few others I had in mind. Did you pick the bridesmaid dresses you want to try on?"

Becky held up a couple of them. "I guess we can try these."

After we did a mini fashion show, Nicole finally decided on one of them and we all agreed. Then we decided to grab some dinner.

We went to a nearby restaurant that seemed less crowded, but in Pasadena, every restaurant was busy. Ordering dinner went pretty fast for a Friday night, but *getting* our dinner was a whole different story.

"Jenna, you've been checking your phone every minute. What's going on?" Nicole asked. Her face filled with concern.

Sliding my phone back into my purse, I gave a fake smile. "Nothing. It's work."

"You've never said that before," Kate said. "We know when something is wrong. You're not good at hiding things."

"Something's wrong in paradise. What happened?" Nicole asked as everyone leaned closer.

"It's my fault. I told Max I needed time, but I really didn't mean it. I was upset," I explained. I told them about the lawsuit and everything that happened at Stellars and since then.

"Jenna," Becky started to say. "You can't allow his past to get in the way of the future. Sometimes falling in love means letting go of the past. His past is the past. It's not as if he had sex with every female at his company. For Christ's sake, he was just being a typical horny male with no ties to a relationship. There is nothing wrong with that. He completely adores you and I know with every fiber of my being, he wouldn't do anything to hurt you, not on purpose."

"I know," I sighed. "It's just—"

"He withheld information from you when it should have come from him," Kate interrupted. "I understand."

"I see what you're doing," Nicole blurted. "You're playing games. He pissed you off and now you're punishing him, but it looks like you're punishing yourself too. Go tell him you'll take him back and just withhold sex. That's what I do." Nicole snorted. "Believe me, it works every time."

"I didn't think of that."

"Of course you didn't," Kate stated. "But at the same time, I bet you're making him miserable. He's probably thinking all sorts of nonsense, like you're thinking right now. I don't know why we tend to act childish when it comes to relationships. At least when you're married, you're stuck in one house and forced to communicate; but when you're not, you could drag out this unnecessary misery way too long."

"And don't let that what's-her-face come between you and Max. This is exactly what she wants. I'm sure she did her homework on you and Max. And if I'm right about her, I bet she's done this to other men," Becky commented.

"Max has got to find a way to get out of this. If he goes to court, it will ruin his reputation, along with his company. Even if he's proven innocent, the damage will have already been done. Going to court pretty much means there is enough evidence against him. People will judge him and draw their own conclusions." Nicole shook her head, looking glum. "I feel bad for him."

Sometimes anger, hurt, and pride get in the way of a person's mind, preventing them from behaving rationally. It was great to have wonderful friends who cared enough for me to tell me what I needed to hear, not what I wanted to hear. I knew I was acting immature about this, but to hear it from my best friends only confirmed it.

Becky's last words before dinner stuck with me. "I bet she did this to other men." Then I recalled the conversation I heard in the break room, when those two women mentioned a rumor that it wasn't her first time. I needed to speak to one of them.

Chapter 32
Jenna

It had been a week since I last saw Max. I thought for sure he would have come after me by now. I had to go see him right now.

"Ms. Mefferd, what are your thoughts?"

Flashing my eyes in the direction of the voice, I realized I had been in a daze. "Um…" Thank goodness, Matthew stepped in.

"Ms. Mefferd, we are voting on the color of the dress that will go on the front cover. Do you like the lavender or the white?"

Thinking of Nicole's wedding I said, "Lavender. I believe that will be the new black this season."

"Perfect. I agree," Matthew said, standing up. "Great meeting, everybody. Let's get the ball rolling. Meeting is adjourned."

Pushing back my chair, I grabbed my notepad and headed toward the door. A hand gripped my arm and pulled me aside. "Jenna," Matthew whispered. Looking at him up close like this, I could see the resemblance. God, how I missed Max. I had to stop torturing myself and him. This had to end. I felt like I was losing my mind as the anticipation of seeing Max got to me.

Peering up, I answered, "Yes, Matthew."

"Have you spoken to Becca lately?"

"Yes. Why?"

"She's been ignoring my calls and texts. I thought maybe she was sick or something." He paused.

"Becky is fine. Sometimes she goes to her cave and doesn't come out. She's busy with all the reading and editing. She has deadlines to meet."

"Ok, yeah, I'm sure that's it." Matthew released me, then pulled me back in. "Oh Jenna, I don't know what's going on, but Max needs you now. He's miserable and he doesn't fu...I mean he doesn't seem to care about anything."

"Okay," I said, but I didn't really believe him. Max was confident and proud. He didn't need me. I was the weak and insecure one. I mean, I knew he cared about me, but he didn't need me to stand by him to get through this. Nothing could penetrate that thick skin of his. He was determined.

When Matthew released me, I headed straight to Max's office. Now was probably not the right time, but I needed to see him and fix this before it got any worse. Feeling my heart thump rapidly, I had to prepare myself for what Max might say to me.

"Good afternoon," I said to his personal secretary.

"Good afternoon, Ms. Mefferd. I haven't seen you around. You must be busy at your new position."

"Yes, Matthew is keeping me busy," I replied. Instead of carrying on a conversation, I cut to the chase. "Is Mr. Knight in his office?" My heart started to escalate even faster.

"No. He left a message that he would be with his lawyer. He won't be coming in today. He said something about a dinner meeting. Shall I leave a message for him?"

"No, thank you. I will call him later. It was nice to see

you again."

"Have a good day, Ms. Mefferd."

With that, I walked toward my office feeling miserable. I knew Max's schedule like my own. Having to go ask his secretary seemed so formal. He felt like a stranger. I didn't like the feeling at all, and it was my fault.

Passing by the break room, I took a detour to the reception desk to ask where Susan's office was located. Apparently, there were two Susans, so I had to describe her. As I walked to her office, I tried to gather my thoughts about what questions to ask without sounding as if I was interrogating her. After all, Mr. Shaw said not to be the source of any rumors, but this was important. I had to know. I had to help Max, if possible.

"Susan?" I knocked softly. Her door was slightly ajar.

"Come in."

Peering up at me, she looked surprised. Her cheeks turned slightly pink, most likely recalling the conversation she had with her friend about me.

"Jenna, come in." She sat up straight and gave me her full attention.

Sitting down on the other side of her desk, I started with my questions. "I hope I'm not interrupting anything, but I'm here to ask you few questions and I hope you'll answer them honestly. I'm not upset. I just need the truth. When we are through, I'll walk out of here like we never had this conversation."

"I'm not sure what you're getting at. I hardly know you." Her tone was nervous, but then again, I would be too if I were speaking to the boss's girlfriend.

"I overheard you talking about Crystal, and I want to know if you could tell me more about the rumors."

Susan sank back in her seat, looking a bit more relaxed.

"Oh, why didn't you say that in the first place?" Her smile was somewhat genuine. "There isn't much I can tell you, except we all disliked her and stayed away from her as much as possible. I heard a rumor that this lawsuit wasn't her first. I don't know who started it or when it started. Supposedly, she blackmailed someone else. The difference that time was that she took the money. I guess she knew exactly how much that guy could fork up. Now with Max, she knows he has the company, so he's worth a lot more. I'm sorry, that is all I know."

"Do you know what company she worked for before she came here?"

"No. I didn't care to ask, but I'm sure Mrs. Ward would know, since she's the Human Resources Director."

"Thanks. I appreciate your honesty," I smiled.

"I hope it all works out for Max. He's such a wonderful man. He doesn't deserve this."

"Thank you," I said as I left. Susan was right, and I didn't need to add any more to his grief.

Before I stopped by my office, I headed to see Mrs. Ward. She couldn't disclose any personal information regarding present or past employees, but I had to try.

"Mrs. Ward?" I tapped on the open door.

"Ms. Mefferd, come in. How was your New York trip?"

"It was fantastic. Thank you for asking."

"How can I help you?"

"I have a question about a previous employee. I know you're not allowed to disclose any personal information and I wouldn't ask unless it was very important."

"I see. And whom, may I ask, are you referring to?"

"Crystal." The name spit out of my mouth like venom. I had come to loathe that woman because she had caused nothing but grief to so many people.

"You're right. I can't give you any information."

My heart sunk through my chair. The little hope I had faded. How would I find what I was looking for? And where would I search?

"However, Ms. Mefferd, I enjoy working for the Knight family. They are the kindest, most generous, genuine people I know. I'm so glad I never took the job with their competitor. To think, I almost worked for Rave. That is all I can tell you."

As I sat there, I tried to understand why she told me about a job she didn't take, when it dawned on me that she was giving me a not-so-subtle hint. "Mrs. Ward, thank you so much for your time, and may I say the Knights are very lucky to have you." With that, I walked out feeling hopeful.

The first thing I saw on my desk was a sandwich, a heart-shaped Rice Krispie treat, and a bottle of water. My heart burst with elation. There was no one in the office to ask who had brought it. Perhaps Max had cut short his meeting with his lawyer and he decided to stop by? Picking up the phone, I dialed Max's office. It went straight to his secretary.

"Yes, Ms. Mefferd. How can I help you?"

"Is Mr. Knight in his office?"

"I'm sorry, but his plans haven't changed. Could I help you with anything?"

"No. It's just that someone left a lunch for me and I thought it was Mr. Knight."

"I'm so sorry, Ms. Mefferd. It was on Mr. Knight's schedule. I am to bring you lunch any time your meetings surpass your lunch hour. He knows your schedule better than he knows his own," she chuckled. "I have to remind him to attend meetings, but he seems to know whenever your meetings are set."

"Thank you," I said warily. It was all I could say.

"Not a problem. The pleasure is mine. Anything I can do to make Mr. Knight happy."

After we hung up, tears blurred my vision. Max's kindness was not only proven through the testimony of his employees, but through his actions, time and time again. I needed to make this right.

Looking at my lunch, I lost my appetite yet again, something that had been happening a lot this past week. Thinking of Max not only made me happy, but it saddened me as well. Placing the wrapped Rice Krispie treat into my purse, I heard a low hum sound from my phone. It was another call from Luke, definitely not the person I wanted to hear from. I made a mental note to ask Matthew for a new number after the Crystal situation was over, since the company now provided my cell phone.

Letting out an irritated huff, I ignored the call, deciding it was the best thing to do. When I placed my phone back into its slot in my purse, I spotted Ethan's business card. I recalled he mentioned he had worked for Rave before. Perhaps he would have some insight. It was a slim chance, but I needed to try.

Chapter 33
Jenna

If I had gotten to pick the restaurant, this would not have been the place. It was one of Luke's favorite spots, and that alone made me uneasy. Glancing around, I finally found Ethan, and prayed Luke would be nowhere in sight.

"Thank you for meeting me, Ethan," I said, sitting across from him. He wore a gray suit and a pinstriped shirt opened at the collar. Most likely, he'd already ditched the tie. Holding a cocktail, he slid one of the menus toward me.

"It sounded urgent. What's going on? Is everything okay?"

"Yes…well, no. I need to ask you few questions and please don't ask why."

"O-kay." He dragged out the word, looking reluctant.

"Why did you leave your position at Rave?"

"Jenna, this is kind of private. Where are you going with this?"

Instead of answering his question, I fired another. "How did you know I was dating Maxwell Knight?"

"I read it in the newspaper. I didn't know it was you, for sure. I recognized the name, and I knew about the lawsuit."

Satisfied with his answer, I asked another question. "There's a rumor that Crystal, the woman who is suing

221

Max, worked at Rave and that she did the same thing to one of the managers over there. Do you know anything about that?" I guessed about the manager part. Whatever I said got his full attention. His face went pale, and I was sure he knew what I was talking about.

"That's ridiculous. It's just a rumor. Who told you that?" he tittered nervously, trying to dismiss it, but I knew better. His eyes gave him away.

"Ethan." I leaned in closer. "The man I love is about to have his name, and the company his family has worked so hard to build from nothing, smeared through the mud. All because of a selfish, devil of a woman, who thinks she can get away with it by manipulating, deceiving, and lying. She will rip him to shreds in court and none of what she says will be true. In the meantime, I will be thinking about the person who could have prevented this misery. I believe there is good in most people. People with morals who will step up, even if it means that person may lose face, just because it is the right thing to do. So let me ask you the question again. Do you know if Crystal did this to anyone at Rave?"

"I don't know what you're talking about." His tone was dead. Whatever he knew, he wasn't going to budge.

"I'm sorry, Ethan. I didn't mean to drag you out here and then grill you with questions. It's just that I don't know what else to do."

"I'm sure Max has a top-notch lawyer and he'll make sure she doesn't get a dime."

"That's what everyone thinks, but no amount of money is going to stop her. She was offered a big payoff, but she didn't take it. You know what sucks? It's her word against his. Unless we find solid evidence to discredit her, she'll win."

"I'm sure that won't happen."

"How do you know? Can you swear to me that Max will win? Can you honestly sit there and give me false hope? Unless you have a crystal ball that shows the outcome will be in his favor, I'm going to think the worst because I'd rather be prepared for it."

The tears I'd been holding, locked up tightly, burst out uncontrollably. Embarrassed, I wiped them away as fast as they poured. There was nothing to cry about yet the reality of the situation hit me hard. I had been so mad at Max and Crystal that the anger prevented me from facing what could happen in the future. "I'm sorry, Ethan." He handed me his napkin. "I didn't mean to do this."

"You love him, don't you?"

I had never told Max I loved him, even though he'd said it several times to me. I knew I felt something special for him, but it didn't hit me until then that I truly did love him. 'Love' was something I didn't say easily. The word held so much meaning, that unless I was absolutely sure, I would not say it. "Yes. I love him. I couldn't begin to tell you how much. I would do anything for him. I would rather lie or go to jail so he could be free of the shame."

As I smeared away the lingering tears, guilt and sympathy clouded Ethan's eyes. "Tell me, Ethan. How much do you love your wife? If she was in Max's situation, what would you do? How would you free her from that grief?"

"I understand how you feel, but I don't have any information that could help you. Max is a good man. I've had a few opportunities to cross paths with him. He was professional, generous, and one of the few genuine people in that ugly business. I wish I could help you."

Sitting here was a waste of time. The longer Ethan went

on telling me he didn't know anything and lying to my face, the sooner I would do or say something I would regret.

"Thank you for your time, Ethan. I need to go." I stood up, and grabbed my purse and jacket.

"What about dinner? You should at least eat something."

Looking at my watch, I saw it was already eight o'clock. "I've lost my appetite. Please give Kim my regards. I wonder what she would do if she were in my shoes? I just hope this guy will step up and be a real man." Then I had a thought. "Do you think it would be crazy of me to go to Rave and start asking the women there a bunch of questions? Maybe one of them will rat the guy out. What do you think?" I was that desperate. I wanted him to know just how far I would go for Max.

"They'll kick you out as soon as you start asking questions," he stammered. His eyes darted in anger, flickering back and forth.

I couldn't believe he would get upset over my idea. Was he concerned for my well-being or was he hiding something? Leaning into him to show how serious I was, I said slowly and with conviction, "I don't care. I would tear the whole building down, layer by layer, to find whoever could free Maxwell Knight. You know, it's really a shame. The Ethan I knew in college had balls. Either it's the age, or you are scared shitless, but your balls are sagging."

With that uncharacteristic remark, I walked away so fast I almost knocked the waitress down along the way. Feeling heat rise to my face from anger and frustration, my heels clicked away in my hurry to see Max. Then someone grabbed me around my waist. Thinking it was Ethan, I turned into the grasp. I hoped that he had changed his mind.

With one look, my body froze and my heart stopped. "Luke," I whimpered. Turning red after dodging his calls and seeing that smirk on his face, I wanted to crawl away. Something about him made me feel so small and worthless.

"Jenna. I knew you would come to your senses and meet me. I see you got my text and decided to come."

"What? I didn't."

"Come sit." Luke practically pushed me down on the bar stool next to his.

Though I was irritated, it would be a good time to set things straight. Building up every ounce of courage I could summon, I braced myself to do and say something out of character. And it was going to feel good. Someone like Luke deserved every bit of animosity I could give him.

I bore my eyes into his, hoping he would get the point. With a sassy tone, I said, "Luke, I'm not here to see you. I haven't returned your texts or your phone calls because I *don't* want to see you. Not now, not *ever*. I don't want you. How clear can I get?"

"You wouldn't be here if you meant that." His lips curled into a devious smile.

He wasn't hearing me and I didn't want to waste my time. My next stop was to Max's place and I was determined to get there tonight. "I gotta go. Don't call or text me again. Move on with your life."

Luke blocked my way and looked over my shoulder. His eyes kept shifting back and forth. What the hell? What was he doing?

"Jenna. You made me so happy, leaving Max for me." His voice was loud, and what he said didn't make sense.

His arms wrapped around my waist tightly as he pulled me in for a kiss. Struggling, I finally managed to pull away. "What the hell, Luke?" I yelped, using the back of my hand to erase the disgusting taste of his tongue from my mouth. After giving him a dirty look, I started to storm away, but he caught my wrist and swung me to him again.

"Let go of me," I snapped, but Luke was too strong. Curious customers stopped to observe the scene. If I got any louder or if this got out of hand, someone would step in. Maybe the passing waitress or the bartender would intervene. At first, I thought Luke had too much to drink, but apparently, that wasn't the case. The whole scene just blew my mind. I really wished I had asked Ethan to meet me elsewhere. Sometimes fate does funny things and the worst case scenario turns out to be the best when you least expect it.

"Don't you fuckin' touch her, Puke!" a voice bellowed. From the corner of my eye, I saw a fist fly into Luke's face, throwing him against the stool. While Luke fell, he held onto my blouse, causing me to fall with him. Before I hit the ground, an arm around my waist pulled me up and safely into strong arms.

Max. I knew that smell, that voice that beckoned my attention, and that firm grip. Not to mention his unique nickname for Luke. My body easily succumbed to his, sailing me away into a blissful sea of joy. How I had missed his touch, his hold, and his love. I dissolved rapidly in his arms, realizing all the days, minutes, seconds of missing him that my anger and pride stole from me.

"Jenna," he murmured, holding on to me tightly as if I would disappear. I could tell he had been drinking more than usual. I understood. He was under a tremendous amount of stress. "Why didn't you call? I've been waiting for you." His face dug into my hair, breathing me in. "You're supposed to be my forever. I want to be yours,

Jenna. I need you so much, but you left me. You left us."

Turning to him, I saw the bags under his eyes and the sexy stubble on his face, the stubble I loved to run my fingers over. Though he looked incredibly delicious in my eyes, he looked so worn and broken too. Oh my God! I didn't know I could affect him this way. I did this to him. I didn't leave him, but in his heart, he thought I did.

Before I could tell Max I had been on my way to his place, Max flew to his left. "Max!" I screamed. Luke had managed to stand and fight back. As Max stumbled to get up, I guarded him with my body. I hated that Luke hurt Max. It felt as if he had done it to me. If Max wasn't wasted, there would have been no need for my intervention, but I didn't have to worry for too long. Matthew had been close by and pounded Luke with an even a stronger blow. "Don't touch my brother, asshole."

"What's going on?" The bartender came around as the customers nearby scrambled for safety.

"Nothing." Matthew said. "We were just leaving." Without a word, Matthew threw some cash on the table, grabbed Max's arm, and started to haul him toward the exit.

Standing there dumbfounded, I looked over my shoulder to see Max slumped over, obeying Matthew's order with the most hurtful eyes looking back at me. It pained me greatly to see him this way. It hurt even more to realize he was walking out the door thinking I didn't want him.

For the first time, I saw Max's vulnerability. He had always been my rock, the one that held us together, but now he was lost. I didn't think he needed me, but I had been wrong. I didn't know our time apart would cause him so much heartache. I finally realized that if he had said the words I had said to him, I would have felt the same. The ball would have been in his court and I would not have gone against his wishes. Going to his place tonight was probably not a good idea after what had happened. I would have to wait until tomorrow.

Turning back to Luke, I gave him the most evil look I could. "You bastard. You knew he was behind me."

"Looks like there's trouble in paradise," he gloated, dabbing the blood off his lips with a napkin. "I told you he was no good for you. You'll come running back to me when they throw his sorry ass in jail."

I don't know what came over me, but I had become more aggressive these days. On an impulse, I smacked him hard across his face. The palm of my hand stung like hell, but I didn't care. It was worth the pain. It wasn't something I would normally do, but it sure felt good to do it. "That was for Max and the kiss you took without my permission. If you ever come near me again, I'll call the police and get a restraining order."

Luke mumbled a few words as I walked away. Just before I shut the door behind me, I looked to where Ethan and I had sat. My one connection to a possible witness to help end this lawsuit was gone. *Gone.*

Chapter 34
Jenna

Lying on my bed wearing Max's T-shirt, I rubbed the lack of sleep from my eyes. Matthew had texted me to let me know he had taken Max to his place. He suggested I talk to Max the next day, since today they had a long meeting scheduled with his lawyer. It was the longest Saturday of my life and the day had barely begun.

Thinking of my meeting with Ethan again, I grabbed my cell phone from the nightstand and dialed Mr. Shaw's cell.

"Hello."

"Hello, Mr. Shaw. This is Jenna Mefferd. I'm so sorry to bother you on a Saturday morning, but I needed to tell you something important that may help Max's case. To make a long story short, I overheard a rumor that Crystal had done this before. She used to work at Rave Magazine, and I think—"

"Ms. Mefferd. Please don't say or do anything else that might jeopardize this case. We are fully aware of Crystal's past. We are working on it. I appreciate your wanting to help, but please let me do my job."

"Of course, Mr. Shaw, but do you know who that person is?"

"Ms. Mefferd…"

"I know. You can't disclose that information. I didn't mean to pry."

"That's okay. I assure you, Max is in good hands and I will do everything in my power to stop this from going to court, if possible."

"I'm sure he is. It's just that—"

"You're doing your part by attending our sessions. We've covered a lot of ground, and there might not even be a need to meet again. I thought you did much better the last time we met. If all goes well, we won't be going to court. Of course, if you do find any new information, you are welcome to let me know. Have a nice day."

Feeling a bit better about Mr. Shaw's efforts, I stared at the ceiling as thoughts ran through my mind. Of course, Max would hire only the best.

"Jenna, come eat something." Becky's words went in one ear, out the other. "If you don't get your sorry butt out of bed, I'm going to spoon feed you."

Knowing Becky would keep her word, I paced toward the kitchen.

"So you'll talk to him tomorrow. Everything will be fine. He's not going to push you away when you apologize for acting like a big baby."

"Oh, now it's all my fault?" I plopped myself on a chair at the dining table. Becky had made me an omelet and a cup of coffee. "Thank you."

"No. It's both of your faults. He should have told you, but at the same time, you shouldn't have punished him this long. It's been more than a week. It must have been driving him out of his mind, thinking all sorts of crazy stuff. I know it would have made me nuts."

"Matthew told me not to see him today because of their busy schedule. I'm going there tomorrow to set this straight. I'm sure Matthew will let him know." Becky stiffened when I mentioned Matthew. "Are you sure there is nothing going on between you two?"

"No, why would you say that?"

"Just wondering."

"Before I forget, we have a second fitting for our bridesmaid dresses. Nicole texted and left the date. If you haven't already, you may want to check on that. I'm going to be out of town for a book convention. You know, the one I go to every year. I'm leaving in a couple of days, and I'll probably visit my parents for a little while too. I really hate to leave you at a time like this."

"Becky, go. I'm fine."

"Relationships are difficult. If they weren't, then everyone would do it. But seriously, if relationships went on without a hitch, there wouldn't be any need for couples counseling or divorce court. Life would be boring and there would be no make up sex," she winked. "And Jenna..." she paused. "Sometimes falling in love means letting go of the past...his past."

"Okay." I nodded. I knew she was right.

"I need to go pack."

"I'll clean up. Thank you for breakfast."

"Always a pleasure, my dear." Becky turned when she got to the door. "Oh, and go have some great make up sex tomorrow." Her brow arched, giving me a playfully wicked smile.

"Becky!" I exclaimed. "Hey, I almost forgot. Matthew asked me why you haven't returned his texts or calls. He's wondering if you're mad at him."

Becky's expression became stoic at first, then her lips slowly fell to a pout. "I'm always mad at him."

Stepping out of the elevator, my pulse became unsteady. Max and I needed to get things straightened out, so why was I so nervous? I didn't know what I was afraid of. I couldn't even put it into words, but I had to think this through. Seeing the door slightly ajar, raised my hand to knock when I heard voices.

"Whatever you need, I will be there for you." It was a female's voice, and that alone made my heart sink. Someone else was comforting my Max when it should've been me. Guilt consumed me, fast and hard, and all I could do was stand there, contemplating what to do.

"Thomas and his team are working long and hard. They may have something to discredit Crystal. We may not even need to go to court, but this is all hearsay," Max sighed heavily. "Never in my wildest dreams could I have imagined being in this situation."

"Oh, Max, darling. You know what you need right now? You need a good lay." Her tone was flirty, and I imagined her dirty hands touching Max on his fine chest. Who wouldn't want to?

"You know I'm not with anyone right now," she continued.

Oh God! Cringing from her words, I wanted to disappear. As heat flushed through my body with jealousy, I waited for Max's response.

"You know I'm taken…I think."

"You don't sound so sure."

"You really need to leave," he ordered. "I have work to do. Crystal may have broken my spirit, but damn her to hell, she's not taking anything else from me."

"Like I said before, all the models will testify on your

behalf. You've been nothing but kind to us, making sure we are always treated well. You're always a gentleman. It's the least we can do."

"Thank you for stopping by, and for your support, Ella. Thomas will contact you if he feels it's necessary."

At the sound of a smacking kiss, I wanted to go in and let her know I was here before she tried anything else. It wasn't that I didn't trust Max. I just didn't want her hands on him any longer. Even knowing she was about to leave, I was still caught up in eavesdropping as the door swung open.

Sucking in air, I was embarrassed as both of their eyes set on mine in shock. Ella was beautiful, with long brown hair and a slim body; she looked exactly how a runway model should look.

"Jenna? What are you doing here?"

Max's words stung me deeply, sounding as if I had no business being there.

"I came to talk to you." My courage faltered. "I left you a message and texted to let you know I was coming."

"I left the phone upstairs." Max turned to Ella. "Ella, this is Jenna."

"Ah, the 'one.' It's a pleasure meeting you." Ella was sweet, despite the fact she tried to jump into bed with Max. After shaking my hand, she walked out the door.

"Hope to see you both at the London Fashion Show." With an air kiss to both of us, she made her way to the elevator.

Instead of welcoming me in, Max left the door open while he walked inside. Closing the door behind me, I placed my purse down on the kitchen counter and headed to the living room. Max's shirt and the blue tie I bought him for Christmas, were tossed on the sofa. This was not like him at all.

Max faced the grand window, where the beauty of the city shone below. Looking down, he could get lost and forget about what was in front of him — me. He had his arms stretched out and his palms planted flat against the glass. His chest rose and fell slowly. As his toned muscles straining under the sleeves of his T-shirt distracted me, I wondered what he was thinking.

Feeling my nerves wavering, I laced my fingers together to keep my hands from trembling as I gathered the courage to speak, but Max beat me to it.

"If you're here to gather your things from upstairs, you've come at a bad time. You could've come when I was out. That way, I wouldn't have to see you walk out of my life." Pain radiated from Max's soft voice.

He thought I was leaving him. Oh my God! How do I fix this? "Max, I didn't come to take my things. I came to apologize. I was upset, hurt, confused, and I needed time to catch my breath. You and I, well, it all happened so fast, and then all this stuff with Crystal. You didn't trust me enough to tell me about your past, or the things you did with her. A part of me felt like I wasn't good enough for you."

Max slowly turned his head, furrowing his brows. "Have I ever made you feel worthless?" he asked softly, looking drained.

"No, Max. But what am I supposed to think knowing you and Crystal did things you and I have never even tried? I've been so insecure. I'm afraid that I don't satisfy you, and one day you'll leave me because I don't fulfill your needs."

"You give me no credit, Jenna. I'm not that kind of a man. I'm glad we're communicating, but I'm beginning to think you don't know me at all. It took every ounce of willpower not to break down your door and bring you back here myself. But I wanted you to come when you were ready, on your own terms."

"It's not you, Max. I know you're a good man. It's me."

"Then what do you want?" He asked sternly.

That question could make or break us. I knew what I wanted, so what was I waiting for? "I want you, Max. I want us. I'm sorry for being immature and stubborn. I'm sorry I put you through hell while I worked things out. I always knew what I wanted, but—"

"But..." he repeated my word. "You didn't come faster because you knew I would be waiting for you." He sounded angry, and it made me shudder.

We were heading in the wrong direction, but he was right. I took my time because I knew. Maybe I was too late. "No," I stammered. "I didn't mean to hurt you. I don't know why, but I tortured myself too. But you have to understand that I was hurting. When I found out that Crystal had the same car, how do you think that made me feel? How do I know I'm not just another girl you'll get tired of eventually? You told me that you kept things from me to protect me, but how did I know you weren't hiding them instead?"

"You're right. I didn't realize I hurt you until it was too late. I'm sorry for the things I should have done. I should have broken down the door and made you see how much you mean to me, instead of waiting for you to come to me. That was childish of me. For the record, I never leased a car for Crystal. She negotiated that in her contract." Max exhaled a deep sigh. "I've missed you, Jenna. No one will ever love you as much as I love you. It's not possible. I love you more than my own life. I would never hurt you."

Just when I thought everything was going to be fine, his eyes darkened, filled with anger. He looked furious. "But you walked away from me. You walked away from us. There are times when you realize you've been defeated and sometimes you have to let go, so I'm letting you go."

What? Did I hear him correctly? He didn't want me anymore? I was so stunned that it took a minute to register what he'd said. When the reality hit me, the voice in my head screamed...*No!* As tears stung my eyes, my heart dropped to the floor, and my body quivered inside from his words. Suddenly the air was too heavy and thick, and I could hardly breathe. His words sucked the air out of my lungs, as the shock shattered my world.

"You're letting me go?" I whimpered, hoping I had heard him wrong, but when he spoke with the same angry tone, I knew he meant it.

"You fuckin' left me when I needed you." Trembling from his tone, his words cut so deep that it destroyed me, but again, he was right. I had pushed him away and slammed the door in his face. Oh God. What have I done? I've ruined us. Max had never used foul language at me before. Once again, that showed how upset and beyond angry he was.

"I know, Max," I confirmed wearily. "I'm sorry. I'm sorry for acting immature. I should have been there for you. You needed my support, my understanding, my forgiveness, and my love, but instead I turned away."

Unable to handle the heart-wrenching wound, and knowing this was the end for us, I headed for the kitchen to grab my purse as tears dampened my cheeks. At that moment, overwhelming regret kicked in. I had waited too long. I let my pride and insecurity get in the way of a blooming relationship. I wanted to crawl into a hole and sob until I felt nothing, until I forgot Max and what I'd done to us. Before I walked out of his life, I needed to tell him how I truly felt.

"I know I haven't said the word before, but I can say it without a doubt. I am in love with you, Maxwell Knight. I love you, and I want you to be mine. I want to belong to you, and only you. Do you hear me, Max? I love you. And I will say it a million times and shout it out to the world to make you hear me."

As my words flew out of my mouth fast and loud, Max's eyes sparkled and his blank expression turned into raw hunger. His stride was long and fast, with a purpose. Oh God! He was coming for me! My body pulsated in response to him.

Before I'd lost any more of my dignity, I wanted to run out the door. When I reached the doorknob, Max swung me around.

"Jenna, we are not done, nor are we broken. I had to see how you would react. I needed to know. Now I see you truly love me."

Confused, I peered up at him as I wiped my tears.

"No matter how many times you tear us down, I will build us back up. I will be patient with your insecurities and lack of experience in relationships. I will continue to show you time and time again, how much you mean to me. I will wait for you. You are everything to me. That is the reason I can't let you go."

I felt as if I had breathed in the sweetest air. He awakened me, making me feel high. His words went straight to my heart. He had torn me apart, but then he put me back together with his love. Max continued speaking, as his hands weaved through my hair, pulling me closer to his lips.

"I'm going to enjoy punishing you for what you put me through, but not in the way you think. I would never hurt you. I'm going to punish you with my lips, my tongue, my hands, and my body. You'll be begging me to stop. I'm going to make you feel every single bit of worth. I'm going to strip you down naked to your soul, so you'll feel everything I'm feeling. Until you know how much you mean to me and how much you turn me on. Until you understand how much I love every part of you, your beautiful body, your heart, your mind, and your soul."

"I still wonder why me, when you can have anyone?"

"Why not you, Jenna? Don't you get it? I'm in love with you. Only you. No one can control who they fall in love with. Just the sight of you drives me wild. And God help me, because I can't control myself around you."

His passionate words, hungry eyes and body so close to mine, made me lose all control. I slammed my lips to his so hard that it hurt. It felt as though we were kissing for the first time and we couldn't get enough of each other. God, he tasted so good. I had missed kissing him, devouring him. I needed him. *Now.*

Max responded with the same intensity and passion. His stubble pricked and scratched my lips, but I didn't care. When his arms tangled in the strap of my purse, he slid it off my shoulder. "You're not going anywhere."

As he sucked my lip, he yanked my sweater off. "Sorry, babe, I'll buy you a new one." We both watched in amusement as several buttons bounced as they hit the ground. With a short chuckle from Max, I was lost in his endless kisses to my face and neck, all the while undressing both of us.

He scooped me up so my legs dangled over his forearm. Along the way, he grabbed his tie. Midway up the stairs, he stopped and placed me down. His eyes pierced mine, fiery, domineering, and possessive. "Say it again. Tell me you love me." His tone was gentle, yet demanding.

I took a step up so we could be eye to eye. Taking pleasure in brushing my hands across the incredibly sexy stubble covering his face, I lovingly looked into his eyes. "I love you, Maxwell Knight. I will never love another man as much as I love you."

Max radiated a smile I hadn't seen in a while. Then his eyes laid on me tenderly, but with desire. "Sit," he ordered. "I said I would punish you and you know I don't back down on my word."

Seeing Max stroke his tie enticed me, leaving me to wonder what he was going to do with it. Sitting down in the middle of the stairs, I tilted my head back, but Max had already kneeled down to me. Moving swiftly, he not only tied my hands together, he tied them to the poles on the stairway too. I had never been tied up before but holy shit! This was beyond anything I'd ever experienced before.

Max gave me a sexy wink while he spread my legs apart. "Enjoy your punishment." Then with one long stroke of his tongue on my clit, I exploded. Arching my back as I took in the pleasure of being consumed by him, I wanted to touch him. I wanted to run my hands over his back and through his hair. I wanted to touch any part of him, but I couldn't.

The throbbing, aching need got worse when he leisurely glided up to my breast with his tongue as he nipped and sucked on my nipple, producing both pleasure and pain. Every caress and every kiss from Max scorched through my veins like a blazing fire, igniting again and again. I was smoldering between my legs from missing him. I ached with the realization of almost losing him. I was soaking wet. I needed him like I needed air, and I was both hungry and thirsty for him.

"Max, I want to touch you," I breathed, unable to focus as he sucked and nipped at my nipples, while his fingers teased the hell out of my clit.

"You like this, don't you?" He licked my ears as he spoke and gently stroked his dick on my clit. "I didn't know you wanted to play rough. I've got more to show you, but I'm going to expose you to things one at a time, so you can dream about it and anticipate what I'm going to do to you next."

His words drove me insane and I wanted him inside me desperately. "Please, Max. Let me go. I need to touch you."

"How do you think I felt when you didn't call me? You denied me what I wanted and needed most. I'm going to enjoy torturing you like this. I hope you are ready, babe, because I am going to feast on every part of you."

He was not joking. He slid his fingers inside me slowly, in and out, while his lips and tongue tasted me from head to toe. Not a single spot had been missed. "Max," I cried. I needed to touch or grab hold of something as I climaxed, as his hand vibrated faster. I couldn't handle it any more. "Please...Max," I begged, flinging my head back in ecstasy.

"You want me inside?" Taking his fingers out, he lightly straddled me, teasing me beyond the point of endurance. As he caressed the side of my neck with his lips, his hands roamed over my breast.

"Yes," I whimpered. "I want you inside me."

Max pressed his body harder and snarled his words in my ear. "Sorry, this is where I say no. You have no idea how much I want to be inside you right now, but not yet. I've only just begun with your punishment."

"Please, Max," I begged, pressing my body forward to his. "I can't take it anymore."

Max heaved a heavy sigh, looking at me with longing, hungry eyes. "Shit, Jenna. Stop squirming and stop looking at me like that. I'm so turned on right now, I can't hold it any longer." Then Max thrust inside me and I burst like fireworks.

Twisting my wrists, I held onto the pole of the stairway for support as he rocked inside me, making me gasp for air. As the intensity increased, my breathing became even more ragged and heavy.

"You've been bad, Jenna," Max panted, smacking my behind lightly. "Very bad. You left me hanging, high and dry." Unexpectedly, Max pulled out without a word, turned me over, then started to pump me hard from behind. He gave me all he could give, and I lost myself in Max's ecstasy.

Just when I thought he'd had enough, Max pulled out and untied my hands. As he thrust inside me again, he lifted me up. My legs secured around his waist while his hands supported my bottom. "We need to get protection," he said, as he climbed the stairs in that position. Every step he took, he plunged deeper inside me, pleasuring me even more. He knew exactly what he was doing.

Max placed me on the cold bathroom counter, but I was so hot, it was almost a relief. With his hands on either side of me, he gave me a long soft kiss and pulled my bottom lip with his teeth. "I'm not done with you yet. I'm going to show you everything I've got. I'm going to make love to you with my eyes, my lips, my hands, and my words. I'm going to own every inch of you and show you all that you've been missing."

Max was amazing, making me feel every bit of my

worth to him. It was then that Max's past became just his past, and I finally realized that I had always been his future. I was never going to let Crystal ruin us again.

It was the best make up sex in history.

Chapter 35
Matthew

It was never easy going there, and no matter how many times I visited, the pain stayed the same. They say time heals all wounds, but I say time just makes it bearable. Still, I hoped that day would be a different story. As I sat on the grass next to Tessa's gravestone, a warm breeze brushed against me. I'd like to think it was a blessed greeting from her.

"Hey, you," I said, tracing her name with the tip of my finger. "Sorry I haven't been here in a while, but Max needed me. He had this huge lawsuit, but it's over now. Some chick had accused him of things he didn't do, and if the case hadn't gone in his favor, it would have broken him and probably our company too. Luckily, this guy Ethan stepped up. He used to work at the same company as this bitch, Crystal. Who would have guessed he was Jenna's good friend from college? Talk about a small world. Max always said Jenna was his lucky star.

"Ethan was a manager at Rave Fashion Magazine. Apparently Crystal blackmailed him too. But she took his payoff money and nobody knew anything about it. When she went after Max, she knew he was loaded, so she wanted to take him to court. Thank goodness for good, decent people. I'm assuming his wife knew about it, since she didn't leave him. Ethan was lucky for sure." I talked to Tessa as if she were sitting by my side.

"Relationships can be hard, but you already knew that. You and I went through some rough times, didn't we? The part that kills me the most is that we can't always fix them. You and I won't ever get our second chance. I'm sorry, sweetheart." Choking back the words, my eyes started to water. Letting out a deep breath, I continued.

"The reason why I'm here is to get your permission or something like that." Unexpectedly, a tear escaped the corner of my eye. "Tessa, I'm never going to forget you. You were a part of my life, but that's in the past. I grieved for you for all these years. Every second, every minute, and every day I lived in darkness, so cold and alone. You left me broken and dead inside. Hell would have been a more pleasant place to be, but I know you wouldn't want me stuck in a place like that. That's not living.

"You see, something wonderful and unexpected happened. I met someone. I really care for her and I think she cares for me too. I think she may be the one, but I don't know how to let all this guilt in my heart go. When I'm with her, I don't think about you as much. I know this sounds awful, but it's true. She's the only one who has given me hope. She makes me want to live again. She is my light at the end of the dark tunnel.

"So, what do you think?" I chuckled lightly, and felt a sense of peace. "I promise I'll never forget you. It's impossible." My lips quivered, feeling the ache slicing deeper. "You were my first and you would've been my last, but sometimes fate has other plans, and no matter how hard we try to understand the reason behind it, we just can't. We have to accept it, move on, and do what we can to survive. So that is what I'm trying to do. I know you understand this, because I would want the same for you."

Wiping the tears that I promised to shed for the last time, I placed a dozen red roses against the stone. "Happy Birthday, Tessa. I'll always love you. You'll always be in my heart, but it's time for me to move on." My hands trembled, as the guilt came rushing back in again, knowing someone else might possibly replace her; replace her touch, her smile, her laughter, and her love. "I'm not sure when I'll be back, but I promise I'll visit again." My stomach tangled into knots and my muscles tightened. I needed to leave. Shit! How many times must I go through this? How many times would I tell myself I needed to stop going there if I was going to move on?

With one last glance back, I walked away knowing exactly what I needed to do.

Becky

My excuses for leaving town were not valid. Jenna needed me, but I knew she would be fine. Me, on the other hand, well, I didn't know if I would ever be fine. I had to get away from Matthew. Perhaps the distance would help me clear my head and my heart.

I told Jenna I was going to a book convention, but I really wasn't. I didn't completely lie, though. There was a book convention, but I had decided to skip it. I hadn't lied about seeing my parents either, exactly. They were vacationing in Hawaii. They asked me if I wanted to join them, and though the offer was appealing, I wanted solitude instead, so I told them I would doggie sit.

Kicking back on the lounge chair by the pool, I picked up the e-reader Matthew bought me for Christmas. Shit! I wanted to be Matthew-free, but everything he touched or we'd shared reminded me of him. Not just the e-reader, but chopsticks, my robe, ice cream, cotton candy, Starbucks, eggs, my panties, my bookshelf, dogs, Victoria's Secret...hell, even my damn computer. Argh! I was trying to run away from him, but his memories followed me everywhere.

My phone buzzed on the table, and I saw it was Matthew. He kept calling and texting me, but I hadn't responded. I had texted him just before I left to let him know I was really busy, thinking he would stop bugging me. Obviously, he didn't care how busy I might be.

Allowing Matthew's call to go straight to voicemail, I got up, stripped down naked, and jumped into the heated pool. Not only did I want to swim, I needed a distraction and this was it. Since my parents' home was in the middle of nowhere, no one would see me skinny dipping.

Matthew

The news of the lawsuit dismissal spread fast. Max wanted to celebrate the good news by catering lunch for everyone. Jenna and I were the last ones to head to the break room. This was the perfect opportunity to casually ask her a few questions. Swinging my chair from my desk, I turned to her. "Hey, Jenna. How's Becca?"

After doing something on the computer, she turned to look at me in surprise. "Becca? Oh she's great."

"She must be really busy."

"That's what she said."

I don't know why, but Jenna looked nervous. Was she hiding something from me?

"So, where is she?"

Jenna looked dumbfounded. She wasn't good at lying

and I laughed inwardly at the sight of her face flushing.

"Huh? What do you mean where is she?" She swallowed, trying to play cool. She started heading for the door. Sneaky! She tried to avoid me, but I moved faster. Blocking her exit, I stood in front of her. If anyone saw, it would look like I was trying to hit on her. This would probably start another ridiculous rumor.

"Jenna, I know you're hiding something from me." My tone was gentle, yet stern.

She gave me that innocent face, blinking her eyes and flashing her adorable smile. "I have no idea what you mean." She tried to squirm around me.

"While you were at Max's place, I went to yours. I knocked, no I pounded on the door this morning. I even called and texted her." I leaned into Jenna's personal space and gave her my most serious look. "Now… where… is… she? She's been avoiding me and I have no clue what I did. I need to talk to her."

Jenna's eye grew wide and her lips parted with the brightest smile. It was the second biggest smile I had seen, apart from when her eyes were on Max.

"I knew it," she exclaimed with a twinkle in her eyes.

"What do you know?" I chuckled.

"Don't tell her I told you." She waited for me to agree. "She's in San Francisco."

"San Francisco!" I said a bit too loud, losing my composure. "What the fuck? What is she doing there?" I was extremely concerned.

"Relax. She's at a book convention."

"Why didn't she tell me?"

"I don't know, but I'll text you the information."

"Thanks, Jenna." Knowing this, I wasn't going to wait any longer. The truth was I needed to see her now. I needed my Becca. Pulling Jenna into my arms, I gave her the most heartfelt hug. "I'll be out of town till tomorrow. I'll text Max to let him know where I'm at, so don't tell him just yet."

"Don't tell Max what?"

Releasing Jenna, I heard my brother's voice behind me. Caught red-handed, I teased him a bit. "That Jenna and I are running away together."

"You're full of shit."

I wish I could have taken a picture of my brother's face. Even knowing I was joking, he pushed me out of his way and practically fell into Jenna's arms.

"I came to rescue you from this dictator. I was waiting for you in the break room. Now I'm glad I came; I can't even trust my own brother. I've got to protect what's mine," Max chuckled, then he claimed her with his mouth.

"Gross." I let out a laugh. "See you guys later." I didn't need to see that. With a slap of my pocket to make sure I had my wallet and cell, I called my secretary.

Chapter 36
Matthew

Holy shit! How the hell was I going to find her when she wouldn't answer her goddamned phone? Tons of authors sat chatting with fans and signing at endless tables. As I searched for her, my thoughts wandered. What had I done to get her pissed off at me like that? Sure, we slept together, but it didn't seem like it frazzled her at all. We were friends, getting to know each other. Though in the back of my mind, I'd always wanted more from her, I couldn't think about it at that point. But now, I was ready. Shit! I hope I didn't mess it up.

As I looked around, I let out a chuckle when I saw the ladies wearing T-shirts that read, "Books! The other soul food," and "Book hangovers, a girl's worst nightmare." I laughed even harder when I saw one that read, "Book boyfriends are better because they are always there when we need them." That reminded me of Becca and I sighed. She deserved better than me. I continued searching, becoming more and more anxious. Every second gone felt like another second lost, and the chance of making this right dwindled.

After a seemingly endless quest, and having all those ladies stop to stare at me, I finally found an information desk. "Excuse me. I'm looking for Becky Miller." The young lady looked up with a beaming smile.

"Hi. Can I help you?" Her eyes were flirty. Usually when a beautiful girl asked me that question, I flirted back, but not today. I finally realized I wasn't interested in anyone but Becca. I was in trouble. Besides, when I wanted something, I wanted it right away. And to top it off, this girl was frustrating me. I had already told her I was looking for Becky Miller.

"I'm looking for Becky Miller. She's an agent. Where can I find her, please?" I tried to be calm and patient, but the longer she looked at her list and the longer I had to wait, the faster I lost it. I was about to snatch that clipboard out of her hand and look for it myself.

"I'm sorry, but there is no Becky Miller here."

"What?" My mood turned irate and my tone grew angry. Taking deep breaths, I managed to calm down. What the hell did she mean no Becky Miller there? "Can you please look again? Perhaps you might have overlooked it."

The poor gal looked nervous as she scrolled down her list. Shaking her head, she looked at me again. "Sorry. I don't see her name."

"Thank you for your time," I said quickly, dialing Jenna as I walked away.

"Hello, Matthew."

"Becca's not here. She's not at the book convention." My voice rose in urgency.

"Becky told me she was going to stay at her parents' place. Maybe she decided not to go to the convention. I honestly don't know, Matthew."

"Can you text me her parents' address, please? Thanks. Bye."

Getting a taxi wasn't the problem; it was my anxiety. I hadn't thought this through. As the car headed to the address Jenna sent me, my thoughts ran wild. What if her parents were home? What if she doesn't want me? What the hell was I doing? Contemplating whether to go back home or not, I couldn't get myself to tell the taxi driver to turn around. Before I knew it, we arrived.

"Thanks," I said, handing him the fare as I stepped out. "Keep the change. Actually," I turn to him again. "Could you please wait here for a few minutes? I may need a ride to the airport."

Staring at her parent's house, I raked my fingers through my hair and headed to the front door. Feeling all sorts of butterflies in my stomach, I rang the doorbell. No answer. I pressed it again with a sigh. Still no answer. I stepped back from the door, about to head back to the taxi, when I heard my name.

"Matthew?"

It was the sweetest sound I had heard in a long time, though all the barking almost drowned it out.

I had seen Becca without makeup before, but for some reason she looked different. She looked absolutely beautiful. She was all natural. Just the way I liked it. "Surprise." I beamed a nervous, geeky grin.

"Hold on. Let me put the dogs in their room."

Becca left but quickly came back.

"What are you doing here?" Becca swung the door wider. Her wet hair hung over the shoulder of a long white robe. It reminded me of the time she did her lap dance for me. That was enough to get me heated up. Most likely she had taken a shower, but in the middle of the afternoon?

I waved to the driver to let him know I didn't need his service anymore, and then turned to face Becca, debating about how to approach this. "I had to see you."

"Come in. Is everything okay?"

"Everything is fine." Stepping inside, I glanced around and listened for sounds that would indicate her parents were home. Since there was no sign of them, I cut loose. "Why didn't you answer any of my phone calls or texts?" My voice wasn't loud, but it expressed my hurt and anger.

Becca's eyes flashed to the wooden floors. "I don't know what you mean." She tried to sound innocent, but I knew that tone.

Standing in front of her, she gazed at me, her eyes bewildered and holding something else that saddened me. Had I done this to our friendship? "Did I do something wrong?"

Before I had the chance to ask her another question, her eyes grew fierce and she spoke loudly. "You shouldn't have come. My parents will be here soon. Besides, I'm leaving in a couple of days. We can talk somewhere else. Are you here on a business trip or something? How did you get this address, anyway?" Becca was finally coming to her senses after the initial shock of seeing me.

Two could play at that game. Pressing my body forward, I challenged her back. "I'm not answering any of your questions until you answer mine first."

"Take a hint," she growled. In an effort to shove me, Becca placed her hand on my chest, but before she pulled it back, I grabbed it. When she tried to yank it away, I wrapped my hands around her waist, and pulled her to my chest. Her wet hair against my face cooled me down, but the need to have her drove me crazy. I wanted to strip the robe off her and take her right there in the living room.

I don't know how long we stood there, but I enjoyed having her in my arms. So much that my hands had a mind of their own and started idly rubbing her back. Feeling her mold into my body created an overwhelming sensation, and I forgot where we were. That was the way it was with Becca. I utterly lost myself in her. When she moaned lightly, I broke out of my daze.

"Becca, I need an answer," I whispered. She didn't respond, and I hoped she was equally lost in my embrace. I pulled her back enough to see her face. Her expression told me she wanted to say something, but was afraid. "It's okay. Tell me how you feel."

"I feel nothing," she stammered and escaped my hold. Chasing after her, I passed the kitchen, the hallway and out onto a nice balcony. Becca stopped near the pool. "Matthew, I told you to go away. I don't want to talk to you now. I'm busy. And my parents are on their way home." Becca took a few steps away from me.

"I got that part," I said out loud, but I stayed put. I was getting aggravated. There was no way in hell I'd go back home feeling like this. If she didn't want me, then fine, but I could see it in her eyes that she did. The way she responded when I held her—she wanted me too. "Damn it, Becca. I'm not leaving. In fact, I'm going to start taking off my clothes and let your parents see me naked in their pool."

That got her attention. "Are you crazy?" she yelled. "I'll call the cops."

Brushing the thought off, I took off my shoes, socks and sweater while Becca stared at me. She seemed to be enjoying the view, but I'm sure she thought I would stop.

"Okay, okay! Stop! I stopped returning your calls because I don't want to be your friend anymore. We can't be that close. How will it look when I start dating someone else and you want to hang out?"

Having Becca talk about dating other guys did not sit well with me. My blood pressure shot up and in my head, I just punched some imaginary guy in the face. "Friends can hang out." I took a step closer to her when she retreated. Shivering, I tried to maintain my composure. I was beginning to wish I hadn't taken off my sweater.

"I don't think so. Not since we…" she paused. "Do you sleep with all your *friends*?"

"What are you talking about?"

"At the restaurant. The day I ran off telling you I had something important to do. Well, I saw you. I saw how you cuddled with that girl. You probably slept with her too. Actually, I'm pretty damn sure you did."

That got closer to the truth. My Becca was jealous and I loved it. "Really? You saw her?"

"Yes, I did," she said with conviction.

This time instead of retreating, she held her ground as I took a step toward her. Her confidence level built, and she was sure I'd disappoint her. "You mean the brunette with the long hair, hazel eyes, about twenty-one?" Becca's eyes grew wide, looking pissed off or hurt, I couldn't tell. I continued. "And who happens to be my favorite cousin and happened to have been eating in the same restaurant?"

Becca looked totally stunned. "Your cousin?" She took a moment to digest the information I threw at her. "It doesn't matter. We need to stop. One of us will get hurt and it will probably be me."

I didn't let her talk anymore. Without thinking of rejection, I crushed my lips onto hers and held her tightly. It happened so fast, she had no idea it was coming.

My body temperature shot up. God! She felt so good. Since Becca didn't try to push me away, I wrung my hands through her hair. Devouring her lips and tongue with mine, I realized more than ever how much I missed her. No words could describe how much.

"What was that for?" she asked, dizzily fluttering her

eyes open when I pulled away. I loved how my kisses did that to her. Not only that, she couldn't take her eyes off my chest, her eyes flickering back and forth, trying hard not to stare.

Gazing into her eyes with sincerity, my hands fell on her back. "I don't know where we're going with this. All I know is that I've missed you like crazy, and I wouldn't be able to handle it if you dated or kissed someone else. I want to be more than your friend, Becca. I'm sorry I have some baggage, but I promise it will get better. In fact, I'm letting the past go so I can have a future, hopefully with you. You've brought me back from the dead and given me the life I'd lost. You made me whole again. All I needed was you."

"I'm not her," Becca said wearily. "I can't replace her."

"I don't want you to." I paused, gathering my thoughts. "You know what I did just before I came here? I went to Tessa's grave and told her I was moving on." I nodded when I saw the uncertainty in her eyes. "I told her I found someone and that it was time to let her go. You are not Tessa, and I wouldn't want you to be. You're my beautiful, sexy firecracker. You put every Victoria's Secret model to shame. You're the one who makes me smile, who can't use chopsticks, who delivers wild, hot sex, who makes me want to be a 'book boyfriend,' and who can give one hell of a lap dance. Becca, you are the one, and I'm so glad I've found you."

"I don't know," she said softly.

"We need to take this one day at a time. If you give me a chance, I'll make sure that for the rest of your life, you'll never regret your decision. I need you, Becca. I've been miserable without you. I don't want to be without you another day. I want to be the one putting your book boyfriends to shame."

I absolutely stunned Becca. I think I got her when I talked about her book boyfriends. She not only froze in place, but hope danced wildly in her eyes and her lips slightly parted. She was positively speechless. When she regained her composure, she threw me totally off guard.

"Take off your pants," she demanded, her eyes gleaming with an obvious plan in mind. Knowing Becca, it was a devious plan for sure.

"What?" I said, chuckling as I started to step out of my jeans. I enjoyed sex anywhere, and in any position, but not usually on the hard ground. I gave into her order anyway.

"I owe you one." Biting her bottom lip, she gave me a sexy hot smile. "Time for payback."

She meant to throw me in the pool. I didn't have time to avoid it, but I grabbed her robe as she pushed me in, and she fell on top of me. I had prepared myself for the freezing water, but in fact, it was rather warm.

Becca screamed, her head emerging from the water, and she wiped the hair out of her face. Thank goodness, we were at the shallow end. The thickness of her robe would have been too heavy for her.

"You deserved that," I laughed aloud, pulling her closer to me.

Becca's eyes beamed happily, biting her lips playfully. "Did you mean everything you said?"

"No," I said without thinking things through.

She tried to pull away, looking hurt, but I wouldn't release her from my hold. My firecracker struggled to break free, twisting and pulling. "Hold on. That came out wrong. Yes, I meant every single word I said. I said no because there is so much more I want to say, but I can't seem to find the words, so I'll have to show you instead." Capturing her eyes, I dove in for a slow, lingering kiss. Her arms ran over my chest, around my shoulders, then to my back. Hearing her moan softly excited me, and I wanted more.

After I untied the robe, I slithered my hands inside and realized she was completely naked under it.

Chapter 37
Becky

I wish I could've taken a picture of Matthew's surprised expression. He had no idea I had been relaxing in the pool totally naked just before he came.

"Becca, you were waiting for me, weren't you?" How he could say those words and make it sound so sexy was beyond me.

"You wish," I teased, surrendering into his hands as they explored my body, then peeled the robe off me.

"Yes, you were, and now, I'm going to make it up to you."

Before I could say a word, his lips pressed to mine as he guided my legs around his waist. Holy shit! His pants were off and he was hard and ready for me.

"When do your parents come home?" he asked between sucking my tongue.

"Oh, my parents. I uh…I lied," I mumbled, kissing him back.

"My kinky Becca. You're lucky I can't spank you under the water. Instead I'll make you suffer some other way."

What did he mean by that? I didn't have to wait long, as I soon found out what he meant. With a deep inhale, Matthew ducked under the water and next thing I knew, his tongue and lips slipped between my legs, devouring me. Lord, have mercy! I went completely limp as I threw my head back.

Rising out of the water, Matthew brought my bottom up, exposing me to the cold breeze, tantalizing my body even more. With my hands anchored to the edge of the pool, my body floated while taking in the pleasure Matthew offered.

After letting go of my legs, Matthew pressed me into the wall. His eyes filled with desire. "Have you ever done it in the pool, Becca?" he asked, spreading my legs with his knee.

"You would be the first…if I let you," I flirted.

"Want me to beg? I will, but I'm better at showing, not asking."

Matthew dunked himself back under the water. His tongue and lips sucked and teased the hell out of my clit again. Unable to take it anymore, I pulled on his hair to bring him up for air. "You win."

Breathless, Matthew's eyes glistened greedily as he positioned his body for me. Mere moments after I parted my legs, he thrust inside me. It felt tight when he first entered, but after, it just got hotter in the pool. Matthew draped my legs around his waist again and started pumping deeper. I swear I thought we were going to rock out of the pool.

As the water splashed and waved across the pool, I opened my mouth to his lips, feeling myself climax. Oh God! He felt amazing. When he pressed me into the wall again, his arms protecting me from the cement, he gave me all he had.

To answer Matthew's questions, I had never had sex in the pool before, but yes, oh God, I would do it all over again with him. When his energy had been spent, we continued to embrace each other.

Matthew pulled back and rested his head on mine as he ran his hand through my hair. "Come home with me tonight," he pleaded.

"My flight back home is in three days."

"You were going to stay away that long?"

Feeling guilty, I nodded. I couldn't look at him. I punished the both of us, because of a misunderstanding. I was afraid to get too close to him, in fear of having my heart broken. It was definitely easier being on the other side and giving advice. It made me think of Jenna.

Matthew tilted my head to meet his eyes. "I can understand why, but don't ever take off like that again. I was out of my mind, going crazy. I'm ready for us. I don't want to lose you again."

"Okay." I nodded.

"After we get out of this pool, I want you to go inside and pack. Don't worry about the flight home. I'll take care of it."

"Matthew…I couldn't."

"It's on my parents. How do you think I got here?"

"What do you mean?"

"I used my parents' private jet. Although they don't know I took it." Matthew bit his lip with a frown, looking like a little boy about to get in trouble. How could I resist that expression?

"Okay," I agreed, and Matthew beamed the happiest smile. "But before we go, I have to take the dogs to the pet hotel."

"Sure. Not a problem."

Wait 'til I tell Jenna. She'd be stunned that Matthew and I were actually dating, and she would flip out when she realized I hid it for so long.

Jenna

After all the drama, the heartaches, and especially the madness of the lawsuit out of the way, it felt good to get together and celebrate all the upcoming occasions. Becky and I arrived at the bar first, waiting for Nicole and Kate.

"I'm so glad Max didn't have to go to court," Becky said. "Who would've thought Ethan would save his ass? This is totally fate. It goes to show you, sometimes miracles do happen to good people."

"I know. What a relief! I don't even want to think about the what-ifs."

"Well, I'm just glad you and Max made up. And you stopped being so stubborn."

"How about you? Hiding your relationship from me. I can't believe you didn't mention one word about Matthew all this time. But I had my hunches."

"Hunches? What are you talking about?" Becky snorted, taking a sip of her cocktail.

"For starters, you wouldn't take his calls. And Matthew looked like he was going to lose it when he asked me where you were," I rebutted. "Now who was the one being stubborn?"

"It was different."

"I'm just happy for you."

Becky curled her lips, giving me a dream-like smile. "Sorry. I didn't tell you because I wasn't sure what was going on. I promise I'll talk to you about it all later. I don't want Kate and Nicole to know just yet. And by the way your package came."

"Package?"

"You forgot already? Make sure to swing by our

apartment before you go to Max's place. You can try it on him." Becky arched her brows.

"Oh!" I said, blushing as I stared down into my drink. "*That* package," I mumbled, smiling.

Becky turned her head. "Nicole is here."

"Becky…Jenna." Nicole squeezed, draping her arms around our shoulders. "Thanks for coming. Did you have your last fitting?"

"Yes, we went together after work."

"Great. I'm glad you both love the lavender color. I think it's perfect for a spring wedding. Don't you?"

"Perfect," we both agreed. "Let's go get our table."

"We can't get one until we're all here," Becky reminded.

"No need to worry. Here comes Kate." Nicole waved.

"Hey." Kate smiled, giving us each a tight squeeze. "Sorry it took so long. The lady who was fitting me took forever. She said I lost weight. I was so happy. It's been so difficult to lose the extra pregnancy weight."

Nicole waved, letting the waitress know we were all there. After we were seated at our table, we ordered, and soon after, the waitress brought our drinks. "Let's toast," Kate said, raising her cup. "Here's to friendship, Nicole's wedding in April, Max's lawsuit being dismissed, and Becky's new lover, who just happens to be Max's brother."

Becky's eyes grew wide and she lowered her jaw. "How did you—" Becky turned to me. "You told them?" Though she was completely surprised, she wasn't mad. Thank God!

"I hinted. Although they're not very good at taking hints," I scoffed.

"Why didn't you say anything?" Nicole asked. "And to think, we're supposed to be friends."

"Just hit my glass, will ya?" Kate demanded.

After the toast, Becky chatted about how her relationship with Matthew began. She didn't hold anything back; she never did. Talking about relationships and sex came easy for her. It was fun hearing about their hot and steamy encounters and their make up sex in the pool. When she mentioned the private jet, I realized Max never told me about it. Hmmm? Not that it was important.

Our topic of conversation changed when our dinner arrived. "Where would you like your bachelorette party to be?" Becky asked Nicole.

"No need to ask her. I've already started looking around," Kate said, twirling her pasta with her fork.

"Where?" I asked.

"Vegas, baby. And we are going to have the time of our lives," Kate exclaimed. "Though, I may have to bring Kristen with me, and my mom, so she can watch her. There is no way Craig can take care of her alone for the whole weekend."

"We don't have to go all the way over there. I don't mind just hanging out and having dinner," Nicole said, looking guilty for the trouble she thought she was causing.

"Are you kidding? You planned an awesome party for me," Kate said excitedly. "Now it's my turn."

"And we'll help," Becky said, pointing to the both of us.

Nicole nodded with a smile. "Okay. That really sounds like fun."

"I'll drive," Kate offered.

After setting the date, we finished dinner while chatting about how much our lives had changed in the past year. Kate and Nicole left after we paid the bill, but Becky and I decided to hang out at the bar. It had been awhile since the two of us hung out alone together, like we used to.

"I still can't believe it. I mean, I love that you're dating Matthew, but who knew?" I giggled.

"Yeah. Who knew Matthew would be interested in me?" Becky raised her brow.

"Hey! It should be who knew you were interested in Matthew? Don't sell yourself short just because he's good-looking, rich, successful and Max's brother..."

"You can stop right there," Becky snorted. "He's pretty amazing so far. Let's see where it takes us. One day at a time." Becky sighed.

After an hour had passed, we decided to head home, since we both had to work the next day. Becky headed to the ladies room one last time. Looking down into my purse to dig for my car keys, I got off the barstool and almost ran into someone. "Excuse me," I said. When I looked up, I froze and lost my breath. Not again!

Crystal glared at me. Not an inkling of surprise showed on her face. She knew I was there and she came specifically for me. With the blink of an eye, I dropped my keys back into my purse and tried to weave around her when she grasped my arm.

"I might have dropped the lawsuit, but that doesn't mean Max won't run back to me. You won't satisfy him the way I did." Her tone was cold and challenging. Others around us not only shifted their eyes to us in curiosity, they listened intently to our conversation.

I was tired of hearing all her crap. She had caused enough trouble and almost came between Max and me. The old Jenna would have sulked away like a coward, but the new Jenna was not only pissed off, I wanted to hurt her like she hurt us.

As anger boiled inside me, my fists tightened and I wanted to punch her in the face. I stopped myself since that wasn't ladylike. Besides, I didn't want her suing me. Who knows what she would pull. She would most likely find a way to hurt me, plot some type of sick revenge.

Just as I was at the breaking point, Becky came back from the restroom and stood behind me, rubbing my arms to calm me down. Having Becky by my side gave me the courage to say what I wanted to say.

"You know, I'm tired of all of your threats. I don't need to satisfy Max because he's too busy satisfying me," I stammered. "So, if you think Max is going to run to you, you'd better think again." My eyes shifted to her hand still holding onto me. "You can let go of my arm now. I'd like it back," I ordered with a cool, calm tone. I decided she wasn't worth my time or my energy.

"You're just a new toy. He'll get tired of you," she hissed.

"No. You were a toy. I'm something more. I'm his future." Becky placed a cup of water in front of me. "And you know what? I'm also terribly clumsy." It happened so fast, even I was surprised how quickly I acted. With no time to think of the consequences, I took the cup and tossed the water on her.

"You bitch!" she yelled, wiping the water off her face.

"You're lucky it was only water. Next time, something else will hit your face." After slamming the glass on the bar, I walked away with Becky's arm around me. Laughing and feeling exhilarated, we pranced out of the restaurant.

"Oh my God, Jenna! That was epic. I didn't think you understood what I was trying to tell you to do with the water glass. You *do* have an evil side."

"You ain't seen nothin' yet." I smirked. The cold air swept my hair away from my face, cooling me down as we exited, and headed toward the parking lot. Slapping Crystal would have been wrong, but dumping water on her was the next best thing.

"Too bad Nicole and Kate left early. I can't wait to tell them what you did." Becky kept staring at me with an awed expression on her face. "Going to Max's tonight?"

"Yes," I said, keeping my stride with hers. "But I'm going to go get my package first." I might have built up courage to do something I wouldn't normally do, but talking about sex or thinking about it would always make me blush.

"I wish I could see the look on Max's face," Becky snorted. "He's going to thank me tonight."

Chapter 38
Jenna

With my heart beating out of my chest, I stuffed the items from the package into my bag and headed to Max's place. I can do this, I told myself, as I unlocked his front door. The colorful city lights glowed against the night in the darkened room. Though there were no stars out, the lights alone were picturesque, like a painting you could stare at forever. No matter how many times I saw it, I was mesmerized.

Trying not to make a sound, I took off my jacket and heels, taking in the warmth from the heater and quietly paced forward. With each step I took, my courage faltered. Until I saw Max sitting on the bed with his back to me. He wore his usual white T-shirt and black cotton shorts and sang along to a love song. I had never heard him sing before.

As I stood there listening to his beautiful voice, chills ran through me. I think I fell in love all over again with the wanna-be rock star who had become my best friend, my lover, my something wonderful. I wanted to show him what he meant to me. I had to put my shyness and my insecurities aside, because Max stripped those away from me every time he made me feel beautiful and sexy through his words, his touch, and his love for me.

When the song stopped and Max turned to the door, he jerked back and dropped his iPad. His hand went straight to his heart. "Jeez, Jenna," he panted lightly. "You scared the life out of me. You're like a little mouse! Make some noise when you come in next time."

"I'm sorry, Max," I laughed and headed toward him to give him a kiss on his lips. Those lips, his lips, were meant to kiss only mine. "I didn't mean to startle you. I wanted to surprise you, but I think I was the one who got a surprise. You have an amazing voice."

"Oh, that," Max mumbled, suddenly looking shy. "I don't sing in public."

"Well, I'm not public," I commented, running my hands along the curve of his biceps.

"How about I change the subject? I can make you forget what you heard," he said, kissing me passionately. Max pulled back and smiled, leaving me in a daze.

Stumbling a little, I looked at him with lustful eyes. "It's not enough, Max. I want more," I said with my sultry tone. He rewarded me with the most delicious, naughty grin. Just before he pulled me onto him, I tugged his T-shirt off and pushed him back onto the bed. "No, no, no. No touching," I ordered, and reached into my bag to take out the first item.

Letting him watch, I seductively took off my long coat and revealed a sexy, black negligee. This one was even hotter than the one Becky bought for me for Christmas. Max lit up with a huge, hungry grin, obviously enjoying his view. Locked on his eyes playfully, I slowly crawled like a lioness after its prey over his body. I took both of his hands and pinned them above his head.

"Jenna? Did you take something?" Max chuckled. "I love what you're doing to me, but this is…"

"The new me," I answered for him. "You make me feel

sexy and I'm going to show you just how much." I smiled as Max swelled underneath his shorts. That always got me aroused. With the black satin tie in my hand, I bound his hands together, but not too tight. I fumbled with the tie, my inexperience showing.

"You want to punish me back, Jenna?"

"Don't talk. Let me enjoy." Starting at his lips, I nibbled down to the side of his neck, then from one shoulder to the other, while slowly rocking myself on him. When Max groaned, I ground against him even harder, and I sucked his tongue just as fast and hard.

Max turned his face to the side, looking completely unglued, but still he managed to speak. "I love what you're wearing, but what if you had gotten pulled over by a cop?"

I could tell he was trying to untie his hands while he distracted me. "Then for sure I wouldn't have gotten a ticket. I'd just have to show him what was underneath my coat," I replied without hesitation, no hint of embarrassment from saying what I wouldn't normally have been able to say.

"You naughty girl," he said, biting my lip. "Untie me so I can touch you."

I didn't respond or do as he asked. Instead, I ran my tongue down his chest, tasting and enjoying every inch of him. When I went further down to his groin, Max growled and arched his back. Snatching my body with his tied hands, he pulled me back up to his lips and kissed me hard. "Let me go. I need to touch you." His tone was low, serious, and caveman-like.

"Now you know how I felt," I stated. Grabbing more items out of my purse, I placed them below my feet so he couldn't see them. Guiding his hands to the side of his head, this time I blindfolded him.

"Jenna," Max chuckled. "I'm going to assume this was Becky's idea. Am I right? Do I need to thank her?"

"Shhh! You talk too much. Now enjoy." Tugging his shorts off, I poured the lotion over my hand. From the first contact, Max made the most pleasurable sound. Oh, how I loved making him feel as good as he did for me. Stroking steadily, I let him kiss me and when I went faster, he bit my bottom lip. When he got even harder, nearing the point of no return, I stopped.

Groaning with pleasure, Max succumbed under my control for the first time, and it was gratifying to know I could make him feel that way.

"My turn. I need to be inside you," Max said. Before I could flinch, I realized Max had somehow untied himself. Taking off the blindfold and the tie completely, he rolled me underneath him.

"Hey! I was having fun," I whined, but Max thrust inside me before I could do or say anything else. I'd lost all sense of reality and time as he pumped away.

Cradling my head with his hands, Max looked lovingly into my eyes. I could see so much in that look—how much he wanted me, and cared for me, even as he pounded me faster.

"You've got me so hard, I can't stop." Max's eyes darkened with passion, want, and the need for fulfillment. I would swear the whole world heard the sound that emanated from me. "Shit! I need to get a condom," he muttered without stopping.

"Don't stop, Max," I begged.

As if I gave him permission, he grabbed my bottom tightly and gave me all he had. When Max pulled out, he jerked and shuddered on top of me. Luckily, there was a hand towel on the nightstand. Max gently wiped his release from us both and cradled me into his arms. As our bodies linked flesh to flesh, I felt his chest rise and fall with mine. Out of breath and feeling as if I had just had an out of body experience, I peered up to his eyes when he brushed my hair away from my face.

"You little sex kitten. Where did you get those things?"

No longer role playing, I became shy. "Online," I answered, feeling my cheeks burn.

"We can look online together if you'd like," Max suggested, almost sounding unsure, as if he didn't know how I would react.

When I agreed, he chuckled happily, and cuddled me tighter. "Next time we have to be careful and use a condom."

"I was going to go see my gynecologist and get on the pill."

"You're not on the pill?" Max's angry tone startled me.

"No." I sat up. "I wasn't involved with anyone sexually, remember?"

Max relaxed when my voice sounded annoyed. "Jenna," he said as he tenderly caressed my arm. "I'm sorry. I didn't mean to raise my voice. More than anything, I want to make you my wife someday, and have a minivan full of children, but not now. I want us to have fun, see the world, and explore each other on every level. Having a baby right now would end all that. Babies are a lot of work. I know you know this."

"I do, but even though you thought I was on the pill, you used a condom."

"It's a precautionary measure. I've always used one, and I always pull out even when I use one, but I guess with you, I wasn't as vigilant."

"Don't worry; I'm sure we're fine." I plopped back into

271

his arms, snuggling. "I'll get on the pill."

"You don't have to," Max caressed my cheek. "I'll use a condom."

"No. I like to feel all of you." I laced my fingers through his hair, gazing at this handsome man, admiring his perfect features.

"I knew you had a wild side. It just needed a little encouragement. You really are my sex kitten. Seeing that side of you drives me crazy. It's like I'm helping to mold this part of you and I get to watch and experience as you blossom."

"Want to know what other naughty thing I did tonight?"

Max raised his brows, looking confused. "As long as there wasn't another man involved, I think I can handle anything."

"Don't be silly," I slapped him lightly. "You're the only man in my life."

"Good answer." Max kissed the tip of my nose.

"I ran into Crystal at dinner."

Max stiffened, but began to relax and even laughed out loud when I told him what had happened.

Chapter 39
Becky

"I'll get it," I yelled. Looking through the peephole, I opened the door when I saw a delivery person. A cute college guy held out two large vases filled with the most beautiful red roses and a little card sticking out of each bouquet.

"Becky Miller and Jenna Mefferd?"

"Yes, I'm Becky." Taking the vases from his hands, I headed to the dining room table. After depositing the beautiful flowers on the table, I reached into my purse, grabbed five bucks, and handed him a tip. I remembered how hard it was to make ends meet in college. "Here. Thank you."

"Wow! Thank you and happy Valentine's Day."

"Thanks," I said and closed the door.

"Becky, who was at the door?" Jenna asked, and then stopped in front of the roses.

"One is for you and the other is for me," I pointed, recalling a comment Matthew made a while back. He said I deserved bigger flowers, and he did not disappoint. Our apartment began to smell like a beautiful rose garden. Seeing Jenna take her card out of the envelope, I did the same.

Becca,
I'll pick you up at 4. Be ready to take that robe off.
We're going skinny dipping. See ya later, firecracker.
Be prepared for MY fireworks!
Don't forget to pack as we've discussed.
Matthew

I swallowed and looked at Jenna who was smiling from ear to ear. "What does your card say?"

Jenna handed her card to me as she continued to smile. Walking to her room like she was floating on air, I wondered if I did the same. Her card read:

Jenna,
Be my Valentine tonight.
I'll pick you up at 4, as per our conversation.
I can't wait to TKLS. Bring a sweater.
Don't forget to pack as we've discussed.
Love,
Max

"What do the initials stand for?" I asked out loud.

"Touch...kiss...lick...and suck," Jenna yelled back from her bedroom.

"Oh." It was all I could say, taken by surprise at her words.

When the doorbell rang, Jenna opened the door. Not knowing who would come first, I peeked out of my bedroom door. When I saw Matthew, my heart fluttered. The butterflies in my stomach would not rest, leaving me nervous and giddy at the same time. Looking absolutely edible, Matthew wore dark slacks, a pin striped shirt, and a dark brown, suede jacket.

I had no idea where we were going for dinner as I glanced at what I was wearing. Jenna and I both wore form-fitting black dresses, but not too casual looking. We were a perfect match.

After Matthew gave Jenna a hug, he spotted me. Grinning, he came for me. "Becca," he whispered in my ear, squeezing me tightly. "I've missed you." Matthew exhaled a deep breath, then took a whiff of my perfume. The simple touch electrified me.

Matthew had been out of town on a business trip for the last few days. He had just come home last night, but we exchanged some hot texts while he was gone. "Hi," I said, releasing from his hold.

"Wow. Both of you look so beautiful. I think I'll take the both of you out tonight. Max can go on a date by himself."

Jenna giggled and blushed. "Thanks, Matthew. Maybe next time."

"I don't think so," Max said as he walked in, twirling the apartment key on his finger. Max had his own set of keys to our place. Embracing Jenna and giving her a kiss, he said, "This one is mine and I won't share her even with my own brother. But Matthew is right. Both of you look absolutely gorgeous. You'll be turning heads and Matthew and I will enjoy making all the guys jealous."

"Let's go," Jenna said while batting her innocent eyes. Max was so taken with her, she could tell him to drop his pants right then and there and he would for her.

I'd been seeing a whole new side of Jenna, and I loved it. She was taking charge instead of living her life like a back seat driver. She wasn't afraid to express her thoughts and feelings anymore, becoming the woman she was always meant to be.

Life experiences mold us into who we are today. Sometimes it's not in a positive way, like when those experiences make us fear, lose hope, or crush our dreams. Jenna's ex-boyfriend might have crippled her. What he pulled could have made her lose faith in real love and trust, but Max has helped her heal. He chipped those broken layers off, in more ways than she'll ever realize, and for that, I was grateful. I couldn't be happier for my friend.

Chapter 40
Jenna

Listening to soft music in the car, Max drove with one hand while the other hand held mine. Whistling along to the song, his shoulders were relaxed and he looked happy. He looked so handsome in his dark suit and tie, I couldn't take my eyes off him. All the time thinking, this amazing man is mine.

Max kept my hand after he helped me out of the car. I took a whiff of the ocean breeze. After grabbing our overnight bags, I walked beside him toward the most amazing house. It looked like one of those homes you'd find in a magazine, and I was completely in awe.

The pristine white mansion was two stories high, with tall windows. Various roses lined the path leading to the front of the house, making it smell heavenly. "What are we doing here?" I asked, thinking how ridiculous my question was. Reading the note, I had assumed we were staying at a hotel.

"It's my surprise. I'm not about to share you with strangers at some restaurant. This is our place for the night. Happy Valentine's Day, babe." After a soft, long kiss, he opened the front door with the key, gesturing for me to walk in first.

Stepping on the white marble floor, I gazed up at the

huge, crystal chandelier, watching as each teardrop shape sparkled like a diamond in the sunlight that poured in through the long windows. To my left and right were stairs, curving to meet at the center of the second floor. Directly under the chandelier, right in front of my view, was a large table with a colorful arrangement of flowers that added the perfect touch.

A man walked in, dressed in a simple black suit, and took the bags from Max. "Good evening, Mr. Knight,"

"Hello, Brandon. This is Jenna."

"Brandon, hello," I smiled.

"Hello, Ms. Jenna. I will be at your service today. We will be out of your way this evening." With a quick nod, he headed upstairs with our bags.

"We? Are they staying till dinner?" I asked. Not that we needed anyone else to be here. Max was all I needed, and I could take care of things. I wasn't used to having someone at my beck and call.

"Well, they'll leave right after dinner is over." Max wrapped his arms around me as he kissed my forehead, and then whispered. "I wouldn't want him to hear how loud I'm going to make you scream tonight."

His words blasted pleasant shivers through me. I don't know how he could do that to me every time he talked dirty, but I didn't want him to ever stop.

"How loud, Max?" I asked, looking at him with my finger in my mouth, giving him the most enticing look I could give.

"Jenna…" His voice was low and hot. Oh man, I loved how he growled my name, as if he was going to punish me. "You want to skip dinner and eat dessert first?"

Max guided my finger out of my mouth. Just before it went into his, I stopped him. Walking backward, I sucked my fingers, pulling in and out seductively, and I found myself on the other side of a massive grand piano. I couldn't believe what a tease I'd become. I liked this new side of me, and I was sure Max did too.

"You're so lucky I have a plan tonight or I would have you naked and sprawled out on that piano, in front of Brandon and his staff," Max grunted, taking several steps toward me.

Pulling out my finger, I halted. "Staff?"

Max chuckled, his eyes sparkling with humor. "Yes, staff. Turn around Jenna. Meet Molly."

Holy crap! I swallowed nervously, gulping down the air, and sure enough, there was Molly. She was a plump, friendly looking woman. I couldn't help myself as my face flamed in heat. I parted my lips to greet her, but nothing came out.

"It's nice to meet you, ma'am. I'll be out of your hair in a second, but I wanted Mr. Knight to know that dinner is ready and if he doesn't want to miss the reason why it was to be served outside, he'd better go quick."

"Thank you, Molly." Max nodded.

It was as if they were talking in a secret code. The reason? What did they mean by that? Max hooked my arm and led me out the front door.

"Max? Where are we going? Why are you in such a hurry?"

"I want it to be perfect." After walking along the sidewalk, we went up the stairs. The next house was quite a distance away, so I assumed this was a private beach. Max stopped and covered my eyes with the blindfold I had used on him.

"Max. What are you doing?"

"Jenna, I don't want to miss this opportunity, so please,

just do as I ask and stop asking questions. It's a surprise."

Feeling all sorts of excitement rush through me, I couldn't wait for whatever Max wanted to show me. Trying to walk blindfolded was almost impossible, even while Max had his arms around me. Just as I was getting used to it, he scooped me up.

"Max! Put me down," I demanded, though I didn't mean it. In fact, I loved being in his arms. Shortly after, he placed me down and I could hear the sound of soft waves. "I hope you're not planning on going skinny dipping." I giggled.

Max didn't answer me but started speaking again. "Jenna, I'm going to take the blindfold off, but you have to promise me to keep your eyes on me."

"Okay. I don't think you're giving me much choice right now," I said.

The blindfold came off and I blinked to adjust my vision. Max embraced me so fast, I had no time to move. When he started to sing, I didn't feel the need to do anything but listen to the words he was conveying to me.

Perfectly spellbound by his sexy voice and the words of Elvis Presley, he continued as he swayed us to his rhythm. "I can't help falling in love with you." The words to the song hit me in waves as his voice resonated straight through to my heart and soul. He filled me, reaching deeper, expanding my heart and I shuddered in his arms as that feeling spread through every single nerve in me.

His voice was full of passion and love. Why he decided to sing me this song right here, right now, I had no idea, but it didn't matter. I could listen to his voice any time, day or night. His voice always compelled me to surrender to him.

Sliding his hands to my cheeks, he locked his eyes on mine with adoration. His sternness and sincerity told me he meant every word. "You're my heart. It beats because yours beats. You're my lungs. I breathe because you breathe. You were right Jenna; you're not public. You're my everything, and I will sing to you for the rest of my life if you want me to."

His eyes continued to reach deeper, and I didn't know what to say. In fact, I couldn't believe what was happening right before my eyes. He turned me toward the ocean. We were actually on a cliff, overlooking the beach. The most amazing view of the horizon stretched out in front of us. The sun was just setting, giving its magnificent blending colors of yellows, oranges, and reds.

This vision absolutely hypnotized me, and I understood why he was in a rush. He wanted to share this precious moment with me. "Max," I whispered, reaching for his hand without peeling my eyes off the horizon. "I don't know what to say. This view is so perfect. Sharing this with you makes me want to cry happy tears."

"Babe," he laced his fingers through mine. "Look on the sand, to your right."

"Huh?" I asked, shifting my eyes to where he directed. OH...MY...GOD. Was this real? Thousands of candles lined up to form letters, spelling out the words. I threw my hands over my mouth. I didn't want Max to see me cry, but I couldn't help it. Tears pooled in my eyes, but I blinked and wiped them away, and then I read the words in my mind repeatedly.

I was in shock. I couldn't speak. It felt like a dream, only it wasn't. My hands shook. I think my whole body shook. These tiny fireworks crackled and popped in my stomach, tickling me from the tips of my fingers, down to my toes. Then the big ones ignited, filling me up with an overwhelming sense of euphoria, and I exploded with happiness.

"What do you say, babe. Yes or no?" Max asked sweetly. His eyes never left mine, waiting for me to soak in what I was seeing.

More tears wetted my face. With my lips quivering, I turned to Max. He was down on one knee, holding a box with the most beautiful solitaire ring I'd ever seen. It looked to be a three-carat diamond, mounted high on a simple white gold band. Or maybe it was platinum. All I knew was it sparkled and shimmered in the glow of the sunset as we stood on that perfect spot.

"Jeanella Mefferd, you're the only woman I want to spend the rest of my life with. I'm going to spend every single day making you feel loved. I want your body, heart, and soul filled with everything I can give you. From now on, February 14th will not be Valentine's Day for us. From now on it will be the day I proposed to the most beautiful, amazing woman in existence. I want the whole world to know that Valentine's Day is ours now. Will you marry me, Jenna? I will spend the rest of my life making sure you never regret saying 'yes'. Be mine, because I want to be yours. I want to give you forever."

What else could this wonderful man say? "Yes, Maxwell Knight. I want to be yours forever," I managed to say while my lips trembled. The tears I desperately tried to hold at bay came pouring down. I didn't think I could possibly love him more than I already did, but he proved me wrong.

Max stood up, kissed me tenderly, and held me tight. A soft breeze caressed us as we stood against the backdrop of the most beautiful sunset.

"We can take our time, babe. I'll leave it up to you to pick the date. If it were up to me, we would've been married yesterday." His eyes twinkled, looking so happy. I loved that I could make him feel this way.

Pulling away from me, he took out the ring, shoving the box into his pocket, and placed it on my finger. "I think I did a great job guessing the size of your finger."

He sure did. It fit perfectly. "How did you guess?" I asked, admiring as it shone, still not believing Max had just proposed to me.

"Babe, I know every mole, every curve, and every scar on you. I bet I know your body better than you," Max said, pulling me into him.

"And do you like what you see, Mr. Knight?"

"Yes, soon-to-be Mrs. Knight. I'm planning to do more studying tonight, but I have to warn you. It's going to be a very extensive examination."

I shivered from both the breeze that had gotten colder, and the thought of what Max was going to do to me tonight.

"We should head back. Dinner is waiting for us."

"Was Molly your sunset keeper?"

"Yes, she was. I'd asked her to keep an eye out and let me know when it was at the most perfect point. I also prayed for no rain. I only had one chance."

"How about the candles? I'd like to enjoy them a little longer." They glowed brighter since the sun had almost sunk from view.

"You'll be able to see them from the backyard. That's where we're having our dinner.

"Did you tell your parents and Matthew about what you were planning tonight?"

"Yes, I did. Oh, and before I forget to tell you, I asked your parents for their permission to ask for your hand in marriage the night I met them."

"You did?" I asked, feeling completely stunned. No wonder my mom looked so excited and acted a bit off that night. I thought she smiled way too much during our get-together. Now it all made sense. "How did you ask them?"

"I told your parents how much I loved you." Max laced his fingers through my hair. "I told them I would provide for you and take care of you through the good and the bad. I promised that I would never look at or love another woman. And I would give them a minivan full of grandchildren," Max chuckled. "I think they loved that part. I'm pretty sure that sealed the deal."

"You're sneaky," I said, wrinkling my nose. "But I love that you are. Thank you for being who you are. I don't know what I did to deserve you." Meaning every word I said, I molded into his arms with a gratified sigh. Max thought of everything tonight. It was definitely the most romantic night of my life. I will never look at Valentine's Day the same ever again.

Chapter 41
Max

I took Jenna back into the house. She never once complained about the cold, but she shivered in my arms. Her hair looked a bit wild from the breeze, making her look sexy as hell, but I didn't tell her. I just enjoyed my view.

I wasn't sure if proposing this early in our relationship was a good idea, but I didn't want to wait another day. Besides, when was it ever a perfect time to propose? You do it when you think the time is right, but who knew about these things. I never wanted to propose to anyone until I met Jenna.

As we ate dinner on the balcony, under the heat lamp, Jenna couldn't stop staring at the candlelight. Seeing her smile and in awe of everything I did for her tonight confirmed I had made the right decision. The thought of her saying "no" did cross my mind. However, after what we'd been through this past month, I knew our love for each other had grown. I guess this would be the arrogant side of me, but how could she refuse?

Knowing Jenna, I may have to wait a year to get her down the aisle, but I was fine with that. I wanted her to feel comfortable. Scaring her off was the last thing I wanted to do. If I was patient with her, we could work out the kinks, the trust issues, and her insecurity.

"Are you cold?" I asked, seeing her tremble as I took a bite of my steak.

"I'm fine," she said, taking a sip of her tea and pulling her black shawl over her shoulders. Her new black dress had a touch of lace around the neckline and looked fantastic on her. With her hair in soft curls, though the curls had straightened somewhat due to the breeze, she looked edible, and I couldn't help thinking about the things I planned to do to her later.

The diamond earrings and necklace set I had bought for her for Christmas twinkled at her ears and neck. They looked lovely on her, and I'm glad I chose them. A woman like Jenna deserved all the finer things in life, though she would disagree; all the more reason I wanted to do it for her.

Her eyes sparkled in the candlelight, just like her ring. I loved seeing her this happy. Knowing Jenna as well as I did, I figured she would want something simple yet elegant, and that is what I bought for her. She couldn't stop staring at it, though she tried to pretend she wasn't.

As I took my last bite, I noticed she only ate half her dinner, and I knew why. She must be feeling as giddy as I was.

"Babe, eat your dinner, or I'll have to feed you myself."

Jenna let out a slight giggle, looking at me wickedly and deviously. "I'm not that hungry. I can't think about food when I'm thinking about getting you naked in bed."

Holy shit. Then her finger went straight to her mouth purposely, and she gave me that innocent, sexy grin that made me come unglued. That look that can make me do anything for her.

Jenna was a lot more flirtatious these days. She was getting more comfortable, and opening up more. I knew there was a wild, sexy goddess in there. I just had to help her ease into her new skin. Absorbing her words, I gulped down my last sip of wine. Though I had poured some wine for Jenna, she hadn't even taken a sip.

Leaning into her, I gave her a challenging stare. "You want to make that come true?"

"I dare you to," she teased, holding up an asparagus stalk, gliding her tongue on it with a long stroke. As I watched, I could swear I felt her tongue on my dick.

It took every ounce of restraint not to clear this table and take her right here.

"You know what would make me eat more, Max?" she continued. "If I could eat my dinner off your naked body."

That did it! She had no idea how much self-control I had been utilizing since the minute we walked through that door. Jenna gasped when I pushed back my chair. Did she think I wasn't going to take her up on her offer? Knowing Jenna, that's exactly what she thought.

"Come on, I'm taking you up on your offer right now," I said, as I swatted her ass. I flung her over my shoulder. It happened so fast she didn't know what hit her.

"Max!" Jenna laughed out loud. "Put me down."

"Don't move. I'll drop you." The way she was wiggling, I might lose my concentration. "If you don't listen, I'm going to spank your ass all the way to our room," I said in a forceful tone, giving her a good smack on her ass again.

"Max, don't forget my plate," she giggled.

She didn't know I was already holding it. She also didn't know I had a can of whipped cream upstairs and I was planning on licking it off her. "Prepare yourself, babe. You're not getting much sleep tonight."

Chapter 42
Matthew

Becca looked absolutely stunning in her form-fitted black dress. She looked relaxed as I held her hand while driving. When we reached our destination, I told Becca to stay seated, as I ran around the car and opened her door for her.

"There are so many boats here," Becca gushed, gazing around, looking amazed.

"We're in Long Beach. The best place to look at them," I commented, embracing her in my arms as we headed to our yacht.

I had purposely taken my time getting here. I wanted Becca to see the amazing view, and I knew by the look on her face that she was in awe. Her eyes gleamed and her smile said it all.

White lights dangled from poles along the dock, highlighted by the moon. The sound of the small, anchored boats rocking against the water was hypnotic, and the music that emanated from one of the boats gave a soothing feel.

Lightly shivering in my arms, I pulled Becca tighter. "You cold, firecracker?"

Becca gave a hardy laugh. "I hope you don't plan on calling me firecracker in front of other people."

"Why not? Unless you want me to call you love, babe, sweetheart, sunshine...."

"Okay, stop," she snorted. "You can call me firecracker when we're alone. If you promise, I'll show you what a real firecracker can do in and out of bed. But I rather you call me Becca."

She was talking all hot and flirty, so how could I resist that offer? "Agreed. Better hold on to that thought. Here we are."

Becca's eyes were wide as she stood there taking in the beauty of our magnificent, three-leveled yacht. How could she not be? I was in awe every time I set eyes on her, and I'd been on that boat a million times. "Welcome to the Ellen Knight, named after my mother. My dad gifted this to her when our company took off."

"Wow. I don't know what to say. Thank you," Becca said softly, unable to peel her eyes off the yacht.

"Let's get on board." Holding Becca's hand, I led her inside. She was grinning from ear to ear and it got even bigger when she set her eyes on our private dining table, adorned with candlelight and flowers.

"Good evening, Mr. Knight, Ms. Miller."

Becca looked stunned that Carlos, our personal chef, knew her name.

"Good evening," Becca replied.

"Please watch your step. Mr. Knight, I'll be back with the wine." With that, Carlos disappeared.

After I helped Becca settle into her chair, I sat across from her. The cool breeze gently tousled her hair. Being under a heat lamp, we were able to enjoy the view on deck, instead of having to eat inside. So many boats sailed that night. I had planned to do just that after dinner, so Becca and I could be truly alone. She had no idea what was coming.

After Carlos poured the wine, he slipped out of sight. I lifted up my glass. "To our first Valentine's Day together, and many more to come."

Becca clinked the glass. "To a new beginning." After she took a sip and placed the glass down, she let out a soft sigh. "Thank you, Matthew. Everything about today is amazing. I've been on Valentine's Day dates before, but this is something else. You've gone out of your way to make me feel special."

"Firecracker." I lifted her chin to set my eyes on hers. "You are special to me in every way. You're the only one who made me want to move forward, and I'm going to do everything I can to show you exactly what I mean."

Becca gave me a huge smile. "Thank you." That was all she could say. I think I just put out the fire in my firecracker.

Becca

Matthew made me blush big time with his compliments. I don't know what I did to help him move on, but I was glad it worked. Everything about that night was fantastic. I would dream about it for a very long time.

After dinner, Matthew gave me a tour of the fabulous yacht with its elegant leather seats and fine wood cabinets. The television was state of the art, and everything else was nothing but the best. His mom was sure spoiled, but it was also sweet of her to allow him to use it for tonight.

"When you're ready, you'll have to meet my parents," Matthew said out of the blue. "I mean when we're both ready."

"Matthew, remember one day at a time. I don't want

you to get sick of me so quickly," I joked.

"Never," he said, whisking me into his arms.

When he let go, I jerked back. "We're moving?" I started to panic. "Where are we going and who's driving?"

"Relax. Carlos not only cooks, but he is fully qualified to pilot this boat."

Matthew wrapped a blanket around us, planted a kiss on my forehead, and led us out. We headed into complete darkness, but the light from the other boats was a reminder we weren't alone. From afar, they looked like stars, floating on the wave of the ocean. At times, it felt as though we were aimlessly drifting through the universe without a destination. It was magical.

Matthew reached under what looked like a secret compartment I hadn't noticed before, and took out a walkie-talkie to speak into it. "Carlos, make sure to steer away from all the other vessels and then you can return to your cabin. Please do not disturb us unless it's an emergency. If you do, fair warning, you may see me naked," Matthew laughed.

Matthew saying the word naked caught my attention. When I flashed my eyes at him, he winked at me. After he put the radio away, he pushed a button, and soft music filled the air around us. Leaning into each other, neither of us spoke as we stared at the magnificent view.

"Ready for tomorrow's trip?" Matthew asked.

"I can't believe I'm going to the London Fashion Show," I said excitedly. "I'm so freakin' excited I can hardly contain myself."

Matthew snuggled into me, chuckling. "I love it when you're excited. It makes me happy to see you happy."

"You know what else makes me excited?" I asked in a flirty tone, running my hands across his hard chest, the chest that made me gasp for air every time he took off his sweater at the apartment.

"I can take a guess." Matthew bit his bottom lip. Seeing him flirt back made me lose it. "I bet I got you excited when I first took off my sweater."

He was right, but I wasn't going to feed his ego. "You think so?" I glued my eyes to his. "I bet I got you excited when I dumped the plate of leftovers on that sweater."

Matthew's eyes grew wide with humor, recalling the incident. "I bet you got excited when I told you to wash it off. And then your eyes rested directly on my crotch."

I don't know why recalling our not so friendly, heated conversation turned me on, but I had nothing to say after that because he was damn right. Without any further hesitation, I sealed my lips on his for a quick kiss and backed away. "Happy Valentine's Day."

Matthew didn't respond at first, taking his time staring at me with the look of longing. His look said, 'I'm going to take you. Now.' Then he closed the gap between us, pressing his chest against my breasts, his hands not touching me. Pulling his face into the side of my neck, he whispered, "I want to make love to you under the stars."

When I nodded to confirm, Matthew slowly peeled off my clothes, layer by layer, as if I was the most precious gift. Tenderly, he continued to worship my body as he stripped off his own clothes. He took his time kissing every single inch while we cuddled under the blanket.

Feeling like I was going to melt any minute as his hands, lips, and tongue explored me, I quivered. I could no longer stand on my own two feet. Suddenly, he spun me around. Instinctively, I gripped the handrail for support and parted my legs as I eagerly waited for him. With one hand on my breast, the other on my thigh, he entered me from behind.

I moaned as I exploded. Matthew gingerly rocking back and forth only increased my yearning and pleasure started to build again.

"Matthew, you're driving me crazy," I panted.

"Patience," he said, savoring my neck. "We've got all night. You're mine. I'm going to fuck you all night long." With each spoken word, he slammed into me.

Holy shit. His words drove me to the edge. I liked it rough and hard, including him talking dirty to me. Matthew knew what I wanted, and he certainly delivered. I don't know how long we were out there, but it seemed timeless under the dark sky. It was just the two of us, devouring each other.

Out of breath, I released a heavy sigh when Matthew pulled out. Then he scooped me up, and headed into the cabin. After passing a few doors, we entered a bedroom he hadn't shown me on the tour and I was speechless again. Warm candlelight gave an enchanted feel, and the bed was covered with rose petals. I'd always dreamt about something like that. Never did I imagine I would actually see it.

"You're amazing," I said, embracing Matthew with all of me.

"If I am, it's all because of you."

Matthew kissed me tenderly and led me onto the bed. No freakin' way. We were having sex on a waterbed. We rode with the waves and enjoyed every second. We looked into each other's eyes, but it felt more like we reached into each other's souls. I found the connection I longed for in that look, in that kiss, and in that smile as we made love. I would never forget that night.

Jenna

"Come on sleepy head," Max said, embracing me and gently placing a kiss on my forehead. "Up you go."

The breeze slapped my face, forcing my hair over my eyes. It was early in the morning and the sun hadn't broken through the clouds yet. "You didn't tell me we were going on a private plane."

Max brushed my hair out of the way. "This isn't just any plane, babe. This is my parents' private jet. I'm borrowing it for our London trip."

"What other toys do you have that you're not telling me about?"

Max gave me a sexy grin and twitched his brow. "Wait 'til we get home. I have other toys I'd like to share with you." Then he smacked my behind, nudging me up the stairs to the plane.

"Ouch." I giggled, and turned when I heard my name.

"Jenna!" Becky was speed walking while Matthew lagged behind, holding their luggage.

"Good morning, Max." Becky greeted him with a hug, and then squeezed through to get to me. "Jenna!" She was so loud. I thought she had lost her mind. "I want to congratulate the both of you." Becky had tears in her eyes as she hugged me tightly. "I'm so happy for you."

Matthew must have told her. When she released me, I couldn't help but tear up as I looked at her beautiful, content face. I hadn't seen that look in a long time. Becky looked over her shoulder to spot Matthew, and then turned to Max. "Congratulations! You've just made the best decision of your life."

Max chuckled lightly. "That would be the second best

decision. The first one would be that I never gave up on us. Now ladies, if you don't get yourselves onto the plane, it will take off without us and we'll be more than fashionably late to the London Fashion Show."

"Yes, sir." Becky nodded, tugging me right along with her. I knew the reason. She wanted to see my ring, but as we climbed aboard, the beauty of the décor overrode that thought. From the finest technology to the comfortable, spacious leather seats, and all the amenities anyone could ever hope for, it was like a five star mini flying hotel.

After we had our fill of the interior design, Becky pulled me toward the bathroom, while Max and Matthew were up front, getting drinks and breakfast trays ready for us.

"Let me see, let me see" Becky squealed, holding my left hand. "Oh my!" she gasped, dropping her jaw. "That is one huge, beautiful, rock. It's blinding my eyes," she snorted. Her gaze shifted to my eyes sincerely as she held both of my hands. "I don't know where to begin, my friend. I'm so happy for you. You deserve all the happiness, but this confirms that someday soon, you won't be my roommate anymore. I'm going to miss you. I feel like you're leaving me already." She wiped the tears that flowed down her cheeks. "These are happy and sad tears. I can't wait to share this with Nicole and Kate."

"Oh…Becky," I sniffed as my lips quivered, and tears streamed down my face as well. "Don't worry. It's going to be a long engagement. Not only are you my best friend, but you've been like a sister to me from the moment you took me in. You made me laugh, you made me feel good about myself when I was lost, and you definitely picked me back up when I was down. You've helped me through rough times more than you'll ever know. I'll never leave you.

How can I leave the one person who has meant the most in my life? You're my sister forever, Becky. Don't ever forget that!"

Becky snatched me so fast I sucked in air. Hugging me tightly, I thought she was going to crush me. "I feel the same," she bawled.

"Then be my maid of honor," I said.

Becky pulled back, opening her eyes as wide as she could. "Hell, yes!" she shouted. "I better be the one." Then her excitement settled. "It will be my honor. I humbly accept," she said, as she made a feeble attempt at a curtsey. We both busted out laughing, causing the tears to flow even more.

"Everything okay back there?" Max asked. "We need to take off."

Wiping away the evidence that we had been crying, Becky and I headed to our seats. Later, when we had the chance to talk again, we could exchange the details of our Valentine's dates. I knew she was dying to know the details of how Max proposed. I couldn't wait to tell her.

Epilogue
Jenna

We stayed at one of the most exclusive hotels in London. Certainly, no other one could compare with the views and luxury of The Lanesborough. The four of us shared a suite that was about 4,000 square feet. There were four bedrooms, five and a half bathrooms, two living rooms, a kitchen, and a dining room.

The floor-to-ceiling windows gave sweeping views of Wellington Arch and Green Park. Not only did we have our own 24-hour butler service, but a complimentary chauffeured Rolls Royce Phantom, too.

Besides the excitement of the hotel, the shopping and dining were a dream come true for both Becky and me. Though we didn't have a lot of time to shop around, she and I pitched in together to buy souvenirs for Nicole and Kate. It was a lot colder than in California, but Max had already warned us to bring thick coats.

The London Fashion Show was beyond what I imagined it to be. Max looked relaxed, compared to our last show. Perhaps I had made him nervous back then. Thankfully, he sent others he trusted to represent Knight Magazine so we could relax and enjoy the show. As for Becky, she could hardly contain the excitement of her first time in London and at a show.

It was a short trip, but so amazing, we would never forget it. Having Matthew and Becky with us was an added bonus.

"Did you tell your parents about the engagement?" Becky asked from the kitchen.

"I did. They're really excited about it, but they knew Max was going to propose. He had asked their permission behind my back."

"Max is such a gentleman."

"Yes, he is," I agreed, recalling the night he proposed: the candles that spelled out "Marry Me", the romantic dinner, the sunset, the way he sang to me, and...Oh God, the whipped cream he ate off my body.

"What are you doing?" Becky asked, looking over my shoulder, glancing at the calendar that displayed on my phone. I had forgotten I was looking at it before my thoughts shifted to Max.

"I can't remember my last period. I mean...I spotted, but it was very light. I think it was the stress of lawsuit and all."

The sofa cushion shifted when Becky plopped next to me. "You're being safe, right?"

It never changes; any mention of sex made my face flush. "Yes, Max always uses a condom." I paused. "Well, except for a couple of times. Like on the stairs and..."

"Stairs?" Becky's eyes grew wide. "You wild thing, you."

I covered my eyes with my hands.

"Nothing to be embarrassed about, Jenna. If Max only had sex with you on the bed, I would think he was boring. This is just more proof he's smoking hot. Where else?" she snorted.

Squinting my eyes and biting my bottom lip, I said,

"On the kitchen counter."

"Wow, Jenna," Becky said excitedly. "I never knew. Okay, you can stop there. I don't even want to know anymore. I could bet next you're going to say in his office, and that would be insane. But it's his company after all."

When I gave her my innocent smile, she shook her head like she was scolding me playfully. "You dirty girl. I can't believe what Max has turned you into."

"I know," I giggled, then stopped laughing. "Seriously, I had been keeping track so I can go on the pill. I have an appointment this Friday." I counted the days in my head, trying to figure out when I started to spot.

Becky rushed into her room, and then came out with a small box.

"What is that?" I asked.

"Come here," she gestured, and handed the box to me. "It's a pregnancy test."

"I'm not pregnant. There is no way that I am." My voice was definite, with only a little hint of uncertainty. "Max never came inside me. I know there is a small chance he could've leaked, but I know when I ovulate."

"It doesn't matter. A small chance is still a chance. Just take the test. At least then you won't have to worry."

"I'm not worried. And why do you have this?"

"Oh." Becky's cheeks turned pink. "I had a little scare a while back. I was late, and I was on and off the pill. Probably not a good idea."

"Oh. Well, thanks." It was all I could say as I walked away, closing the door of the bathroom behind me. After reading the instructions, I took one packet out, peeled the seal, and placed it under me as I peed on it.

How much was enough? I had no idea. I drenched it, placed the cap over it, and set it on the sink. A chill froze me in place. The thought of being pregnant never occurred to me. We were safe except...but I was sure I wasn't ovulating.

Oh God! What if I was? We're not ready. I'm not ready. Max didn't want kids yet. The thought of having his children...our children...exhilarated me, but what if I had a difficult time getting pregnant like my mom had? What if I couldn't even have children? As all these thoughts rushed through my mind, I didn't know if being pregnant would be good news or bad news.

Hearing nothing but my heart thumping like it was going to jump out of my chest, as every second moved toward that one-minute mark, I dragged my hands through my hair and tried to calm my nerves. Tapping my feet while sitting on the toilet lid, I wondered if enough time had passed. I forgot to bring a timer with me, so I started counting in my head.

My muscles tightened, my lungs constricted, and I drew shallow, raspy breaths. I had never been this nervous in my entire life, except for when I thought Max was going to leave me, but this was different. This could be a life-changing moment. Not just mine, but Max's, his family, my family, our friends...the list went on and on. All sorts of thoughts spun in my head, as I waited for the results.

Figuring it was about time, though I had lost count, I picked up the stick with my trembling hand. I saw the first line... then...

I swung the door open. "Becky..."

Book 3, Something Forever

M. CLARKE

My Clarity
(New Adult-For 18+)
Told from Alexandria's point of view.

When we got home, I thought Lexy would have left, but she stayed. I headed straight for the bathroom to take care of my wound. Lexy followed behind me and leaned against the door.

"Sorry, Alex. I shouldn't have brought you there. I thought it would help get your mind off your dad." Her tone was apologetic at first, and then it became filled with excitement. "But wasn't it fun?"

"I did have fun, Lexy," I confirmed. I didn't want her to feel bad for doing something thoughtful. "I'm glad you took me. I've never been to one of those before. It was exciting. But do the cops come every time?"

"No. Sometimes we get lucky. They change the location every time. The guys who were taking the money are the ones who arrange it all. Either someone ratted the location or the cops played a hunch this time. If you get caught, they'll throw you in jail and let you out the next day."

"How do you know?" I asked, pumping liquid soap in my hands, and then running them under the sink. Thankfully, I only had minor scratches.

Lexy gave me a sly smile and handed the towel to me. "Cause Jimmy got caught before."

"Really?" I said, laughing as I hung the towel back on the rack. Our laughter was cut short when we went to the living room and saw Seth and Elijah walk through the door. Elijah was still huffing mad. His jaw muscles were tight and his lips were pressed in a thin line.

"Out!" Elijah was short and to the point. He made everyone jolt.

Thinking he meant me as well, I started heading to my room. I didn't want to be around him either.

"Alex, where do you think you're going?" he said softly, confusing me.

I stopped when he called my name. Without answering, I went to the kitchen instead and waited for him. I heard harsh whispers, as if they were arguing and didn't want me to hear, but it didn't last long.

"Good night, Alex. See you tomorrow at work," Lexy said.

"Good night, Alex," Seth said next. "Go easy on her." I heard him say to Elijah. Why would he say that?

"Bye," I said loudly without a thought to walk them out the door.

Feeling restless, my heart hammered faster as I took out the milk carton and a bag of chocolate chip cookies. It was late at night, but I just felt like having something. After pouring milk into the cup, I took out a cookie, as I watched Elijah walk in.

Though his shoulders were relaxed compared to a minute ago, I could see the worried look in his eyes, but not for long. "What are you doing," he chuckled lightly, apparently finding humor in what I was doing.

"Dunking my cookie in my milk. Haven't you ever done that before?"

"No."

"Oh, then you're missing out. Want some?" As I wondered if he would maintain his calmness, I took a bite.

"No thanks. Not right now. I'm not a big fan of milk." He paused for a second, dragged his hair back with his fingers, and released a short, sharp sigh. "Look. I'm sorry I got angry earlier. It wasn't toward you. It was toward the situation and Lexy. She shouldn't have brought you there."

After I swallowed, I retorted. "Why not? You've seen the crowd. Why can't I be there?"

"I can't believe you're asking me that question?" His face tilted, angling his brows at me, as if I should have known better. "Have I seen the crowd? Have *you* seen the crowd?" He blinked rapidly, rattling off his words, but his piercing, beautiful brown eyes and long lashes were distracting me. "There are gang members, gamblers, drug addicts, not to mention the cops."

"I didn't know about the cops, and who put you in charge of me anyway?" I challenged.

"I did."

"I don't need you to take care of me just because I'm Jimmy's cousin. I wish everyone would stop doing that." My tone went up a notch.

"That's not the reason."

"Then what is? Oh, and I didn't see any gang members or drug addicts. Although I wouldn't know what they look like." I dunked the cookie again and took another bite.

"Exactly. And have you ever been in a jail before?"

"No." Biting my cookie helped me deal with how he continued to distract me. Something about the way he was being so protective and how he was staring at my mouth, oozed sex appeal.

"Exactly."

"Stop saying 'exactly'. Have you?"

He didn't answer. I'd guessed that was a yes, and before he could walk away from me, I pointed at him with the half eaten cookie in my hand as I asked another question. "How about the other students and your friends? They were all there too. Aren't I good enough to be there?" I don't know why, but anger boiled inside me.

"No...you're not!" he stammered, startling me. As he took a step toward me, I backed away and bumped into the cabinet.

His words were like a dagger to my heart. He did not say that to me, making me feel worthless. How dare he?

With his hands planted on either side of the cabinet just inches away from my face, his body was way too close to mine. I couldn't help but stare at the tattoo that curved as his muscles flexed. His broad shoulders and his hard, defined chest were too much for me to handle, especially recalling how he looked without a shirt on.

Blistering, heated energy ignited in the space between us. I was drowning into his smell...into him...into that cage he created around us, and I wanted to dive into his arms. Lowering his head and brushing his lips against my ear, accentuating one word at a time, he murmured. "You. Are. Better." Then he paused. No movement...completely still.

I don't know how long we stood like that because a second seemed like an eternity, and I had no control over what I was feeling at this moment. After a soft intake of breath, he continued. "I don't know what I would have done if something were to happen to you."

His words quickly soothed me, making me melt in awe. I tried not to choke on the chewed up cookies still in my mouth. I swear I felt the warmth of his breath against my neck and I wanted so badly for him to devour me right there. The heated feeling got worse when I saw his lips heading toward mine with a slow hesitation. My heart went into overdrive as the room spun around me. We were now face to face as he stared into my eyes with want and need.

Never taking his eyes off me, he rested his hand on my shoulder, and then gingerly slid down my arm, giving me pleasurable tingles...EVERYWHERE. Afraid to move the tiniest of my muscles, I felt locked in place. I was enjoying him way too much and I didn't want it to end. When he finally reached my hand, he pulled it up to his mouth and made the most pleasurable groan I've ever heard.

Looking exhausted and dazed, he shifted his eyes to the cookie in my hand, and mumbled slowly, "I think I'll have that cookie now."

Nothing registered until I saw his lips part, and my fingers disappeared in his mouth. OMG! My pulse skyrocketed, and I whimpered from the warmth of his tongue and the sensation that shot down my arm. My fingers were very wet sliding out of his mouth. I even felt the feather-light graze of his teeth; and I could swear every single muscle in my body became limp.

His jaw worked quickly, chewing. It was the sexiest thing I'd ever seen. He made eating a cookie SO hot. After he swallowed, he turned the other way, picked up my cup of milk, and chugged down whatever was left.

Looking like he just couldn't believe he drank milk, he placed the cup down. "Good night, Alex. Don't ever go racing without me," he ordered, and then he left.

What just happened? Milk and cookies will never be the same for me…EVER.

M. CLARKE

About the Author

International Bestselling, Award Winning, Author M. Clarke resides in Southern California. When she started reading new adult novels, she fell in love with the genre. It was the reason she had to write one- Something Great.

74521095R00173

Made in the USA
Columbia, SC
18 September 2019